Geoffrey Peppiatt is a former scientist and physics teacher. Apart from his family, his interests include playing squash, writing, gourmet cooking and collecting just about anything. With his wife, June, and cat Marlowe, (a.k.a. Bear), he splits his time between New York and Pennsylvania.

With love to my wife, June and my amazing children, Simon, Samantha and Jonah.

Geoffrey Peppiatt

SHALLOW WATER

An Agnes Trout Mystery

AUSTIN MACAULEY PUBLISHERS™
LONDON • CAMBRIDGE • NEW YORK • SHARJAH

Copyright © Geoffrey Peppiatt 2022

The right of Geoffrey Peppiatt to be identified as author of this work has been asserted by the author in accordance with sections 77 and 78 of the Copyright, Designs and Patents Act 1988.

All rights reserved. No part of this publication may be reproduced, stored in a retrieval system, or transmitted in any form or by any means, electronic, mechanical, photocopying, recording, or otherwise, without the prior permission of the publishers.

Any person who commits any unauthorised act in relation to this publication may be liable to criminal prosecution and civil claims for damages.

This is a work of fiction. Names, characters, businesses, places, events, locales, and incidents are either the products of the author's imagination or used in a fictitious manner. Any resemblance to actual persons, living or dead, or actual events is purely coincidental.

A CIP catalogue record for this title is available from the British Library.

ISBN 9781398453319 (Paperback)
ISBN 9781398453326 (Hardback)
ISBN 9781398453333 (ePub e-book)

www.austinmacauley.com

First Published 2022
Austin Macauley Publishers Ltd®
1 Canada Square
Canary Wharf
London
E14 5AA

Many, and extra, thanks to June for her support and expertise.

Chapter 1

The sky was stroked with amber, grey and orange as the fading sun slipped behind distant hills clad in hazy greenery and purplish grassy slopes. Aggie was driving at a time that she enjoyed and which was blessed with the evocative terms dusk or twilight. It was a late Fall evening with minimal traffic on the road.

In fact, as she skimmed up the curving wide hill between roadside banks that were thick with trees and undergrowth, she felt her eardrums pop gently with the pressure changes caused by the climb and noticed only one set of distant headlights piercing the darkening vista behind her. The rented Camry crested the hill and hummed down the long gradient on the other side when flashing, flickering bursts of light about a mile ahead caught her eye. As she approached the source, she could see without a doubt that the light was produced by flames emanating from a parked truck on the hard shoulder of the roadside.

As she drew closer the flames were accompanied by small flurries of sparks pushing up into the descending darkness.

She eased cautiously alongside the truck and saw that the flames were climbing up the rear of the cab, having appeared to have gained a firm hold on the cables and other material there. Glancing up at the cab, she saw an inert forearm, the upper part of which sported a red checkered material, pressed against the glass.

She pulled onto the hard shoulder some way in front of the truck, leapt out of her car and ran towards it, vaguely aware of another car stopping on the other side of the center median. In moments, a man and a woman were hopping over the median wall and running to where Aggie was assessing the situation.

After looking up at the cab, she clambered up the shiny metal steps to the cab door handle, the heat from her right being bearable but gaining in intensity. Flames were just inches from her face and arm. As she grasped the handle, she heard someone yell, "Call 911" just before a tall man climbed swiftly up alongside her. Together they hauled on the cab door which swung open and was pushed to one side, allowing the arm of the motionless driver to flop down like a dead fish while he remained solidly ensconced behind the wheel. Aggie grabbed the arm and her fellow rescuer gripped the shirt collar and both pulled in unison resulting in all three tumbling backwards onto the paving, the weight of the driver spread across the two of them.

Aggie was acutely aware of landing on her butt and an elbow, air being violently expelled from her lungs by the impact and weight of the driver who was solidly built. Her companion coughed up a couple of choice expletives as they extricated themselves and scrambled upright. He was thin and fit looking with fine grayish hair and rimless spectacles which were askew on his aquiline nose. Professorial was the description that flitted across Aggie's mind.

He said in a rich, tenor voice, "Let's get him away from here." Aggie grunted a positive response and they proceeded to drag the driver, who had lost a sneaker, away from the truck and towards Aggie's car. They were joined by the tall man's companion, a small, dark haired, dark eyed woman in a bright floral dress and a white cardigan, who helped somewhat decorously with the task. All three were breathing heavily by the time they had pulled the driver to safety.

Aggie fetched a hoodie from her car and put it under the driver's head. She noted that he was a bulky individual with a heavy, lightly stubbled pale face topped with rumpled, thinning brown hair streaked with grey. His arms, the site of major tattoos, and the whiteness of his exposed neck, stood out against his shirt, the collar of which was substantially torn.

As she straightened up, a car pulled up onto the shoulder some yards to the rear of the truck which was now aflame to the top of the cab and had begun to pop glass from the windows. Two men emerged and ran up to the group, the smaller one of whom called out, "Can we help? What happened?" Aggie, uncharitably, thought that it was obvious, but said, "Truck on fire. Something wrong with the driver."

The same guy walked over to where the unconscious driver lay on the ground.

He was of medium height, thin and wore an expensive looking dark suit with an open necked white shirt. His black hair was sleeked back in a fashionable way. He bent down and placed his fingers on the driver's neck.

"Got a pulse."

Aggie said, "You a doctor?"

He raised his eyes and looked at Aggie. They were blue and cold.

"No. Just checking."

The other man moved forward. He was larger, also dark suited, with a dark blue open necked shirt and was somewhat swarthy with cropped grayish hair.

He looked very fit. Just then, as he was about to speak, flashing lights came into view over the hill accompanied by sirens and more flashing lights. Within seconds, the scene was awash with firemen, police and a medical team.

It was an hour before all the details and practical issues had been resolved satisfactorily. The fire had crept into parts of the cab but it had been rapidly extinguished by the firefighters. The driver had been carefully examined and was showing some signs of recovery as he was transported away in an ambulance. Copious statements had been taken from everybody by two scrupulous cop note takers, the scene having been cordoned off and very light rubbernecking traffic having been diverted around it. Aggie's natural curiosity had gleaned a couple of the names of the participants who had been compelled to partake in this tableau. The tall, academic looking man who helped her tug the driver from the cab was Paul Wright while the truck driver seemed to be of Polish extraction, his name being Jakob Kowalczyk. The latter came from a thin wallet found in the back pocket of his jeans by an enterprising cop. The smaller of the two men who had shown up late in the proceedings had the name of Strum. All in all, the whole episode was wrapped up fairly well and comprehensively by those who had assumed authority but, for Aggie, one or two facts did not totally hang together. Yes, the driver could have passed out for several reasons. It happened. But the fire was a problem.

How did it start in such a strange place – just behind the cab? And, it was a bit of a coincidence that it started at about the same time that the driver passed out.

Stranger things had happened of course but, even so, Aggie's curiosity was piqued. She had managed a look at the charred area behind the cab but there was not much to be seen – just damage and mess. The two men had also drifted over to the cab and checked out the same area. Nobody commented on what they had seen and, if the cops were wary of the situation or even curious about it, they did not show it or mention it.

Eventually, everyone was released of their desired presence and, after perfunctory goodbyes, they all left the scene. Aggie was suffused with a flat, anticlimactic feeling, a sort of emptiness after all of the frenetic action she had been part of. A man's life had surely been saved by swift action on her and others' part. That was a good thing, in fact, a wonderful thing. Now, though, everyone was moving on in their lives. She found herself heading back to New York and home. She had visited an old college friend in Pennsylvania who seemed very happy with her home, husband and three children. Aggie was pleased for her and, after trying to visualize herself in that position, gave up quickly and turned her mind to work – solving cases. Although, she was currently working on two divorces and not really solving anything. Fall evenings are pleasant, enjoyable times in the city. Yellow, orange and reddish brown leaves are beginning to flutter onto the sidewalks. Patrons of burger, ethnic and fish restaurants park out at sidewalk tables and traffic hums everywhere. Mounting numbers of limo taxis, yellow cabs, buses, delivery trucks, personal cars and bicycles are filling the streets and avenues as they negotiate parking lanes, bicycle lanes, bicycle racks and wayward pedestrians, replete with hand held smart devices. This massive competition for space is inevitably heading for an anti-chaotic book of rules and complex legislation.

None of this crossed Aggie's mind as, submerging herself back into the city, she dropped off the rental and made her way to her apartment. She was in no rush to buy another car yet, having lost two during one of her last cases. She rather liked hiring as needed, which was not often enough to jar her finances, and she had decided to let fate lead her to her next transportation adventure. She was soon letting herself into her brownstone apartment through the door with the fancy double locking system, a legacy of her recently acquired friend, Jonathan Black. Occasionally, she had burdened herself with the thought that her apartment had assumed a Fort Knox quality because of the barred window to the fire escape and the high tech nature of the door locks, both a manifestation of her last case, as was the mild pain she occasionally felt in the a/c joint of her shoulder. As to all of the security, she was beginning to consider hitting the retro button and restoring her apartment to its former vulnerability – at least in terms of debarring her window. After all, lightning wouldn't, or couldn't strike twice – or could it? For now, it seemed to be a waste of time to even think about it. Time to relax, eat, have a glass of wine and peer into the near future.

She ordered Chinese delivery and was soon accompanying the food with a glass of decent Malbec while watching the local TV news. Nothing surfaced about the truck fire, of course, because there were no deaths or anything catastrophic enough for the news cycle. After a second glass of wine, Aggie decided that any peering into the future was not an option and went to bed.

Chapter 2

The next morning Aggie felt refreshed and semi invigorated after a good night's sleep. It was some weeks now since the conclusion of her last case which had left her feeling exhausted and a little vulnerable, a very unfamiliar feeling for her and one which took some work for her to overcome. But, on the positive side, she had picked up a new friend – the calm, intellectual yet enigmatic Jonathan Black, who had literally saved her life or, at least, a watery exit from it. She had taken him at face value, ignoring any questionable baggage that may, or may not, be floating around in his past. She was almost certain that it was there but so what.

She did not need to know. Most people had baggage anyway. She did know that he had two close friends with, perhaps, a military connection in the past, one of whom resided in Seattle. Jonathan visited him once or twice a year as he did not seem to want to come to New York. The other friend was the affable and talented Cedric who had almost magically installed her security system and had also been on hand to save her from proximate physical harm during her last case. She and Jonathan had kept in touch over these past months by cooking dinner for each other on a semi regular basis and enjoying each other's conversation, humor (mostly Jonathan's) and company. Aggie defined her own culinary skills as reasonable but she thought that Jonathan was in the Master Chef ballpark. Where this very comfortable and easy situation was going she had no idea but it was stimulating, fun and a little mysterious. She began to mull over her current cases as she sipped her coffee, replete with creamer and munched on some cereal and whole milk. She had given up on the fat free, 1% and 2% kicks for milk. Once a day, so enjoy it had become her mantra.

Her first case, a divorce client, was about as straightforward as it could get. It concerned a 43 year old profligate wealth management consultant who embarked on affair after affair as if there was no tomorrow. What was the point or motivation? It took all kinds. His wife needed to confirm what did not need confirmation, at least as far as Aggie was concerned. There were no children and there was no pre-nup. The assumption had to be that, with irrefutable evidence of her husband's philandering, his wife would be hitting him pretty hard in the wallet area, which was as it should be. It felt sordid as many of these cases did. It was sordid. And sad. But there it was. Aggie had taken on the case just before she had decided that she needed a Caribbean breakaway and now, it was almost wrapped up.

That trip had been a masterful idea. She hadn't treated herself in quite this way before. It was out of season for St. Bart's but it had been very restful and rejuvenating. She had loved the adventurous small plane trip from St. Martin's to the island over green seawater winking in the bright sunlight.

The plane, which had only a half dozen passengers, had skimmed over a hill road by what seemed a few feet before landing on the tiny airstrip. She had rented one of several hilltop apartments overlooking St. Jean's bay, with an outside kitchen and a communal swimming pool. She had caught up with her reading for a few days by the pool, had swam twenty or thirty pool lengths a day and made friends with three stray cats, feeding them daily. She had graduated to a local beach which had very few sun worshippers on view, most of whom were nude. She had gone topless and soaked up the sun, clearing her mind in a Zen like way and listening to the small waves brushing gently up the shore. Tranquility was an understatement.

One late afternoon, when the heat of the day was fading to livable temperatures, she became aware of a man standing a few feet away from her, clearly looking for an introduction. He was tanned, well built, bikini clad and could have been any age between 25and 45 years old. They chatted, she saying that she was a writer looking to recharge her storytelling, he claiming to be an artist although, during their time together, Aggie never saw a painting or any artistic accoutrements.

In any event his main, if not only, interest seemed to be sex, which was perfectly acceptable to Aggie. He was quite good at it, which Aggie thought he should be, if he spent most of his waking hours so engaged. For her, the experience just added to the all-round dynamics of a good, regenerative vacation. Fortunately, all of this was towards the end of her sojourn because the only sign of a brain that the guy seemed to have was located somewhere near his six pack. All to the good for a while but, by the time she left the island, the flame had dimmed and sputtered into insignificance. Still, the whole trip had been a glorious break in her lifestyle.

Her second case, which had come up after her return to normal life, was also a divorce scenario. Her client was a stay at home dad with three children and a healthy investment income, whose wife was an airline flight attendant. He was convinced of her infidelity but he was also a pathological liar which had not taken Aggie long to figure out. Still, these days many people seemed to have trouble grappling with the truth. His lying had no effect on her case and how she conducted herself but it was disconcerting. This investigation was much more complex.

Obviously, lots of opportunity for his wife but Aggie had, so far, found nothing untoward. Plane crews had partying reputations whether they liked it or not but, for the most part, that seemed untrue. It was certainly possible to party with all of the overnights but the back and forth travel routine, unforgiving hotels and constant clothing changes were, in fact, largely unenviable. They worked hard, were often tired and were not always treated well by the public.

She had reported back to her client in the negative but he insisted that there was something there, asking her to continue her investigation. She pulled out both files as she sipped her second cup of coffee at her kitchen counter, leafing through her notes which she had not yet committed to her iPad. Ringing, or rippling, from her cell phone broke through her reflections. She picked it up and scanned the screen which offered up 'unknown caller'. Most of the time she would ignore these calls because they often turned out to be glorified sales calls.

Once in a while, though, she would answer them to tell the caller in no uncertain terms, that further calls were unwelcome. She picked up.

"Agnes Trout. Who is this?"

A somewhat raspy male voice with an unidentifiable faint accent said,

"Is that Agnes Trout?" With a sigh, Aggie said, "I just said it was. Whom am I speaking to?"

"Are you the woman who stopped for the truck fire?"

Aggie immediately recalled the truck burning on the highway.

"Yes I am. I stopped to help a guy stuck in the cab."

The caller exited a long breath. "That was me. I am the guy from the cab – the driver."

"Ah. How are you doing?"

"I'm OK, I think. No after effects really. Just some minor burns and smoke inhalation. Nothing to worry about."

Aggie paused for a moment. "Polish name, I think. Jakob wasn't it?"

"Correct ma'am. Jakob Kowalczyk."

"Yes. Well Mr. Kowalczyk, I am sorry to be direct but why are you calling? First, how did you get my number?"

"Oh. I asked the cops for the names and numbers of a couple of the people that helped me."

Aggie said, "You went to the cops for that?"

"No. They came to me. I am still in the hospital. They needed stuff. You know, details. I asked them then. Said I wanted to thank people."

"Right. Well, that makes sense."

Aggie thought that this must be a thank you call. Nice thing to do. She said, "I was glad I could help. Just lucky to show up at the right time. You'll be out soon then. Out of the hospital?"

Kowalczyk said, "Yes. I will." There was a lengthy pause. Aggie took a swig of coffee. She broke the silence.

"Are you OK? I mean, was there anything else?"

She felt a little as though she was brushing him off when he was trying to thank her. She hoped that it did not seem that way. She added, "You'll soon get back into things. It was a nasty experience and, you know, it will take time to get over it."

"Yes. Look, actually there is something else. I looked you up and I think that I need your services."

Aggie felt mild surprise. "Really. You looked me up? What sort of services were you thinking of?"

Kowalczyk sounded slightly nonplussed. "You are a private investigator aren't you?"

"I am." Again, there was the sound of silence. Aggie came up with two simultaneous thoughts. What can have happened to this guy to need me? And, uncharitably, can a driver afford me? She added, "So, what's up?" Kowalczyk said, "Well, basically I want to know who is trying to kill me."

Aggie said, "What?" Then images of the cab fire rushed across her mind. Suspicious?

"What do you mean? What makes you think that someone is trying to kill you?"

"I don't think they are – I know they are. Look, I was drugged or, at least given something that knocked me out after a while – while driving. Plus, the cab fire didn't start on its own." Aggie paused. This was too big a leap.

"Wait, how do you know that you didn't just fall asleep? Or, maybe the fire started and the fumes got to you."

"No, no. This is not my imagination. This is real. The hospital told me that I had ingested a drug – forgot the name of it but it doesn't matter – it gets into the system and knocks you out. I don't do drugs."

Aggie said, "Do you take regular medication for anything? You could have messed up the dosage."

Kowalczyk paused. "No. Well, just a statin. Harmless. Right." He continued. "And then there is the fire. You don't get fires starting in that location. It just doesn't happen."

Aggie said, "OK. You're making a case. I'm still not convinced but here's the thing. I'll meet you and we'll talk it through – see where you stand. It could still be that you are wrong. When do you get out of hospital?"

"I think I've got another night and that's it. Observation."

"OK. How about tomorrow morning. Say, 9.00 am. I'll come to the hospital. We can take it from there."

Aggie thought that was a bit of a trip but never mind. Kowalczyk sounded relieved.

"Sounds good. Thanks for doing this."

He gave Aggie the name of the hospital.

She said, "See you then."

They hung up.

Aggie had chosen to put off Kowalczyk and his problem until the next day because she needed to catch up on her cases and her life before committing the time to him. Plus, she wanted time to do some research on him to see if she could dig up some background noise that would explain what was going on. In the meantime, she felt that calls to Jonathan and her occasional lover, Jack, were in order to touch base after her Pennsylvania trip. She tried Jonathan first. He came on after two rings.

"Hi Aggie. How's things? The traveler returns, good trip I hope."

"Hi Jonathan. Yes, it was good. Caroline is doing well, the kids are fine and we did a lot of catching up. She is working from home, setting up exhibitions, that sort of thing."

"Sounds good. Interesting anyway. Well, at least you have kept in touch."

"Yes, it was nice to see her. As you know, it's been two years – lot of water and all that. Sometimes that sort of thing stops working and you wonder why you made the effort."

"I know. But you sound happy about this… effort. Worthwhile wasn't it?"

Aggie sighed.

"Yes it was. I can feel things drifting a bit, though. Anyway I'm glad I did it."

She paused.

"Had some fun on the way back though."

"Oh-oh. More adventures? What have you been up to?"

"Nothing much. Rescued an unconscious truck driver from a burning cab. The usual."

"What? Aggie, say that again!"

Aggie laughed.

"Yep. I did. Truck was on fire. Guy was out of it. I pulled up and got him out along with another guy who came by."

With concern seeping into his voice, Jonathan said, "Are you OK? That sounds more than a little dangerous to me."

Aggie replied, "Yes, I'm fine. Bit of singeing here and there. I suppose it was, dangerous. I hadn't really thought about it."

"Trust you to be in the wrong place at the right time! What happened to the truck?"

"Oh, cops and firemen showed up. Put the fire out and carted the driver off to the hospital."

Jonathan said, "Ah, never a dull moment. Must be your flair for the dramatic."

Aggie smiled, checking her coffee mug, which had a few dregs in the bottom.

"There's more."

Jonathan laughed.

"Of course there is. Why wouldn't there be? What more?"

"The driver called me."

"The truck driver?"

"Yes. He thinks somebody is trying to kill him."

"Really? Why did he call you?"

"He got my info from the cops. Found out that I was a PI. Wants to hire me."

After several seconds of silence Jonathan said, "Aggie this is going a shade too fast for me. Can we meet up and talk?"

Aggie responded quickly. "Talk about what?"

"Look, I just like to know what is going on – that you are OK. No more than that."

"Of course I'm OK, Jonathan. It's what I do."

He sighed. "I know. I know."

Aggie continued. "In any case, I'm seeing this guy tomorrow."

"Tomorrow? Where?"

Aggie said, "He's still in the hospital, so I'm going there."

"One request."

"What's that?"

"Let me drive. Give you time to think. We can have a chat to."

Aggie paused a beat. She did and she didn't like being cared for.

"I don't know about that. I can manage."

"Well, I know that you can manage. But I could be stimulating, lofty company for you. You could relax. And, you know that I am a masterful driver."

With a modicum of resignation, Aggie said, "I'll think about it."

The idea certainly had appeal. Being driven in the Highlander was a comfortable experience.

Jonathan said in an upbeat voice, "Good. I sense progress being made. I'll gas up just in case."

They rang off.

Even though reticent, Aggie thought that there was a pleasant ring to the premise. Jonathan was good, thoughtful company and she enjoyed his flurries of intellectual repartee. But, and there was always a but, the conversation had left her feeling unsettled, so she put off calling Jack, not wanting to go through any more recounting or explaining. She put a slice of multigrain bread in the toaster and stared at it vacantly until it popped up. She then spread a minimal amount of butter on it, gulped down the remaining coffee which was cold and, munching on the toast, headed to the bathroom for a quick shower. After that, some truck driver research was on the menu.

Chapter 3

Jakob Kowalczyk turned out to be the son of Polish immigrants, aged in his mid-fifties, apparently unmarried. Since he had some kind of faint accent, he must have come to the US at an early age Aggie thought.

Although, was it possible to grow up with your parents speaking another language without picking up some kind of accent? She didn't know but it seemed feasible.

He ran a trucking business with, it seemed, three eighteen wheelers with the aid of two partners, both Americans – George Mason and Budge Waters.

They were both married, the former with three daughters and the latter with a son and a daughter. So, he had money, probably didn't need to drive but did anyway.

No indication as to whether either of the partners drove any of the trucks.

Tough life Aggie thought but, evidently, worth it, although she understood it to be a highly competitive business with plenty of inherent knowledge needed.

There were all the financial transactions involved in acquiring or leasing the trucks – no way of knowing which of these options the guy had gone with. She had no idea of insurance costs, overheads like truck breakdowns, eighteen tires and fuel costs.

Plus, how did one arrange for return journey pickups to make a trip worthwhile or profitable? Then there were personnel considerations.

Stop, stop she told herself. There is no need for any of this. No more second guessing – just see the guy, find out what's what and move on from there. For the same reason there was little point in researching either of the partners or their families until she knew if there was to be an undertaking on her part. Also, in that case, the two guys who floated into the scene somewhat fortuitously would have to be looked at. Sunlight was piercing the part of the living area where she had deposited herself on her couch. As she climbed to her feet and stretched, she caught sight of dust on some of the flat surfaces and floating, tiny bits of debris drifting through the shafts of light. Cleaning would have to wait. In fact, it was nowhere on the agenda.

Anyway, no matter how often she cleaned, it always needed doing again almost before the cleaning materials had been stored away. For the time being she decided to text Jack so that, at least, he would be up to date with her travels.

Texting or emailing were not among her favorite means of communication, being impersonal and somewhat emotionless. Today, though, texting would have to do – it served a purpose. In her business, telephone calls provided more information in terms of tone, nuances and spontaneity. In Jack's case she would make up for it later. The day was already leaking into the afternoon and so Aggie decided to make a trip to the gym for a solid workout.

An hour and a half later, feeling much invigorated she headed back to her apartment to contemplate dinner (French Toast),TV (Endeavour) and some reading (Peter Robinson). First, she called Jonathan and accepted his offer to drive her to the hospital the following day, arranging to be picked up early in the morning.

Late in the evening, Jack responded to her text. He was working late, as usual, was more than shocked by her latest escapade and hoped to catch up with her in a day or so to hear more. She retired relatively early, reading herself into a dreamless sleep.

Chapter 4

Aggie arose early the next morning, showered and dressed comfortably in sweats and sneakers. She took in a little of Morning Joe on TV with some coffee and cereal and felt ready to take on the day. Jonathan had texted that he was on his way and so she shook her wet hair into place, grabbed her bag along with a notepad and headed downstairs. Jonathan, smoothly decked in jeans and a cashmere sweater was waiting, engine quietly humming in the cool morning air. The journey took just over an hour, during which the conversation was light and companionable, Jonathan seeking a few more details about the truck fire incident. At one point, towards the end of the journey, he noted with some amusement, "I couldn't help noticing that your nose is no longer reflecting light in all directions."

Aggie smiled, knowing immediately that he was referring to her nose stud which she had removed recently.

"You are correct. Fancy noticing that. I'm done with it. Did it for some kind of personal statement, the meaning of which I have now forgotten."

"Well, statements have their place. That's all good."

Aggie said, "And in case you wondered, my body is not littered with tattoos – pointing arrows, butterflies – not my thing, although I have thought about it once or twice."

"Ah. All welcome and interesting information."

Shortly after this, they pulled up a driveway bordered with grassy areas and copious floral bushes, towards the hospital. They drove past a couple of parking lots for long term and larger vehicles to a well-marked and large visitors parking lot. They climbed out of the Highlander and headed into the main lobby of the hospital where they found the reception area and a large semicircular counter behind which sat one male and two female receptionists. Behind them were several occupied desks with computers and a general air of calm activity.

Aggie chose the middle receptionist and stated the basics of her visit which had, it appeared, been listed by the truck driver. She was given a visitors tag to wear for her visit and directed to the third floor. Jonathan said that he would wait in the reception lobby which had ample comfortable seating. Aggie made her way to the elevator bank and was soon on the third floor, showing her tag to an attendant and being directed to one of several rooms down a well-lit hallway with a shiny floor and cream colored walls. She entered the room which had four beds, one of which was curtained off, the truck driver being the first one on her right. He was sitting up in bed with his tattooed, powerful forearms resting on an empty bed tray. His hair was tidily combed now and parted on one side, the thinning element neatly disguised. His brown eyes were bright but wary, as he looked her up and down carefully. He spoke first with the same hint of an accent that Aggie had heard on the telephone.

"Ms. Trout. My savior in person. Nice to meet you."

Aggie responded.

"Mr. Kowalcyzk. Good to see you too. In better shape, I see."

Kowalcyzk raised a tattooed arm and waved it vaguely.

"Thanks for all that you did. It could have been a close one for me."

"You're welcome. I had plenty of help which made the difference."

Aggie paused as they eyed each other.

"What's all this about then? You said on the telephone that someone was trying to kill you."

"They are. Look, let me give you some background and then we can go on from there."

Aggie walked to the side of the bed and settled on a utility wooden chair which put her at a slightly lower position than Kowalczyk. She turned to him expectantly.

He began.

"I own J.K.Trucking Inc., a trucking company, along with two partners."

As she took out her notepad and pen Aggie said,

"Your initials for the company name?"

"Yes. Because I own the major share of the company. I started the whole thing twelve years ago. I'd driven trucks before and was on my own. My wife had divorced me – never at home, or so she said. In a way, we had become strangers and so it seemed inevitable that we broke up."

There was no trace of emotion in his voice. It was matter of fact. He could have been talking about selling a car.

Aggie said, "Children?"

"No. Never seemed on the cards."

She said, "Go on."

"Well, I was at a bit of a loose end and so I had the idea of trucking for a living, as my own boss. I started small. It took two years before I acquired an eighteen wheeler and began to make really good money. Business built up and I soon realized that I needed help and capital. To cut a long story short, I picked up my two partners and now have three trucks and a thriving business."

As Kowalczyk said the words two partners, Aggie noted a thinly veiled derogatory tone.

She said, "Your partners names?"

"George Mason and Budge Waters."

Again, a touch of derision accompanied their names. A nurse came into the room and went to the kitty-corner bed by the window, drawing the curtains.

Aggie said, "You don't like your partners?"

Kowalczyk looked surprised.

Aggie offered, "Your expression is less than respectful when you refer to them."

"Oh. Well, they are lazy. I suspect that one, if not both of them, is skimming somewhere. Profits are not what they should be – you know the sort of thing."

"Not really. So, no evidence of skimming. Just a feeling, an impression?"

Kowalczyk's face mirrored resignation.

"OK. Yes, just an impression. But I know enough to believe something's going on."

A few moments passed.

Aggie said, "Go on then. About your partners."

"George is married with three daughters and Budge is married with a son and a daughter. The kids are all in their mid to late twenties. Neither partner does any driving but Budge's kids do, on occasion, when we are short."

Aggie leaned back in her chair and flexed her shoulders.

"What do they do then, these partners?"

"The short answer is nothing. They have put up money and they take out a share of the profits. They have other things going on. They have money. My business is just an investment. Partner is a misnomer. It's not unusual. I just expect more."

"OK. You mentioned that someone is trying to kill you. Would you start from the beginning and tell me why you think that?"

Kowalczyk took a deep breath and settled back against the pillows.

"First, let me say that the other day was not the first time. There.."

Aggie interrupted.

"Let's begin with that. Why do you think that the fire was an attempt to kill you?"

"Well, as I said on the telephone, I passed out just as the fire started."

"Wait. Go back a bit. You were chugging along in your truck – say on the other side of that hill. And…..?"

Kowalczyk sighed.

"I came over the top of the hill and, as I was throttling down on the steep side where you found me, I started to feel dizzy and faint. I thought I might be having a stroke or something. I immediately swung off the road onto the hard shoulder and put on the brakes. The truck had barely stopped when I passed out."

"You don't remember anything? Just feeling ill or faint and then out?"

"That's about it. I began coming to on the road. You know, where you and the others put me."

"OK. Now, I saw where the fire was, after it was extinguished. I was really only aware of the fire when I was pulling you out of the cab. It was of no concern to me where it started or how it started. I was just intent on getting us all away from it. What did you make of the fire again?"

Kowalczyk turned his eyes on her intently.

"Fires do not start in an area where this one did. There are cables and couplings there – nothing that would burst into flame. Apart from that, look at the timing. A fire starts just as I pass out. Too much of a coincidence! It makes no sense unless it was deliberate."

Aggie pursed her lips.

"Supposition."

"What? What do you mean?"

"I mean that this is all circumstantial. It's guesswork. You could have fainted or had some kind of medical issue. Perhaps ate something that did not agree with you – there are any number of reasons for passing out. Then a fire starts and now, you put two and two together."

Kowalczyk looked frustrated and irritated.

Aggie said, "Any electrical circuits just behind the cab there?"

"Of course there are. But not enough current to start a fire. I've never heard of a fire starting in that area."

Aggie smiled to soften her comment.

"Well, I have no need to point out that just because you have never heard of it does not mean that it cannot happen."

There was a prolonged silence until Kowalczyk began drumming his fingers lightly on the bed table. The nurse threw back the curtains around the far bed and left the room. That patient appeared to be sleeping.

Aggie said, "Look, you have a point of view. Support it. Give me something else to go on. The only thing that I can see, that might be in your favor, is the timing of the fire – as you have mentioned. What else is there? I mean, did you have dinner with a stranger who might have spiked your coffee while someone was messing with your truck?"

Kowalczyk's expression was enough for Aggie to say,

"I'm being facetious. But I'm asking you to think a bit."

He looked away to the window where spots of rain were appearing.

"There was that other occasion that I mentioned. I suppose you'll put that down too, so what's the point?"

Aggie leaned forward in her chair and raised her eyes to Kowalczyk's.

"I'm an investigator. I gather facts and information and use them to investigate but I only do that if I think that I have a case to apply them to. At the moment, I don't see much to go on. That is, evidence that would support your contention that someone wants to kill you."

The brown eyes ran over her face and were almost expressionless. A hint of annoyance flashed and was gone. Kowalczyk began.

"About a year ago – maybe ten months or so – I was on another hill and started to brake when the brakes began to fail. There wasn't much traffic and I managed to use the hard shoulder and part of the road to bring the truck to rest. It was a frightening ordeal and must have taken well over a mile to stop."

Aggie nodded encouragingly.

"Well, I said the brakes failed but they are air brakes. Obviously, air can leak out of the system and so there is a spring back up system to do the braking. That makes sense and is a safety factor. There are though, various reasons for the spring system to malfunction. There is something called the brake stroke length for optimum braking and, if that is exceeded, then you have a problem. That can happen – I hope I'm not boring you?"

"Not at all- it is interesting."

"Well, too much manual adjustment of the system could lead to failure. That kind of work has to be done by recognized mechanics. Overheating too. Doesn't really matter. The point is I am very careful about maintenance. There is no way my spring brakes would ever be over adjusted."

Kowalczyk wore a triumphant expression.

"I found out later from a mechanic that the braking system had been messed with. Someone had engineered an air leak and doctored the back up system."

Aggie said, "You're sure about that are you? Not your interpretation of what happened?"

"Of course I'm sure. The system is well maintained or it's not. That is – tampered with."

Aggie thought that she only had Kowalczyk's word for that. In fact, for the whole episode. She supposed that he had no reason to lie.

She said, "I'll need the name and contact number of that mechanic. The one who discovered the tampering."

Kowalczyk looked a little surprised.

"I don't have his number with me but I can get it to you. His name is Joseph Steinman."

"OK. If all of that checks out, there may be something there but, still, there could be other explanations for your failed braking system. Not that I know much about braking systems. Any other drivers or any of your trucks have trouble, things malfunctioning?"

Kowalczyk used his hands to push himself up into a more upright position.

Aggie wondered if it gave him time to think.

"No. Nothing that I recall."

"How many drivers do you have?"

"Just me and two others. Plus one occasional and the Waters kids if we are strapped. There is a driver retention problem nationally. It is approaching the critical stage these days. Drivers are looking for jobs with better conditions than they have in trucking."

Aggie said, "I'm not surprised. It's a tough job. So, just to be certain, there has been no mechanical problem with your trucks, other than these two instances."

"No."

"OK. Next, who can you think of that would do you harm? You seem convinced that someone is out there trying kill you. Any idea who might harbor a grudge, want you out of the way or just hate you enough to kill you?"

Kowalczyk's eyes widened.

"No I can't. I mean I'm not the sociable type, friendly or any of that. I have probably upset a lot of people but not to that extent."

Aggie pushed her chair back a little, leaned back and crossed her legs.

"So, we have a couple of events that may or may not be some kind of deliberate sabotage. Even if true, the intention may not have been to do you harm. Plus, you do not know of anyone who would want you gone. No ex-wife, angry partner or slighted lover – nothing like that?"

"You are diminishing my concerns again."

Aggie smiled.

"Perhaps I am but I don't have much to get my teeth into. On the face of it, it is an intriguing concept – only a concept, though. I have just a couple of questions before we finish here."

"OK. Fire away."

They both laughed at the inadvertent comment.

"Do you know the name Paul Wright?"

"No."

"What about Strum?"

Kowalczyk's eyes blinked rapidly as he said,

"Strum?"

"Yes."

"Hm. Unusual name. No, can't say that I do."

Aggie thought otherwise, her interest stimulated.

"The reason that I asked was that two guys showed up at the fire – sort of out of the blue. One had the name Strum."

"Oh. No, don't know him. Hard to forget a name like that."

Aggie looked down at her notes which had now covered several pages in her clipped style of writing. She switched back a thought or two.

"So, to be quite clear, you have had no disputes, lawsuits, contretemps, anything out of the ordinary that might lead to violence?"

"No."

Not wholly definitive but getting there.

"Has anyone been to see you here?"

"No. Only you and that was by arrangement."

Kowalczyk looked slightly crestfallen.

"I did let the partners know about it. Otherwise, there is no one."

"Good. Because, if there is anything in this, other drivers could be in danger. The company being the target and not you."

Aggie closed her notepad, sighed deeply, stretched, pushed her chair back a few inches and looked at Kowalczyk.

"Here's where I am. I want to make a few inquiries; do some research before I make a decision. There could be something going on, or not. What I cannot know is motive and I won't have that unless I can confirm your views about possible attempts on your life or, at least, the sabotaging of your trucks. Are you OK with that?"

"Yes, of course. You mean you will look into it all and let me know?"

"Yes. Give me a few days and I will be in touch."

Aggie paused. She did not use business cards.

"First, you have my phone number. I need the information on your partners and that mechanic. Addresses, emails, phone numbers, all that. Plus, of course, your information too."

Aggie tore a clean page from her notepad and wrote down her work email address before handing it to Kowalczyk. She stood but they did not shake hands, for which she was grateful.

She said, "Take care."

Kowalczyk nodded a thanks and she turned and left without looking back.

As she entered the elevator, Aggie felt satisfied that she had not yet committed to the case, if there was a case. One does not have to like a client to work for them but it helped if one did. She was ambivalent about Kowalczyk, because, although she sort of liked him, she was not comfortable with his assertions about the attempts on his life. Was he paranoid? She didn't know. There was just a germ of a possibility that he was not delusional, but that was all. If someone was trying to kill him, why use a truck? There were plenty of ways. Perhaps, it had to look like an accident but any investigation worth its salt would easily uncover tampering.

But, in the latest incident, nobody in an official capacity seemed to see anything amiss. Guy starts falling asleep, pulls off the road and a fire starts, perhaps during braking. Not overly suspicious. Why would they? She stepped out of the elevator and found Jonathan in conversation with two or three people working behind the counter. All were smiling and, as she approached, he broke away and came to meet her.

She said, "Sorry it took so long. Are you OK?"

"Not to worry – I'm fine. I've been learning a bit about this medical facility. It has 238 beds and has a group of resident physicians across several departments. But, enough about that. Fancy stopping off for a coffee and a sandwich?"

"Great. That sounds perfect."

They soon found a thriving café that was not fast food but offered breakfast fare and pastries. They settled in with a pot of strong coffee and two Danish pastries apiece. They were delicious and after several minutes of agreeable silence while they ate and finished their first cups of coffee, Jonathan said, "Do you feel like talking about it yet? You don't have to but, if you do, I'm here."

Aggie looked at him over the top of her cup.

"I think I do – just to get my head around it all. To see if I believe in the whole thing."

Jonathan remained silent while Aggie summarized the meeting she had had with Kowalczyk with as much detail as possible. When she had finished he looked at her quizzically.

"Would you like my considered opinion?"

She smiled and said, "Please. Go ahead."

Jonathan smiled in return. He was enjoying the camaraderie, the sharing of ideas. "Here's my initial perspective. An overview. Did the first incident happen and, if so, was it deliberate or accidental? That's obvious and important. And easily verifiable in terms of whether it happened or not. Then, the fire incident. Again, deliberate or the coincidental confluence of events. If any of this is deliberate, who did it and why? Don't count out the driver here, leave all of the options open."

They sipped their remaining coffee thoughtfully for a few moments and then Jonathan continued.

"Those are the major concerns. Smaller issues then emerge and would, in most cases, depend on how all of the above transpires. First, did you think to confirm with the medical facility that a drug was ingested by the driver? That is, was he telling the truth? Maybe, that is confidential but worth a try. If it is verified, then who gave it to him – and, incidentally, how? Of course, it also could have been self-administered. Next, insurance. Was the truck insured? If so, was it a reasonable agreement – no red flags? That is something that all three partners would have to be party to. Plus, the two guys showing up bothers me. You thought that the driver knew them or of them. Their appearance does not gel, at least not to me. You might follow up on them."

Jonathan put his cup down and lay both hands on the table.

"Finally, and I may think of more, what was the load? May or may not be relevant but, where was it going to and from and where did it originate? If deliberate, was it intended that the load be destroyed? Come to that, where is it now? Presumably, it survived."

Jonathan leaned back as Aggie put down her cup.

"That's it. Those are my humble machinations."

Aggie's face had taken on a grateful look.

"That is really helpful Jonathan. You've spelled it out perfectly for me. I was trying to get beyond the close up and personal and you have done just that for me."

"Good! My pleasure."

They paid up and headed for the journey back with the thought 'teamwork' flashing across Aggie's mind with no hint of resentment. In fact, the thought was accompanied by a touch of pleasure.

Chapter 5

Back in her apartment, Aggie sat on the couch and wrote up all of her notes on her iPad, including a careful summary of the interview – because that is what it had been – and Jonathan's take on it. On the way back they had talked some more. Jonathan was almost sure that when truck brakes fail, a trained investigator has to inspect the system and file a report with The National Transportation Safety Board, giving the cause of failure. The reason could still be poor maintenance, manual over adjustment, etc. and not malicious but it was worth checking.

Eventually, just before Jonathan dropped her off with a promise of dinner in a few days, Aggie had arrived at a point where she was considering taking on the case as a 'find out if anything is wrong' kind of investigation. Find out a yes or a no for Kowalczyk's assertions. If a yes, then there was a serious situation emerging which might lead to police involvement. That was all in the future. For now, she had all of the required information dutifully supplied by him via email. It was getting past lunchtime already and so, after a hasty repast of squeezed orange juice and a chunk of cheddar cheese, she called Kowalczyk. He was still at the hospital but getting dressed and ready for his discharge.

After a quick, straightforward discussion, they agreed to terms for Aggie's undertaking of the case on the basis of determining whether there was a problem or not – her usual retainer and expenses with a summary either by telephone or a meeting in two weeks to decide whether further work was needed. Kowalczyk had sounded surprised and pleased at the same time, straining, it seemed, to keep any eagerness out of his voice. She decided to get started straight away. After prioritizing, she thought that a call to the mechanic would be first, followed by research on Strum, the guy with him and Kowalczyk's partners and their families. She also planned to call the hospital to see if she could find out more information on the drug ingested by Kowalczyk. That felt like a long shot.

In addition, there was the truck and its load whereabouts and the insurance situation. Somewhere in there she knew she should call Jack also. It all portended to be a very busy afternoon and evening. She picked up her cell phone and called the mechanic.

"Hello"

"Mr. Steinman?"

"Yes. Who's this?"

"My name is Agnes Trout. I'm…"

Steinman's slow, intelligent voice interrupted her.

"If you're selling, I'm not buying."

"No, no. Nothing like that. I'm a Private Investigator. I've been talking to Mr. Kowalczyk who owns J. K. Trucking."

"Yes?"

"Did you know that he had an accident?"

There was a brief pause, then concern.

"No I didn't. Is he OK? Did he crash somewhere?"

"He is OK. His truck caught fire and he barely escaped."

Disbelief.

"What? It caught fire? That doesn't happen unless the engine overheated or something."

"No, it wasn't the engine. It was somewhere behind the cab."

"Well, that doesn't make much sense. How would a fire start there?"

Aggie paused.

"I don't know but it is one of the areas that I'll be looking at."

"Everything go up in flames?"

"No. As far as I know the load survived. Not sure about that. I don't even know what the load was."

"He's been shipping kitchen appliances and bathroom stuff lately but it could be anything. Except food. He doesn't ship anything perishable. You know, refrigerated and all that."

"Right. Now, he told me that you did all the mechanical work on his trucks."

In the silence that followed, Aggie glanced at the window where rain was beginning to spot the glass. Eventually, Steinman spoke.

"He did? What's all this about? Why does he want a private investigator?"

Aggie considered her answer in terms of confidentiality but decided to offer some background.

"Mr. Kowalczyk has had two unfortunate incidents with his trucks – that is while he has been driving. He wants me to look into the circumstances. At the moment I am just gathering information to see if any further incidents can be prevented."

"I see. Are you a NTSB Investigator?"

"No. Nothing like that."

With some relief in his voice, Steinman said carefully,

"I keep the trucks in good shape. Unless I am asked to do something specific. I do regular maintenance about once per month."

"Anything specific in the last few months?"

"No. Just normal maintenance."

Aggie pressed on.

"You found nothing strange about the braking systems."

"Strange?"

"Well, nothing wrong with them."

Aggie wished that she had more knowledge. She knew that she sounded vague.

"I mean, over adjustment of the stroke length, that sort of thing."

"Ah, I see where you are going – the time when the brakes went down about a year ago."

"Yes. I think so."

"Well, Mr. Kowalczyk did have a problem. The inspection called it the incorrect manual adjustment of the brake stroke length. It bothered me because, as far as I was concerned, everything was in good shape when I finished my maintenance."

"When was that? In relation to the failure."

"I would say about two weeks before."

Aggie drew in a deep breath.

"So what could have happened?"

"I don't really know. I assumed that another mechanic had worked on the truck."

"Did you talk about it with Mr. Kowalczyk?"

"No. We rarely meet. I just go in and do my job every so often. Then I email him to let him know that it has been done."

"He didn't discuss it with you to find out what happened?"

"No. As I said, I thought that another guy had worked on the truck – so he would have spoken to him, I suppose. I sort of let it go. Anyway, I fixed it and there hasn't been anything else."

Aggie idly watched rivulets of water running down her window. Kowalczyk hadn't checked it out further then. He must have dismissed it too, until this latest episode.

"So, you would say that Mr. Kowalczyk takes good care of his trucks?"

"Yes."

After a prolonged silence while Aggie scanned her mind for anything more to ask, Steinman broke in.

"There is one more thing."

Aggie responded.

"What's that?"

"Did you know about the tracker?"

"What's a tracker?"

"I found a tracking device on the truck."

"You mean a device for showing its location?"

"Yes."

"Is that normal?"

"Not at all – at least in my experience. Many trucks these days do have built in tracking systems – they are supposed to make better use of assets and faster delivery times but Mr. Kowalczyk's do not. Drivers do not like them."

Aggie made the vocal equivalent of a nod.

"Not that I look for that sort of thing. Just came across it near the transmission shaft. I can see owners wanting to know where their stuff is, you know, if there's been a problem."

"Like missing merchandise, false mileage?"

"Yes. Something out of the ordinary. Normally, you should trust people."

"Have you checked the other trucks for trackers?"

"Yes. Well, sort of. I just checked around out of curiosity. I didn't find any. I mean, I didn't go crazy, nothing obvious."

"Right. And you would know what to look for and where to look."

"Yes."

"Did you wonder about who put it there?"

"Not especially. Assumed it was ownership for some reason."

Aggie paused.

"Thank you for your time Mr. Steinman. You have been very helpful."

"You're welcome. Any time."

They rang off.

Aggie thought that Steinman had been open, if cautious, with her. He sounded like a good, reliable employee. The tracker device was interesting. It did not feel like a Kowalczyk move because, if he had any concerns about his truck locations, he could have installed current equipment to do that. It was probably not too expensive and he, himself, was one of the drivers anyway. So, someone was tracking his truck for reasons unknown at this point. Plus, in the earlier incident, the braking system had been either legitimately but incorrectly adjusted or tampered with.

Her next thought was where were the trucks housed? Were they easily accessible? Also, where was the damaged truck and its load? A closer look at it was looking crucial. She put her thoughts together in her iPad. She would need to talk to Kowalczyk again. During her talk with a Steinman, she had barely noticed an incoming telephone call registering on her iPad. It was there for a few seconds before it disappeared. She checked her cell and saw a missed call from a number that was familiar but not immediately identifiable. Then it clicked. It was from Dwight Forman, the husband of the flight attendant – her second divorce case.

Clearly, a call back was needed and so, reluctantly, because she was steeping herself in the Kowalczyk case, she clicked on the reply button. After only one ring Forman came on. There was urgency in his voice.

"Ms. Trout. Thank goodness you called back."

"OK, Mr. Forman. What's up?"

"Well, there's been a development. I need to talk to you."

Aggie wondered what the mystery was.

"What's the development? You can tell me now."

A pause with an intake of breath.

"Look, I can't talk about it now, especially on the telephone."

"Why ever not, Mr. Forman?"

After a much longer pause.

"I can't say at the moment. Can we meet somewhere and I can explain?"

"I suppose we could. If you don't mind me saying so, this all sounds a bit weird."

"I'm sorry. Perhaps it does but it would not take long. I have a babysitter here with my kids. I could meet you anywhere."

Several scenarios raced through Aggie's mind, none of them wholesome or pleasant. None of this felt right although she was being paid for her time by this client. She decided to go for a public place to meet him.

"Mr. Forman. If this is absolutely necessary, I can meet you in Central Park."

"Perfect. Where in Central Park?"

"There are seats next to the tennis courts for viewers. I'll be on one of those in about thirty minutes."

"Great. Thank you. I'll see you then."

His flat tone belied his words. They hung up. Aggie dropped her cell onto the coffee table and stared at it blankly. What was going on? Had Forman found out something about his wife? Evidence of her infidelity. If so, it had to be new because Aggie had found nothing, not even a hint. So, should she expect lies, false accusations? It would hardly be a surprise. She would soon find out.

She changed into sweats and sneakers and, leaving her Kowalczyk notes together with her iPad on the couch and coffee table, she headed out for Central Park. The rain had cleared up leaving the air clean and the pathways dry and dotted with walkers. Families with children were sitting or playing on the damp grass. She crossed over a road packed with intent looking bikers and runners and strolled towards the tennis complex. There were several empty benches alongside the courts which were almost all in use largely by doubles players of all ages. She chose a seat by four middle aged men pounding a tennis ball with gusto and good humor. All wore hats of some kind. The dampened courts seemed perfect with no dust flying about. She watched for a few minutes and realized that Forman might not show up. If that were the case, what was all this subterfuge about? And then she spotted him walking up the side of the first court towards her position at the back.

He was of slight build. As Aggie looked at him, she thought that he was medium all around. Medium height, unobtrusive though expensive clothing – grey flannels, white sports shirt, a brown jacket and sneakers with a grey ball cap sporting a yellow logo that she did not recognize. He was not especially attractive and, she thought, was someone who could easily disappear in a crowd. He made it to the bench, sat a couple of feet away from her and turned towards her. "Thanks for coming," he offered as he put an arm along the back of the bench and crossed his legs. Aggie did not respond but waited for him to continue speaking.

Chapter 6

He looked at her intently. Aggie held his stare, aware of various tennis match scores being called out after each piece of action and drifting through her consciousness, along with the sound of multiple thwacks of a ball striking strings. His eyes were hooded, the creases in his forehead softened. She decided to open the conversation.

"What's all this about then? Why so secretive?"

"I wouldn't say secretive. More like cautious."

While addressing her, he waved his arms around and leaned forward.

"My wife didn't show up last night."

"She didn't? Was she supposed to?"

Again, he used an arm dramatically to underscore his reply.

"She was supposed to be home around 1.00 am or so."

"You checked her flight times?"

Forman put his hands in his lap, studied them and looked up.

"Yes. I also confirmed that the crew members were aboard the flight. It landed just after midnight."

"Could she have gone to a hotel? Not well or tired, perhaps?"

Two arms again. Aggie wondered if he was on drugs or medication.

"She could have, of course. But she would have called. Anyway, why not recover at home?"

Aggie thought that to be reasonable. Unless she really was having an affair.

"Yes, I suppose so. What, exactly, is it that you want me to do? By the way, have you notified the police?"

Aggie glanced at the tennis. There seemed to be an inordinate number of lobs.

Forman stood up suddenly and looked down at her.

"No, not yet. I'll do that this evening, if she's not back. I'm not asking you to do anything – just information. Looks suspicious doesn't it?"

Aggie looked up at him, puzzled by this whole episode which struck her as unreal, almost absurd.

"Not really. There could be any number of genuine reasons for the delay. Illness, trouble with customs, airport delays, helping a colleague, you name it. But, if you are sure that your wife is missing, you should contact the police. The sooner the better. Waiting 24 hours is not the way to go these days."

Forman raised both arms halfway, hands outstretched.

"OK, then. Fair enough. I'll be in touch."

And with that, he turned and purposefully strode away, back in the direction from which he had entered Aggie's universe. Aggie watched him go. The four tennis players on the nearest court were shaking hands at the net. They looked tired, but happy. Two other players were standing by the fence at the back of the court, looking at their watches. Aggie watched all this reflectively as she digested the last twenty minutes or so. She did not recall Forman ever gesticulating in this peculiar way before. Something was up with him. She hadn't noticed whether his eyes had any indication of drug use but his behavior was certainly odd – much too animated for the conversation they had been engaged in. Maybe he had been taking acting classes! With that amusing thought, she stood up, stretched her legs, rubbed her butt unceremoniously where it had become numb from her awkward sitting position on the bench and strolled thoughtfully away. By the time she had reached her apartment, she had packed this whole episode into the back of her mind to percolate. She was surprised to see that it was already time to think about dinner. Plus, she needed a drink and time away from the clouds of thoughts coursing through her brain. She pulled her cell out of her bag and called Jack at work. To her pleasant surprise, he answered on the second ring.

"Hi Ag. How's things? Trip a good one?"

He sounded pleased to hear from her.

"Hi Jack. Yes it was good. Worthwhile anyway."

"Ah. Do I detect faint praise?"

"No, not really. But I have had a day or so of utter craziness. If you have the time I can tell you about it – but you are still at work I see."

Aggie was not keen to talk about anything at the moment, especially over the telephone. As he often did, Jack read her correctly.

"I am. Leaving soon though. Are we up for something?"

Aggie laughed.

"We are. I was hoping that you would go there."

"Great. Food? Shall I bring something?"

"Please. Your choice. I have wine."

"OK. I'll be about an hour."

They rang off.

Aggie had a bit of time now, so she turned her thoughts to the Forman meeting as objectively as she could and brought her notes up to date. Writing it out from memory made Forman's antics with his body language stand out in her mind with no conclusion being forthcoming yet. She was favoring some kind of drug induced performance which was not a good sign if, as he had intimated, he had just left his kids with a babysitter. He had lied to her several times during their business relationship and so she saw no reason to believe his current story now. She told herself to see what tomorrow brings. She had just finished setting up the coffee table for dinner, the wine and glasses being in the kitchen – a Liebfraumilch and dessert wine in the fridge with a red wine on the counter because she did not know what the meal was going to be – when Jack arrived. He was wearing a leather jacket, blue T shirt, sneakers and jeans. Tall with fair hair awry, he hugged and kissed her while holding a large brown paper bag. He put it on the floor next to the coffee table and tossed her a happy smile and a belated,

"Hi Ag."

He gestured to the bag.

"Health food. Hope that's OK."

"Great. Thanks Jack. Do you want to wash up?"

He nodded.

"Thanks."

Then he turned and headed for the bathroom as Aggie emptied the bag. There were two salads and two giant tuna salad sandwiches. Two bars of Cadbury's Fruit and Nut chocolate completed the contents of the bag. Aggie laid out the sandwiches on paper plates and left the two salads stacked at the side of the table. She fetched the bottle of Liebfraumilch from the fridge along with two glasses and waited for Jack, who soon joined her, minus jacket and with hair freshly combed. Aggie said, "This is perfect. Sandwich or salad first?"

"Sandwich. I'm rather hungry."

Aggie opened the wine and filled the two glasses. They both picked up at the same time, touched glasses and drank deeply.

Jack said, "This is good. Just what I wanted."

They put down their glasses and munched on the sandwiches in companionable silence, part of a well-established comfort with each other. After they had finished the sandwiches, Aggie summarized the recent events. Apart from his concern over Aggie's safety being next to a fire and a possible explosion, Jack listened quietly as they sipped wine, only once adding the comment that truckers were a tough, hardy bunch of men and women and knew how to take care of themselves. Aggie, more out of curiosity than anything, asked about truckers' unions. Jack said that, as far as he understood it, there was once a need for strong unions but most truckers did not now belong to a union, although there were some union jobs. He also added that the best trucks these days were essentially RV's with wi-fi, TV, small portable toilets, beds and more. These days, if a trucker could not find a parking spot for the night – they filled up quickly – there was an app which helped them to find one.

Aggie said, "Really? There is an app for just about everything these days. Even the word, or the abbreviation, did not exist until recently."

Jack sipped some wine.

"True. So what is your feeling about the trucking incident? You must think there is something there or you wouldn't have taken it on."

Aggie paused, glass in the air.

"Not necessarily. It is early days. I'm trying to keep an open mind but my instinct is that somewhere, somehow, the story is not right."

Jack smiled as he picked up the paper plates, took them to the kitchen and returned with new ones. They opened up the salads which seemed to be predominantly Arugula, added the dressing and began to eat. Jack raised his plastic fork and waved it for emphasis.

"Well, the old gut feeling is showing up again then."

Aggie nodded. "That's all it is right now."

They finished the salads, which Aggie thought were excellent, cleared away the plates and containers and sat back on the couch with the dessert wine and pieces of chocolate. The way that Jack had used his fork while talking had reminded Aggie of the afternoon meeting with Forman. She put off mentioning that for a few moments.

"How have things been with you?"

Jack put his glass down and popped a couple of pieces of chocolate into his mouth. After a moment or two he replied.

"Usual. I've been working a couple of cases. Just picked up another. A break-in on 69th. A Brownstone, owners away but housekeeper home. She was roughed up a bit. Only cash, jewelry, silver, small items taken in a D'Agostino bag. Two guys, disguised with some kind of face covers but both young and probably on foot."

Aggie said, "How's the housekeeper?"

"Shaken up more than anything else. Kept overnight at the hospital. Some bruising to her upper arms but I don't think they meant to hurt her."

"So you are talking to the housekeeper and looking for similars? Busy then."

"Yes, I have to get off early tomorrow."

They sipped some more dessert wine which was almost all gone.

Aggie said, "My second divorce case has taken a peculiar turn."

"What happened? Was that the stay at home guy?"

"Yes."

Aggie went through that afternoon's events.

Jack was looking tired and his only comment was,

"You have really picked up a couple of weird cases haven't you. I would watch this divorce guy. Nothing about him sounds kosher to me. I wouldn't see him on your own again, if I were you."

He smiled lazily and added,

"But I'm not am I?"

Aggie said, "Let's go to bed."

Burning trucks and strange divorce cases all faded away into oblivion as Aggie and Jack made love into the early hours.

Chapter 7

Jack left early the next morning to go to work. Aggie felt refreshed and emotionally strengthened to take up her research and pursue both current cases. Jack had looked happy and relaxed and so she assumed that he had taken on similar feelings. Over a cup of coffee and a slice of dry toast, she reviewed her notes. The Forman issue was really status quo. It was more of a wait and see situation which might well resolve itself sometime today. She wanted to build up some research background but she also felt that another look at the truck would be useful which, in turn, meant a call to Kowalczyk. A pity because she did not want to speak to him again so soon. She liked to have time to see where her feelings finally came to rest concerning his story and integrity. Her instincts were almost always spot on and they were telling her that something was amiss. It did not necessarily mean that Kowalczyk was not being forthright but it could be the case. She didn't know yet. So, reluctantly, she put in a call to him. He answered almost immediately.

"Hi Ms Trout. That was quick. Do you have some news for me?"

His tone was flat and Aggie knew that he was not expecting anything.

"Sorry. I'm calling to ask a couple of questions."

Kowalczyk did not sound too disappointed.

"OK. Anything I can do."

"First one – where is your truck now? It must have been towed."

"Oh. Yes, it's still with the towing company. I did have the load transferred though. Security reasons."

"So, it will remain there, I assume, until a claims adjuster can get to it."

Aggie had recently been through the insurance labyrinth herself.

"Correct."

"Could I have the towing company address?"

There was a significant pause at this point which Aggie noted.

"Oh. Of course."

He gave Aggie the company address which was proximate to Paterson, New Jersey.

"Are you thinking of taking a look?"

Aggie was equivocal.

"Not sure yet. I was wondering if the trip would be worth it."

Kowalczyk offered help as Aggie drained her coffee.

"Well, if you do decide to go, just give my name if confirmation is needed."

Aggie responded.

"Thanks. What was the load by the way?"

"Oh. Boring stuff. Kitchen equipment. You know, cabinets, sinks, faucets, counters, that sort of thing. A Home Depot run."

"Right. I was curious about the name of your company. Is there a difference between trucking and hauling? Nothing to do with the case."

His tone became lighter, which was what Aggie wanted.

"Not really. I didn't think about it much. I just liked the word trucking rather than haulage. Trucking is about moving merchandise, sometimes just with one company or business. Haulage is more about what a trucker will do. That's my take on it anyway."

"Interesting. Are your trucks garaged when not in use?"

Kowalczyk was up to the change in topic.

"Oh yes. We have a steel hangar, two in fact. Lock ups."

Aggie asked, "Always locked when not in use?"

"Well that's the idea. I can't say always locked up because I don't know that. I would hope so."

"Good. Well I'm almost done, I think. Oh, there is one more thing. Do you track your vehicles? The ones that you are not driving that is."

Quite a lengthy pause.

"What?"

"Just wondered if you checked on their whereabouts occasionally. You know, electronically or other ways."

Kowalczyk recovered.

"That's a strange question. No, of course not. No need to."

"Just background Mr. Kowalczyk. I need all I can get if you want answers."

"Right. Took me by surprise, that's all."

Aggie thought it was time to wrap it up.

"Thanks. We are done. Have a good day."

"And you. Bye."

They hung up.

Aggie washed up her cup and headed to the couch. She brought her notes up to date and reviewed her new information. She thought that Kowalczyk was careful when she asked about the truck whereabouts, what load it was carrying and her suggestion of a visit to see it. Clearly now, she had to go and have another look at the truck. As the load had been removed she could not physically confirm what it had been and she hoped that it did not become crucial to her investigation. If it did, she supposed that there had to be a manifest somewhere. There was, as she expected, insurance involved but that too did not seem important at this point. Kowalczyk had been adamant that he did not track his vehicles. There had been genuine surprise in his voice although that could have been because she asked the question.

It was worth keeping that in mind. Odds were that someone else had put a tracking device on the truck he was driving. She felt that a trip to the towing company would be useful just to get a new look at the fire damage and, perhaps, an inkling as to what had caused it. It was now late morning and the urge to do anything connected to a case had seriously waned in Aggie's deliberations. Exercise! The thought leapt into her consciousness. A trip to the gym was in order. With burgeoning enthusiasm, she pulled out her workout attire and headed for her gym facility, where she performed a solid kickboxing session and some light weight work. She followed that with half an hour of meditation in a personal 'quiet room'. Back in her apartment, after a shower and a cucumber and tomato sandwich, she sat on her couch with a glass of ice water and gazed at her latest notes looking for the clarity which she had felt was eluding her. She realized that the Forman meeting with its peculiar and odd atmosphere had tainted her thoughts and actions. She carefully put it out of her mind to await further developments and turned her thinking towards the Kowalczyk case. She considered going to the New Jersey towing company that afternoon but it felt like too much. She was intuitively convinced that the appearance of the two men at the truck fire was more than fortuitous, plus the vibes she got from Strum were not pleasant. Tomorrow morning would do nicely for the New Jersey trip with the rest of today being research, beginning with Strum.

Over the next hour or so Aggie found the most likely Strum character was Tig Strum who ran a large Ford dealership in Bergen County with a partner named Michael Westlake. In addition to the dealership setup there was a secondary financial business, or, maybe it was the primary business. As far as Aggie could tell, the company arranged loans or lent capital to small or medium industrial businesses like scrap metal, junk yard car parts, trucking, farm machinery and garages.

The interest rates were high but not in the region of, say, loan sharking. That probably meant that the businesses they lent to could not get reasonable interest rates anywhere else. She needed to know if all of this was legitimate and if the dealership was some kind of front for something else. There was no obvious reason for thinking this way but Aggie wanted to know. She would ask Jonathan or Jack if they could find out. One interesting tidbit of information was that Michael Westlake was well educated. He had a degree in Psychology. She stared at the information distractedly. She thought that it took all sorts but why a dealership then? Probably more viable financially than any educative endeavor. There it was, then. All that she had, unless Jonathan or Jack could come up with something – she was moving towards the former as she would see him in a day or so. The dealership was within striking distance of the towing company and so Aggie began to consider a trip to both on the same day. What she could glean from a dealership visit was uncertain except that she always preferred face to face engagement because something often popped up from it or pointed her in another direction. Surely, anyone called Tig must, at least, be interesting. She needed a break from her research and so put in a call to the hospital that had taken care of Kowalczyk. Eventually, she reached an administrator who, at least, was purported to have the correct access for her query. After some preliminary jousting, during which she introduced herself and explained the circumstances of her mission, Aggie got to the point.

"So, I was trying to identify the drug, or its generic composition, that Mr. Kowalczyk ingested."

The administrator said, "I'm sorry but that information is confidential.

Even to the point of whether there was a drug or not."

Aggie countered, "But Mr. Kowalczyk has engaged my services."

"That may be. In that case he could inform you himself."

"He could but he seems to have no idea what the drug was – just that it caused him to pass out."

"Well, then I'm afraid that you will have to get him to contact us so that he can find out for himself."

Aggie needed just a little more from this contretemps.

"Find out what for himself?"

A large sigh preceded the response, which was heavy with sarcasm.

"Find out what the drug was, of course."

"OK. That seems to be it then."

"Indeed it is Ms.... er Trout."

They hung up.

Aggie was now sure, or fairly sure, from the wording of this conversation that Kowalczyk had taken a drug in some form or other, willingly or not. It struck her as interesting that she had that last thought – willingly or not. It meant that deep down, she was still harboring some ambivalence about her client. It wouldn't be the first time. She often found herself in need of convincing. That was why she was a good investigator. She wrote up her findings and decided on an indulgent late afternoon and evening. Predominantly vegetarian Indian takeout with a couple of glasses of Malbec defined that time followed by a rerun of last week's Bill Maher show.

She always enjoyed his comedic outlook and the way that he approached issues of all kinds unflinchingly and head on. As it happened his final guest monopolized the conversation too much, although the panel, as almost always, was brilliant.

She wound up reading into the early hours. She had just acquired Neil deGrasse Tyson's book on Astronomy and loved the easy flowing, readable writing style used to present an essentially demanding topic. She fell asleep wondering how to imagine tiny intervals of time in seconds, expressed in dozens of zeros after the decimal point.

Chapter 8

Aggie awoke later than she expected, having had a full, restful night's sleep which she valued these days because they were not as plentiful as they used to be. She hurried through her shower and cereal breakfast along with two cups of her filtered coffee – black with sweetener, having, not for the first time, forsaken using a creamer. Just over an hour later, wearing sweats, a white tee shirt and sneakers, she was driving a rental Camry, under a heavy, grey sky with no rain, towards her first stop which would be the towing company. She had considered taking an Uber because it was so easy and comfortable and some drivers were interesting and entertaining, albeit, the cost was now increasing which, she supposed, was inevitable. But, since she planned to have a shot at a visit to the Ford franchise too, the rental was less complicated and cheaper. Without the fun of bringing her own musical playlists with her – her car had been destroyed during a previous case – she had to rely on the radio. Her tastes were fairly eclectic but she enjoyed only some of the musical offerings, catching just one of her favorite performers, Anna von Hausswolff performing Track of Time. With her attention divided between the music and the many fragments of connected thought turning over in her mind, she was barely aware of the fact that she was almost at her destination.

She was now driving through suburban roads with the occasional appearance of a small business, including a brick and tile company, a car rental company and the odd anonymous warehouse, squeezed in between residential establishments. Then, suddenly, there it was – a large compound which was mostly concreted and fenced in by stout chicken wire fencing covered in a black fabricated material which was not quite opaque. The fence was about six feet in height with the covering reaching to within a foot from the top. Fence posts were made of tubular steel. There was no razor or barbed wire in evidence. Trees, in surprisingly good shape, rose from the edge of the paving which ran alongside the fencing.

As Aggie reached the entrance she saw that it was comprised of two substantial gates made of the same wire and tubular steel as the fencing and which were both opened to a ninety degree angle to the fence. One of the open gates was draped with lengths of heavy chain and a hefty padlock. She pulled slowly through the entrance, noting a large hangar type building in one back corner with a smaller building next to it. There was some heavy looking, serious machinery next to the buildings. There were neat rows or groups of vehicles in various stages of damage, ranging from almost demolished to untouched – maybe the latter having been towed for legal infringements. Among these she saw larger vehicles, vans and, close to the back of the compound, a couple of containers or trailers, one of which carried the logo J K Trucking Inc. on it, printed across the trailer in a large arc. There were wide access pathways through all of this surreal metalwork leading to the back corner of the compound. A small one story building near the entrance gate appeared to Aggie to be the most likely source of a reception area although there were no indications of that or, indeed, what the business here was.

She parked next to the building, which had no designated parking spaces, but did have a Silverado truck parked at an angle. She got out of the Camry and walked up to the only entrance, a green door with a single dirty window, covered by a screen door. Aggie drew the screen door outwards amid the sound of squealing, untended hinges and tapped sharply on the door before turning the dented brass knob and pushing it inwards. She stepped through the doorway into a very warm, stuffy room dominated by a very large man in a boiler suit, the top half of which was hanging down. He had flaming red hair and a strong, darker beard that was somewhat unruly and was perched on a metal desk amid sheafs of paper, pens, pencils and several trays with paperweights, pieces of cardboard, measuring devices from rulers to micrometers and unidentifiable objects. The walls were mainly cork boards with papers pinned all over them. The word chaos sprang into Aggie's mind but did not seem adequate.

She said, "Good morning. Sorry if this is inconvenient."

The man said, "Not at all. Good morning. What can I do for you?"

He had a loud, booming voice, unsuited to the small room and had an accent that was clearly New England. Aggie introduced herself and said that she had been hired by Kowalczyk to look into a few issues for him, one of which was to inspect the towed truck that belonged to him.

The man said, " I'm Steve, by the way."

Aggie nodded.

He carried on, "Ah. I understand but I don't know that you have his permission to take a look."

"Well, you can look me up if you have to. And, you could call Mr. Kowalczyk."

He climbed off the desk, shook himself and strapped the top of the boiler suit into place. He was a full foot taller than Aggie and very imposing.

He said, "OK. I won't need to do that. You are only looking. I'll take you down to see it."

Aggie murmured, "Thank you."

She followed him out of the door and walked alongside him on the concrete pathway.

He said, "So that's your business. Investigating?"

"Yes. I like it and as long as I do like it, I'll keep doing it."

"Right, good. What does this guy want you to look at?"

Aggie offered, "Well, as you know, there was a fire. I need to see that to find out, if possible, how it started."

They were approaching the back of the compound, close to large winches and a crane.

"Well, that might be difficult."

"Why?" Aggie queried.

"A woman came by yesterday and took away some stuff."

"Stuff?"

They had reached the burned cab, over in the opposite corner of the lot from the buildings.

"Yes. A bunch of wires and odds and ends from in there."

He indicated the back of the cab which was seriously damaged by the fire. Aggie stared at the area and saw that several cables had been cut and there were just loose ends showing amongst the charred and blackened debris. Nothing of consequence was visible. Aggie turned to the guy, Steve. "You just let this woman come in and do that? You checked me out."

Steve said, "No. it was by appointment. She called first."

"Did she say where she was from?"

"Yes. J K Trucking. What's the matter, then?"

Aggie said, "Well, as you can see, I have no way of checking how the fire started."

"True. Electrical, I would think. But unusual though. When you look at it, what is there to burn?"

"What do you mean?"

"Well, the cab is badly damaged. I mean, sure, maybe it was an electrical short. That would do it."

Aggie drew her eyes away from the cab and looked at Steve.

"But?...."

"What would sustain the fire? Keep it going?"

"Cables, plastic, rubber."

He waved a large arm in the general direction of the rear of the cab.

"Yes, but enough for all of this?"

"Have you seen it before?"

Steve responded, "Can't say that I have but I don't get semis very often. I tow smaller rigs and regular vehicles usually."

He added with a pleasant smile, "Maybe I'm reading too much into it. I suppose it is possible – what happened."

Aggie wasn't sure either way. Could there have been an accelerant? A bit fanciful. She sighed. They then walked over to the container which revealed nothing. It was just blackened and empty. She looked at the side of it with the logo written in an arc and the address and telephone information down in one corner. She wondered idly how difficult it was to put the logo in an arc at the center of the trailer side. The only item of interest on the back of the trailer was a sticker which said 'How am I driving?' Beneath it was a telephone number to call and offer an opinion. As they walked back towards her car she said,

"What was she like, this woman?"

Steve thought for a moment.

"About your height and size, black slicker and ball cap. It was raining then."

"How convenient!"

"What?"

"Oh, nothing. Just not much to go on."

"No, I suppose not."

"Did you get a sense of her age? You know, young or older."

"On the younger side I would say. Your age perhaps. She did drive a Cherokee, though. Nice. Dark green."

Aggie smiled as they reached her car.

"Well, that's something. Thank you."

Steve paused and then took a pencil and a piece of crumpled paper out of one of his many pockets. He wrote a number on it – left handed Aggie noted – and handed it to her with what approached a sympathetic smile.

"OK, then. Call me if I can help."

With that, he turned abruptly and headed for his office. Aggie hopped into the Camry and sat quietly for a few moments absorbing the visit before firing up the engine and heading towards the Ford dealership. About forty minutes later and in deep thought, Aggie found herself turning right at some traffic lights with the dealership ahead alongside the left side of the road taking up over half a block on a gentle downward slope with a stretch of grass dividing it from the road. It was a single story extensive building with rows of plastic brightly colored flags fluttering in the light breeze. Aggie drove across the road and into the complex past rows of new and pre-owned cars, pulling up close to a reception sign and parking. As she climbed out of the Camry, she looked at the cars and, with some amusement, thought of how 'pre-owned' had replaced 'second hand' in the lexicon. It did sound more attractive though. Looking around her, she assumed that there were workshops and storage areas at the back of the building which was the usual way that these places worked. She could see more rows of cars at the side of the building and thought that there were probably more out back. Quite a big operation then. She entered through automatic sliding doors and was confronted by a long counter behind which were seated five reception staff, each partially blocked by a computer. She was greeted by two people at once and chose to speak to a young fresh faced woman.

"I do not have an appointment but I would like to speak with Mr. Strum, if he is in."

Aggie glanced to the side as she spoke where a line of four or five offices stretched down one wall. All were made of glass but the first one had frosted glass up to about four feet above the floor. She assumed that office housed her quarry, or one of them. The receptionist responded.

"Could I have your name please and your business and I will see if Mr. Strum is available."

Aggie smiled to herself. This was a car dealership. She wasn't trying to see the CEO of Exxon. She gave her name and said that she had important personal business to discuss. The receptionist's expression plainly indicated that that information would not be enough. She spoke quietly into a telephone at her side and was shortly nodding her head.

"Mr. Strum can see you in a few minutes. Could you wait over there please and I will call you when he is ready."

She pointed to several armchairs over by a well-lit window area. The thought occurred to Aggie that this was the old make them wait ploy. Well, at least, she would get to speak to Strum. She hoped that, after all of this he was the correct Strum. She did not think that there was much doubt about it. She sat in a comfortable armchair and waited, wondering what she would say. She liked to be prepared but was also a fan of playing it by ear. She was quite sure that Strum would get a look at her before their meeting and so she just stared out of the window, taking in the now calm colored flags. About five of so minutes later the receptionist came over to Aggie and said,

"Mr. Strum will see you now."

She led Aggie to the first office, the one with frosted glass, and showed her through the doorway. It was the guy from the truck fire, sitting behind a large mahogany desk, replete with a blue suit, open necked white shirt and sleeked back hair. Aggie held his gaze as she approached. He looked her over with no expression of approval or disapproval – just a kind of cool assessment. He brought his arms up and rested his elbows on the desk, his hands clasped together. Although he obviously knew her name, she said,

"My name is Agnes Trout."

He responded, "Really."

"Yes. We met at the truck fire a few days ago."

Strum smiled faintly with no hint of mirth.

"Well, met is a bit of a stretch. Same place at the same time."

Aggie paused a moment and said, "Right. You would be Mr. Strum I take it."

Strum said, "You take it correctly. My friends call me Tig. You can continue to call me Mr. Strum."

Aggie responded quickly.

"Did you say Tig or Tick?"

Strum's elbows dropped flat to the desk, his hands still clasped as a flash of irritation crossed his features.

"Tig."

He then spelt out the name in a flat tone, his eyes unblinking.

"What do you want?"

Aggie was still standing as Strum had made no effort to offer her seating. She took the initiative.

"Can I sit or do you want me standing all the time?"

He just waved an arm towards the two chairs in front of the desk and said,

"Sit."

Aggie did so, on one of the chairs.

"Thank you. To get right to the point, what were you doing there? At the truck fire."

Strum's face momentarily assumed a puzzled expression followed by one of annoyance.

"What do you mean? I was out for a drive. None of your business anyway."

"Well, it is now. I am a private investigator and the driver of that truck has engaged my services to look into that fire."

"A private investigator? So what. What has that got to do with me?"

Strum was sitting more upright now, alert and wary.

"I don't know. Maybe nothing. But, you did show up at a somewhat convenient time and I want to find out all that I can about all of those people that were there."

Strum said, "Convenient time? What kind of garbage is that? Think what you like. What were you doing there, come to that?"

"Oh, you know, out for a drive. None of your business."

Strum took his arms off the desk and sat back in his chair, eying Aggie as he did so. He was struggling mightily with the notion of respect for another human being, a woman at that. He seemed to come to a decision.

"OK. What's on your mind?"

Aggie jumped right in.

"Did you start the truck fire. You know, with some kind of smart device?"

Strum looked genuinely shocked, his blue eyes widening in disbelief.

"No. Of course not. Are you crazy?"

Before Aggie could respond he added.

"I could ask you to leave you know. Right now."

Aggie said, "You could. But why would you?"

"Because you have rolled up here unannounced and you are making absurd accusations. There is no reason why I should put up with it. Put up with you."

Aggie read the face. Strum was playing angry. Testing the situation. She made no move to get up and leave.

She said, "How's your partner?"

"My partner? What do you mean?"

"Mr. Westlake. Your partner. I wondered if he might be interested in our conversation."

Strum now fully embraced the concept of respect for Aggie. He still needed time to think. He shifted in his chair, sat more upright and focused the blue eyes on a spot just above Aggie's hairline.

"Look. Would you like a coffee or something?"

"That would be very welcome. Thank you."

Strum put a quick call in to somewhere in the building.

"How long have you been, er, investigating? Taking on cases, that is."

"Several years now."

Aggie nodded around the room.

"What about all of this? How long?"

"Eleven years and counting."

Just then a young guy came in with two paper cups of black coffee, some creamers, a plate of Oreos and two plastic stirrers.

Strum said, "Sorry, didn't get any sweeteners or sugar."

Aggie said, "That's fine." She poured one creamer in and they both sipped a little coffee. Strum looked up.

"What do you really want? I mean, why did you come here?"

Aggie felt that the time had arrived to put some thoughts on the table.

"I'll go back a bit. I came upon the truck burning, as you probably know, found the driver unconscious and got him out of the cab with another guy. You showed up with your sidekick – sorry, partner, just afterwards. It looked to me as if you had been following the truck. On the other hand, your arrival could have been a coincidence. That aside, a fire starting where it did is very unusual. Plus, once started, it does not have a lot of fuel to maintain it. Remember, you checked it out, as did I. Bottom line, maybe a deliberate fire so who started it. That's what I'm looking at." Strum had remained quiet and attentive. He stared into the distance through one of the glass walls. He returned his gaze to Aggie.

"My partner and I run this dealership. It is going well. It is reasonably profitable. There are ups and downs, times when not much happens but pretty good on the whole. We needed more income."

His features almost cracked a smile. The intent was there anyway.

"Doesn't everyone? So we started up a financial operation. People need money. We had accumulated some capital and began lending. That has been doing very well indeed. That income backed up the franchise and then some."

He leaned forward.

"Here's the thing. Some people don't accept their responsibilities."

Aggie said, "They don't pay up."

"Exactly."

"Do you strong arm them? Baseball bats. That sort of thing?"

Strum looked askance.

"I hope you are joking. That is not our scene."

Aggie had a doubt or two.

With a smile she said, "Your partner, though, looks very fit and has the build of, say, a fixer. Or, have I been watching too many movies?"

"Indeed, you must have. He is a very smart guy and, as I said, we don't work that way."

Aggie could not help risking a little dig to test the new found compliance.

"He's the smart one?"

Strum's eyes flashed momentarily but that was all.

"As you say, he is the smart one. On the other hand, I am the savvy one. There is a difference."

"There is. No offense intended. So, where does that leave us?"

"None taken. Well, your driver, Mr. Kowalczyk, is one of the aforementioned borrowers."

"He owes you."

"He does."

"A lot?"

"Depends how one defines a lot. But, yes. A substantial amount when one considers the concept of cash flow."

Aggie now saw strands of her case beginning to fall into place. Parts of it anyway.

"So, Mr. Strum, can I assume that your being at the truck fire was less than fortuitous? I am not implying bad intent here. I am looking for clarification."

Strum put both hands flat on his desk.

"Let's not dance around this. We were following Kowalczyk to see if we could meet up somewhere – maybe a truck stop or an overnight- to discuss the matter of financial restitution. No bad intent implied."

"You were going to confront him?"

Strum said, "Yes, put our case, if you like."

"Would Mr. Westlake have been the one to put your case?"

Strum looked annoyed and amused at the same time.

"Crossed a line there, Ms. Trout."

Aggie responded, "Understood. Not my purview."

She continued. She needed to tie up one more loose end.

"You were a long way back if you wanted to meet up with Mr. Kowalczyk. What if he turned off or something. I assume that you did not know what his route might be."

Strum actually smiled as he settled back in his seat and looked directly at Aggie.

"You know, don't you?"

"Know what?"

"I'm wondering if you are fishing."

"I'm not. What do I know?"

"OK. About the tracker?"

Aggie smiled.

"Yes. I do know about the tracker."

"You mean that we have just been through all of this BS and you knew all along?"

It was not an aggressive response, more with a tinge of admiration.

"No. I did not know all of this. I had ideas and I was confirming them."

Strum said, "Well, if I need an investigator anytime, I know where to come."

"Thank you Mr. Strum. I appreciate that."

"What's next on the agenda?"

Aggie stood, drank the rest of her cold coffee and returned the cup to the desk. The Oreos remained untouched. She knew that Strum was not entirely off the hook. There were still things to check out but the situation had clarified rather nicely.

"This has been very helpful. I can now move in a different direction. I can put my time and energy to good use somewhere else."

She thought that was suitably vague and no less than Strum expected. He stood up also and said,

"Well, good luck with your new direction,"

He made no attempt to shake hands or to move forward around his desk. She had been dismissed but that was OK. She nodded to Strum, turned and walked out of the office, feeling his eyes on her back as she did so. She reversed her incoming path past the front counter, which was bustling with activity and through the sliding doors to her car, which, to her surprise had been washed down. Some kind of courtesy wasted on a rental. She took one last look around, taking in the flags, the tiny drops of water on the Camry and the sign hanging unobtrusively in one of the windows which said, 'We try to please', before opening the car door and hopping in. After she had put on her safety belt, she checked her cell phone and saw that she had two missed calls. The screen indicated NYPD but it was not Jack's number. She fired up the engine and began the journey back to the city, the messages beginning to weigh on her mind. Why would the cops be calling her? What could have happened? Maybe it was just for some information. On one of her cases but which one? Nothing to interest them. If it was a case, it had to be the truck one – Kowalczyk. It felt messy, unresolved to a large extent but she was making progress. As usual, it was the unknown that caused anxiety. She would call when she got back, even though it was now late afternoon. It was only a few minutes later that her cell rang – she had reverted from several different cell ringtones to a normal ring- and went to message. She decided to pull off the road onto the hard shoulder and check things out. She thought how ironic it would be to be picked up by the police while on a cell phone to the police. Did New Jersey not allow cell use during driving? She thought so. There were no messages from NYPD so she called the number shown. After several rings, it was answered.

"Hollis." Short and sweet.

"Hi. I'm Agnes Trout, returning your call. Actually three of them."

"Ah, Yes. I am Detective Ray Hollis. Can I have a word with you sometime today?"

"Well, apart from the fact that you are doing that, I am driving in New Jersey. Some way from the city. Can we do it now?"

"I take it that you are not literally driving."

Rhetorical.

He continued, ignoring her question.

"Well, can my colleague and I drop by to see you when you get back?"

Aggie was concerned.

"You mean at my apartment? What's all this about? Is someone in trouble?"

After a short pause Hollis responded.

"I cannot discuss the matter on the telephone Ms. Trout. I need to see you in person, please."

Aggie pushed back.

"What is the nature of all this? At least, give me a clue. I'm not agreeing to anything without some sort of information."

"I cannot do that Ms. Trout. The sooner we meet the better is all I can say. I might add that I can ask you to come directly here if I need to."

Aggie sensed that this was serious. She was having dinner with Jonathan tomorrow night. This was late Friday afternoon. She wanted time to think. Maybe call Jack.

"It has to be today does it? I'm still in New Jersey. I'll be back about 6.00 or so. But there are things that I have to do."

Hollis said, "That's fair. How about 8.30 this evening."

"OK. My address is…"

Hollis interrupted.

"We know where you live. See you then."

Chapter 9

Aggie reached her apartment just before 6.00 pm, having dropped off the freshly cleaned rental. No 'thank you's' at the car rental agency. She put her keys, iPad and bag on the coffee table and headed for the shower, shrugging off her shoes, clothes and underwear as she went. Thinking in the shower seemed to be imbued with more clarity than out of it. As she shampooed and soaped up, she decided to call Jack as soon as she was dry. She needed some sustenance also and knew that the frozen spaghetti and meatballs in her freezer was the most expedient way to go. Out of the shower, dry and dressed in fresh sweats with bare feet, she called Jack. With a huge sigh of relief, she heard him pick up.

"Hi Ag. What's up?"

"Still at work?"

"Yeah. For a while yet. Is this a social call?"

Aggie couldn't help smiling which stayed in her voice.

"No. Sorry but soon, maybe. I think I have a problem. Well, maybe not but something's up."

She told Jack about the calls and the upcoming meeting.

Jack said, "What's this guy's name again?"

"Hollis."

"Detective Hollis?"

"Yes. I'm not sure where he's from."

Jack paused and said, "Give me a minute."

Aggie heard the phone laid down and computer keys tapping.

Jack came back on.

"This guy is missing persons or, at least, part of his expertise is. I don't know him but if he's coming to you, it's important, serious. You have to be careful what you say to him."

Aggie said, "But I don't know what he wants."

"Well, it's not your truck guy or, at least, it doesn't seem that way. Do you want me to come over?"

"That would seem strange wouldn't it?"

"Nah. Not really. Thing is he might take the interview to the precinct if he is not happy with the situation. He's not going to commit to asking questions unless the circumstances are right for him. It will be one on one with him at some point. I could come over you know. We might find out something."

Aggie responded,

"Do I need a lawyer?"

"Not at this stage. But be careful. No extra information. Don't answer or say anything that you don't want to. In fact, if you are uncomfortable, shut it down and tell him to leave. He will go."

"Sounds a bit serious."

"No. That's when you get a lawyer. But this may be just fact finding."

"I don't know anyone who is missing."

"You won't know until he tells you. If someone actually is missing. Who is his partner?"

Aggie paused.

"I'd forgotten there were two of them. He didn't say."

Jack was concerned.

"Look, I'll come over if you want."

Aggie filled with resolve.

"No. I'll handle it, thanks."

"OK, then. If you're sure. Let me know how it goes. I'll make sure that I'm near the phone."

"OK. Thanks Jack."

"Bye. I'll be waiting."

Aggie put down the phone and sank back into the couch. She felt tired and hungry. Couldn't do much about the first but she could take care of the second. A few minutes later she was tucking into the comfort food. It tasted quite good and she demolished it quickly while thinking of the visit to come in an hour or so. She would have loved a glass of Shiraz but ice water it would have to be. She needed her wits about her. There was no point in second guessing the purpose of the visit so she contented herself with putting out the requisites for some coffee or tea for her visitors – no cookies – and making sure that the visible part of the apartment looked reasonable. Almost on the dot, her buzzer went off and she was soon ushering a man and a woman into her apartment. The man had a baggy, tired looking face, aged before his time, though he was tall and slim. The woman was small, trim and had almost expressionless features with alert grey green eyes and dark straight hair. He took over the introductions.

"I am Detective Ray Hollis and this is Detective Jade Zhou. I assume that you are Agnes Trout."

Agnes said, "You are correct."

She offered them seating. Hollis in the armchair and Zhou on the couch between them.

"Would you like some coffee or tea."

Both opted for black coffee with sugar. Aggie made it three and all soon had a mug of coffee in front of them.

Hollis said, "Nice apartment."

Aggie said, "I like it."

She realized and expected that there would be something of a preamble. She knew that most procedural interviews began with introductions, small talk and a settling in process. She did not herself subscribe to this method too often but allowed the circumstances to dictate her methodology. Hollis continued.

"It appears that you have friends in the force."

"I know some people. Yes. My profession almost ensures that."

"Well, it ensures that you are known. Not necessarily by friends, though."

Aggie bristled internally but did not show it.

"A little harsh wouldn't you say."

Hollis readjusted his baggy features into the semblance of a smile.

"Yes. I'm sorry. By the way, speaking of friends, you should know that I had a call from Jack Coletti just before I left the office. He appears to be one of those friends."

Aggie felt a rush of gratitude. Jack was trying to support her at a distance.

"He is. Now, why are you here?"

It was clear that Hollis was determined to follow his usual way of doing things. They all paused and drank some coffee. He wanted Aggie to keep wondering what all this was about. Zhou had remained silent, watching Aggie from the side. He took a file from a thin briefcase he was holding.

"I understand that you were involved in some shenanigans with a sexual predator and a dentist a few months ago."

"If, by shenanigans, you mean attacked in my apartment here by one guy and nearly killed by the other, yes."

Aggie was remaining calm, waiting for the reason for the visit. Unless this was the reason.

"Ah. I did not mean to minimize your travails, er, ordeals. I was really aiming at levity."

"Bit difficult with that subject matter don't you think. Why are you here?"

Again, Hollis ignored her question.

"Indeed. What happened to those two guys by the way? I am curious."

Aggie knew that it was quite easy to find out about any of this stuff but she played along to see where it was going.

"I believe one is in jail here for a very long time and the other is in jail in London. Or, near London. In the Home Counties."

"Why London?"

"It's where he went to escape the law here. He committed more crimes there. As far as I know, possession of weapons and drugs. Something like that. Said he was set up but he's been put away for seven years, I believe."

Hollis said, "Right. That's good then isn't it."

Aggie added, "Yes it is. I'm happy with it. So, shall we get on with this. Almost an hour has passed and I'm tired."

Hollis and Zhou looked at each other and, after an imperceptible nod from Hollis, Zhou cleared her throat and, in a soft voice began.

"Ms. Trout. You are listed as a Private Investigator. Correct?"

"Listed?"

"Your profession then is a Private Investigator?"

"Yes."

"How many cases are you currently working on?"

Aggie resisted.

"That is confidential information, as far as I am concerned."

"I see. I am asking how many. Not what they are or whom they concern."

Aggie said, "The answer is still the same."

Zhou's eyes blinked and her mouth turned down at one side.

"Are you, for example, dealing with any divorce cases?"

"I might be. Would you care to elaborate."

"You are not being helpful, Ms. Trout."

"Well, you aren't giving me anything to be helpful about."

Hollis interrupted.

"You do realize that we could ask you to come in for an interview, don't you."

Aggie replied.

"I do. And if I did do that, I would ask for a lawyer to be present before I answered a single question."

More exchanges of meaningful looks between Hollis and Zhou. Zhou crossed her legs and leaned towards Aggie.

"Here's the thing. Do you know Dwight Forman?"

The stay at home dad whom Aggie had met in Central Park.

Aggie weighed her answer. She saw no reason not to acknowledge knowing at least the name.

"Yes. I do know the name."

She sensed that they had passed an important point in this conversation.

"As a client?"

"I did not say that."

Zhou's eyes narrowed.

"What are you saying then? Is he a client or isn't he?"

"I'm not saying either way. Is he your missing person?"

She added, "Why don't you answer some of my questions for a change?"

Zhou spoke with a slight edge.

"We are not here to answer your questions. We are conducting an investigation."

Hollis looked miffed.

Aggie said, " Well, thanks for telling me. I thought we were having a friendly chat. Instead of that, I find two detectives in my apartment being aggressive and… She raised her hands in quotes. ..conducting an investigation without any kind of warning."

A heavy silence followed Aggie's calm but forcible statement. Hollis eventually spoke into the awkward silence.

"As you are no doubt aware, because of your connections, we are looking into a missing person situation. We are making preliminary inquiries to see how things stand. It's very early days yet and a summary of information at your disposal would be very helpful to us."

Aggie read the situation. No attempt to reach a conclusion. Playing nice after Zhou had blown it, her feelings getting in the way of patience. No, something was off. Hollis had not gotten what he came for, whatever that was. They looked too eager when she admitted to knowing Forman's name. Time to close up shop.

Aggie said, "Any information that I have is privileged as far as I am concerned. Your preliminary inquiries are done. I am calling an end to this..." her hand quotes again, to rub it in... 'investigation'."

Hollis looked angry, Zhou perplexed.

He stood up, followed by Zhou.

"I'm sorry that you feel that way. We will be in touch."

With that, he picked up his briefcase which had fallen on the floor,

and moved towards the door, Zhou in tow. Aggie jumped up, her bare feet padding on the wooden area of the floor and opened the door. They did not shake hands.

Hollis said, "See you soon Ms. Trout. Not here I would think."

And then they were gone.

Aggie closed the door, took the mostly full coffee mugs out to the kitchen and washed them up as her heart rate settled and she reached some kind of equilibrium. She went into the living area and sat on the couch in a lotus position, putting her hands on her knees. Time to call Jack on his cell – it was nearly 11.00 pm. She sat back, her head on the back of the couch and called him. He answered immediately.

"Hi Ag. How'd it go?"

"Not too well. I pissed them off a bit."

"What happened?"

"Well, they did the usual run around before getting down to it. They were trying to get me to admit to knowing that guy Forman."

Jack interrupted.

"The divorce guy?"

"Yes. The stay at home dad. Three kids and the flight attendant wife."

"What did you say?"

"It got as far as me knowing the name but no more."

"Good. You did the right thing. Until you know what's up give them nothing."

Aggie chuckled.

"Took your advice and thanks for calling them. That was very thoughtful."

"Oh. They told you. Well, I thought it couldn't do any harm and, at least, it would slow them down a bit – not be too hard on you."

"Wow. That was their nice side?"

"Yep. They are apparently a good team. Hollis is very experienced and Zhou is on the fast track."

"I might have put a bump in the road there."

"Why?"

"She blew it, talking investigation instead of fact finding. Got annoyed with me."

"That won't matter. We all make mistakes. She's on the way up and that's what counts."

"Good for her. Not much humor there – in either of them."

"Not a barrel of laughs then."

"No. I think I have to get some sleep. Been a long day."

"OK. You did well Ag. Sit back and see what comes. You may have to talk lawyers but that's way ahead."

"Thanks again, Jack. Bye."

They hung up. Aggie poured that glass of Shiraz and sat quietly as she sipped it, enjoying the taste and the relative peace around her.

Chapter 10

Friday had been a long, arduous day ending with Aggie's stressful meeting with the missing persons contingent. She needed another decent break and so Saturday's events were to be shopping for basics, some gym time and a dinner with Jonathan. No time devoted to clients. Thinking about them and the previous night's visit was inevitable but, the advantage of that was that something useful might emerge in her mind. After her shower and breakfast cereal she called Jonathan. He came on after only two rings.

"Hi Aggie. How are things going?"

"Hi Jonathan. Pretty good. I have a lot to talk about tonight."

"Well that is good. That's what I'm here for."

"Jonathan, I'm calling about dinner. Not doing something heavy are you? I mean, like a roast or meatloaf, something like that."

Jonathan laughed.

"What would you like, Aggie? I have several possibilities."

Aggie murmured, "Something light, maybe."

"How about a gigantic salad. All you can eat. Blue cheese dressing made from scratch?"

"That sounds wonderful. Perfect in fact. Shall I bring wine?"

"No, that's OK. I have Chardonnay and a Moselle."

"I'll get some cheesecake then, for dessert."

"Wonderful. Seven thirty, OK?"

"Great."

They hung up.

Aggie did the shopping with some efficiency, using a list in the right order for the aisles in her supermarket. She was back well before lunchtime which turned out to be a couple of cucumber and mayo sandwiches with some herbal tea. She then headed for the gym and an hour's cycling followed by some weights, all of which felt good. As it happened not a single thought about the previous night's visit entered her mind. With a little spare time in the afternoon, she did work on her notes from the towing company and Ford dealership trips. What came out of the towing company trip was that someone, a woman, had removed evidence from the fire. It wasn't really necessary to think about forensic evidence and how the fire proliferated because the fact that this woman had taken away any indication of how the fire started meant that it was suspect. The fire almost had to have been started deliberately. In turn, that raised the question of who did it?

There were plenty of actors to choose from. The guys from the dealership may not have just been thinking money back. The woman was tied to someone. There were at least six women related to the incident – four in the Mason family, two in the Waters family and the one who showed up at the towing company, assuming she was not one of the six. It was likely that she was connected to someone else in this group, so that meant at least two people were involved. The towing company guy might not have been telling the truth. Aggie realized she had taken him at face value, somewhat disconcerting but understandable because his nature exuded honesty. Of course, the same thoughts could be applied to Steinman too. Kowalczyk was not above suspicion either. This was why she was seeing the whole affair as messy. Not a lot of progress but, at least, she had established bad intentions were involved with the fire. That was a step forward. The Ford dealership guys were involved but she was hoping to eliminate them from having started the fire.

She spent a long time in the shower, her second of the day and dressed in jeans, plain white tee and sneakers with a light hoodie. She took the cheesecake out of the fridge and called for an Uber to take her to Jonathan's now familiar high rise apartment on Amsterdam. He greeted her at the door and she made her way down the hallway past the bedrooms and kitchen to the living room with the huge picture window which she adored. The dining table was set up in front of the view of other lower buildings and the river just blocks away. Jonathan had placed a huge red porcelain bowl of salad in the center of the table with a generous bowl of blue cheese dressing next to it, along with pieces of crusty French baguette on a plate. Aggie could see endive, artichokes, tomatoes, olives, carrots and other fresh vegetables, all of which looked delicious. There were two wine glasses and some silverware laid out neatly.

As always, Aggie faced the view with Jonathan sitting to her right at ninety degrees. Jonathan went to the kitchen and returned with a bottle of Moselle which he opened at the table as they took their seats.

Aggie said, "This looks wonderful, Jonathan. Just what I wanted."

Jonathan replied, "Glad you like it. One of my favorites too. Shall I dish up the dressing or do you want to add it yourself?"

Aggie said, "You do it."

Jonathan poured most of the dressing over the salad and mixed it thoroughly, handing Aggie the servers. After they had put large amounts of salad on their plates, Jonathan poured the wine and they touched glasses and drank deeply.

They ate in an easy silence for a few minutes before Aggie spoke.

"This is amazing. I love the dressing."

"Good. I used Roquefort this time."

"I've been reading the deGrasse Tyson book on Astronomy. It is a beautiful and interesting read."

"The Big Bang version of our current existence?"

"Yes. The universe expanding from…well, almost nothing."

Jonathan smiled.

"Until we have a better explanation. Have to define what nothing is too."

Aggie speared some salad and paused with it in the air.

"That's the problem. Our feeble brains can't imagine what nothing is. Or, for that matter, what a billion degrees, billions of years and ridiculously tiny amounts of time look like."

Aggie paused before continuing.

"If you watch or play sports, you have a good idea of, say, what a millisecond is but dozens of zeros after a decimal point?"

"All one can say is what you just did. Ridiculously tiny amounts of time. And, of course, however tiny that time gets, it still does not define the origin of the universe. What came before that?"

Aggie nodded.

"Exactly. The unknown, unless there is a mathematical way of predicting the origin."

"It will still inevitably be theory but, satisfying nevertheless. Please don't go Donald Rumsfeld on me. We don't know what we don't know, etc."

Aggie laughed, losing the frown that she had developed.

"You just did."

Jonathan drained his wine and poured more for both of them.

"Is it time for some storytelling? Your New Jersey adventures? Or would you like to wait until after dinner?"

They had finished nearly all of the salad and drained the Moselle.

Aggie said, "Yes. I can make a start anyway."

"OK. Let me clear up and fetch the cheesecake. I'll get a Sauternes instead of the Chardonnay, if you are happy with that."

Aggie nodded agreement.

They both rose and took the bowl and plates to the kitchen and the dishwasher. It was Aggie who took the cheesecake from the fridge and placed it on the table. Jonathan brought the dishes, spoons and a slicer. Soon they had loaded plates and Aggie began.

"So much has happened in a few days that I am finding it difficult to put it all together. Well, the opposite really, I am separating out the strands so that I can work on them."

"I'm here to help if I can. When I saw you last you were thinking of taking on the case and I assume that you have done that. At that point, I recall that you wanted to call the mechanic guy and also ask the driver some questions. You were trying to see if the fire was accidental or deliberate. We could start there."

"Right. I am now sure that the fire was deliberate. I'll come to that in a moment."

Aggie summarized the mechanic conversation, covering the brakes and the fire, plus the tracker, the latter piquing Jonathan's interest. She also added Kowalczyk's responses concerning the towing company, the load, the destination of the load and the insurance and garaging facilities. After this, he spoke.

"A wide array of information then. Let me guess. You went to the towing company to see the truck or you looked at the garaging situation. I say that because you couldn't take the load, destination of the load and insurance any further just yet."

Aggie smiled in approval.

"I went to the towing company."

They had finished as much cheesecake as they could manage and so took the wine to the couch where Aggie summarized the towing company trip.

Jonathan said, "So we have a mysterious woman who has entered the equation. And, in doing so, she has indicated a deliberate fire. That was shortly after you spoke to the driver too, I might add. I think you forced someone's hand because that action points us in the direction of arson."

"That's true, isn't it."

Aggie added, "I forgot to tell you. I researched the two guys and found out that they run a Ford dealership in Bergen County."

"You went there. Of course."

"I did. I did not see one of them. The guy I saw was Strum. Rather unpleasant, at least, to begin with."

Jonathan interrupted.

"He succumbed to your winning ways."

"Not quite."

Aggie covered her visit concluding, "So they put in the tracker. How, I don't know but it doesn't matter. Plus, I think they coerce payments on their loans. Just a feeling. I don't think they are very nice."

"Would you write down their names for me. I'll check them out. We are assuming then that, unsavory as they are, they are not directly involved."

"Correct."

They paused to drink some more wine, the bottle half empty now.

"That is a lot of progress. Could be that the gentleman who is funding your investigation is paying to have himself investigated."

"It had crossed my mind but, I suppose that I dismissed it. The hospital indicated that he had taken or been given a drug but not in so many words."

"An educated guess?"

"More than that. I'm sure that he had a drug in his system. What I don't know, is how it got there. He either took it or was given it. I have to keep an open mind about that until I find out otherwise."

"Yes, I suppose you do. It is very tricky to pull off something like that. Take a drug and start a fire with all the timing and care involved. What if nobody appeared on the scene? He would have brought about his own demise."

They both thought of the same idea at the same time.

Aggie said, "The other car arrived at the right moment. Maybe they were parked in an arranged location and just drove up. Still very dangerous though."

"And, your Ford dealers appeared at the right time. Remember they were following at a distance."

Aggie put down her glass.

"That's also tricky. They were a long way back. Still, they could have been back up for the first car in case something went wrong. That would make sense. Oh. What if they deliberately stayed a long way back? So that they could not help out as back up."

Jonathan was amused.

"Lot of supposition there. They would have no way of getting a return on their investment then. Unless they had access to insurance collateral. No, that really is too fanciful without any evidence and very unlikely."

Aggie conceded gracefully.

Jonathan leaned back on the couch. They had both drifted forwards in the excitement of hypothesizing.

He said, "You do realize what you are intimating here don't you. You would be the only person at the scene of the fire who was unaware of the situation. You entered the scenario and, instead of complicating it, you added to the validity of the whole affair."

Aggie sat back too.

"Wow! That is something. How close to the truth are we?"

"Who knows? Proving it or disproving it is not easy. You need to know why it was done, if it was done. Often, the simplest answer is the correct one. Is there money involved? More than likely. Relationships, affairs? I don't see any."

"I'm going to have to look at all of them. The partners, their wives and kids. Not really kids any more, they are adults and two do some truck driving."

"Perhaps start with those two. Truck access. I still think you should look for motive. That would point you to the perpetrator."

Aggie sighed. She wasn't enjoying this case.

"Might save me some time too."

Jonathan added, "I will go ahead with checking out the two guys at the dealership. I will know something within a day or so. If, as I suspect, they are just petty extortionists, you can probably eliminate them. They could have been involved in a peripheral way - back up perhaps, but not planning. Cunning, physical but not bright enough for the sophistication you are looking at here."

"Thanks Jonathan. That will be a great help."

Jonathan poured the last of the wine. They left the remaining cheesecake which Jonathan put in the fridge. When he returned, he asked, "Anything else on the horizon? I sincerely hope not with all of this."

Aggie said, "There is actually. Do you remember my two divorce cases?"

"I do, indeed."

"Well, one of them has taken a weird turn."

"Has to be the flight attendant."

Aggie looked surprised.

"Has to be. The other one was cut and dried wasn't it?"

"You are right. In fact, I had just wrapped it up before my trip. It's been settled for big money. The woman insisted on paying me extra. Sort of bonus, I suppose."

"Good for you. So what about this one?"

"The stay at home dad asked to meet me."

"And you did."

They both picked up their glasses and sipped more nectar.

"I chose Central Park to be on the safe side. I was a bit concerned because I couldn't see what could be achieved by meeting instead of talking on the phone."

Jonathan shifted in his seat, eyes on Aggie.

"Tell me, was anyone with him?"

"No. He came over to me, sat down and told me that he thought his wife was missing."

"Missing?"

"Yes. She had not come home at the expected time."

"What was the time frame for all of this?"

Aggie paused for a moment.

"As I recall it, she was due home sometime just after midnight. She didn't make it and he asked to meet me late the next afternoon. Wednesday, I think."

Some of the finer details were a bit blurry after the wine but Aggie was eventually sure about the day.

"Did he go to the police?"

"He hadn't done so at that point. Said he would do it after our chat."

"Mm. Odd not to report it and to meet you. I mean, it is a bit of a myth to wait twenty four hours. That doesn't really happen. In fact, it might be detrimental to the case. So, that is not significant – he might or might not have known that."

Aggie said, "I did tell him that."

"But why meet you and not talk on the telephone? Did he ask to do that or did it just arise so to speak?"

"He practically insisted on it."

"And all he did was sit next to you and tell you his wife was missing?"

Aggie ran her mind over the event.

"We had a conversation about her flight times, checking she was on board, had landed safely and all of that with me finding alternative reasons for her to be late. Other than having an affair that is."

"That was it? The whole meeting was just that?"

Aggie put her glass down, suddenly feeling a little concerned.

"Basically, yes. He sort of jumped up, said OK or something and took off."

"Well, I don't have to tell you – something amiss there. I can see that you are having thoughts about it now."

"I am. Feeling a bit tired too."

Jonathan smiled sympathetically.

"I'm not surprised. Stay here tonight. The room is ready."

The idea had immense appeal so Aggie agreed almost immediately.

"Before we retire, may I give you an opinion that you might not be happy with?"

"Of course, Jonathan. Go ahead."

"I think that you were being watched in Central Park. I don't know why except that there was no reason to have a meeting there. Logic and experience tells me that had to be the reason for the meeting. Did anything happen when you were there?"

"No. Only guys playing tennis badly. Wait, this guy Forman was behaving strangely. He waved his arms a lot. I thought he was on drugs or something."

Jonathan looked very concerned.

"There you have it. You were being filmed or recorded."

Aggie's eyes widened.

"Oh no. What for?"

"We don't know yet. Let's talk some more in the morning. You need some rest."

Half an hour later, Aggie was sound asleep in the spare bedroom where months before she had recovered from an attack on her life and since had spent an occasional night like tonight, utterly safe and utterly comfortable.

Chapter 11

Aggie was awakened early the next morning by a soft tap on her door. Jonathan called out.

"Will the usual work out?"

Aggie called, "Come in, don't shout."

Jonathan opened the door. He was in jeans and a black tee shirt.

He said, "Just wondering if scrambled eggs and coffee will be OK."

Aggie sat up in bed.

"Sounds perfect. Thank you. I'll shower quickly."

Fifteen minutes later, they were both at the same table as the night before, sipping black coffee and ladling scrambled eggs onto their plates. Jonathan had added some toast to the menu. There was also a small porcelain tray containing salt, pepper, ketchup and HP sauce. Aggie was still in her borrowed robe with wet hair and bare feet. She marveled at how comfortable all of this felt.

Jonathan said, "You slept well, I take it."

"I always do here. Thanks for breakfast. And that excellent meal last night."

"My pleasure Aggie."

After a few moments Jonathan looked directly at Aggie.

"We do have a few things to discuss, you know. I hope that's OK."

Aggie stared out of the picture window taking in the view as she spoke.

"Of course. I know there are loose ends all over the place."

"Not just that. I've been thinking about the next step with this divorce case."

Aggie said, "There has already been a next step or, at least, I think there has."

"What did he do?"

"He didn't do anything. The cops showed up at my apartment."

Jonathan put down his fork, immediately concerned.

"You should have called me. How did that come about?"

He immediately saw the look on Aggie's face and backed down.

"Sorry, I know that you can handle it. Sometimes, though, two heads are better than one. This sounds like one of those times."

Aggie had toast halfway to her mouth but put it down momentarily.

"The cops called me several times during the day on Friday. While I was visiting New Jersey. Eventually, I became anxious about it and called them back."

Jonathan was listening intently.

"They said that they had to speak to me in person but would not say what it was all about."

"Why at your apartment?"

"That seemed to be what they wanted. One of them more or less said that they could bring me in if necessary."

"You mean while they were talking to you at home?"

"Yes."

Jonathan drank some coffee, his face crinkling into a smile.

"Sounds like non-cooperation."

Aggie returned the smile.

"Yes, it was a bit like that. I would not say if Forman was a client. I just said that I knew the name. I had called Jack earlier and he said to say as little as possible."

"Ah. You told him then."

"Yes. Is that a problem?"

Jonathan sighed quietly.

"No, of course not. He was correct. It was good advice. I hope that you followed it."

"I did. They were quite persistent about my admitting that Forman was a client but I wouldn't do it."

"Good."

Aggie added.

"That was what led to the end of the meeting."

She paused.

"It really was an interview wasn't it?"

"Yes. Fact finding preliminaries. What happened exactly – to end the interview?"

"The woman pretty much gave away that they were basically interrogating me, when I asked questions that they had no intention of answering."

"Right. They met you at home because it was comfortable for you and you might be more inclined to be helpful. Also, they could get some background and form an opinion about you."

"What? Whether I am a nice person?"

"You are a nice person. Assess what you are capable of. See how you live.

They would have a file or a report about you. What your checkered past holds, any misdemeanors. That sort of thing."

"My record."

"Yes. As much as they can determine, anyway. Two guys came?"

"A man and a woman."

"She did the talking?"

Aggie drained her coffee distractedly.

"No, actually. The man did. A lot of small talk. Asked me about my recent cases – the dentist and Toomey. I knew that they must have had all of that information but he pressed on. Said he was curious. He seemed to be running over those cases."

"That's interesting. What about them?"

"He wanted to know how both guys finished up. I said both in jail, one here and one in the London area. He did ask about Toomey being in London."

Jonathan began finishing off the last of the eggs and toast as Aggie had indicated that she had finished eating.

He said, "I'm not sure that they would have had that kind of detail about Toomey. How he ended up in jail on drug and weapon charges unless they had contacts in the London area."

Aggie looked at him.

"He did say something like 'all is good then'. How did you find out about all of that?"

Jonathan paused, toast in the air.

"Oh, I kept a watch on Toomey's activities, as best I could. I said that I would do that. Cedric went to London to take a closer look, just in case he planned to came back to the US. It was worth checking on him now and again for that reason. As it happens, in a beautiful example of poetic justice, he masterminded himself into prison."

Jonathan returned Aggie's gaze, heavy with inscrutability.

She said, "What goes around comes around. He deserved all of it."

"Indeed."

He leaned back, folded his arms and looked out of the window.

"Aggie, hear me out on this please. This visit by the police is only the beginning of something. They achieved less than they expected, it seems to me. That was the opening salvo. There must be more to come and I am not exactly sure what the nature of it is."

Aggie nodded, wondering what was coming.

"Next time will undoubtedly be on their turf, that is a formal interview."

Aggie again nodded.

"It makes sense, I suppose."

"What were their names?"

Aggie was unlikely to forget them.

"Ray Hollis and Jade Zhou."

"Ah. Know him or of him. Not her. I believe he is well respected. Been at it for a long time. Now, I know a very good lawyer, occasionally brilliant, in fact. He is perfect for these circumstances ."

"Oh oh. No, no."

"Aggie, this sounds serious. You need protection. Good as you are, you are not good enough to walk through an interrogation."

All kinds of thoughts tumbled through Aggie's mind. Lawyer, cost, unknown serious accusations about to surface, indebtedness to Jonathan, close as they had become. She felt her resistance fading, anyway.

"Well, I don't know…"

"Look, Aggie. This guy, the lawyer, owes me. You will have someone on your side in case you are faced with some heavy hitters here."

She was almost convinced, a sliver of relief finding its way through her body.

"Can I pay him?"

Jonathan sat back and relaxed a little.

"Not needed. Well, maybe something at the end. We will work it out."

Fully convinced now.

"What do I do?"

"The minute that you receive the call, or the visit, you call him and do nothing, say nothing until he has joined you. I will speak to him this morning."

Aggie drank some cold coffee.

"Won't it look bad, guilty that is, to turn up with a lawyer?"

Jonathan spoke earnestly.

"It will look eminently sensible. You are not playing around. You have done nothing untoward and you want to make your case and depart."

Aggie knew that she was safeguarding her situation, trying to eliminate something bad from happening. It made absolute sense.

"Thanks Jonathan. What's he like?"

"Very experienced, disarming, charming, old school, smart. I'm fairly sure that your interviewers will know him. I will call you later today with his information. I am assuming that he is available and not roaming the world. I have to check."

"Great."

They both rose from the table and Aggie helped Jonathan clear up and get the plates, condiments and cutlery into the kitchen.

Jonathan said, "I'll manage this while you get dressed."

She took off to the bedroom and donned yesterday's clothes. Her hair, though a little longer than in recent months, was dry now as she brushed it roughly into place and headed back to the living area. Jonathan had the dishwasher going and was already perched on the arm of the couch.

Aggie said, "Well, I'll be off then. Thanks for everything. Sorry I made the visit so complicated. It took away some of the pleasure. We can have a quiet time at my place next time around."

Jonathan rose, gave her a hug and saw her to the door.

"Couldn't be helped. We covered a lot of ground that was important. I'll be in touch later today."

Aggie murmured her thanks and was soon striding down Amsterdam on her way home. There was a lot to think about.

Chapter 12

Back in her apartment, she dropped her bag and keys onto the coffee table and flopped onto the couch to reflect on all of the latest developments. She decided to veg out for most of the day until she heard from Jonathan. The Forman affair began to loom large in her thoughts. It was taking a disturbing turn when she considered all the facts. For some reason that she was still unaware of, the cops from missing persons were raking over her past, her movements and her current cases, the primary interest probably being the whereabouts of Forman's wife, since nothing else appeared to have happened. That had nothing to do with her, though. She had only been checking on his wife's movements which, as far as she could tell, were wholly innocent in nature, Forman going through some farfetched imaginings about her. Aggie couldn't see why the cops would be interested in her investigation except that some of the information she had gathered could be useful to them in some way. She was now quite pleased that a good lawyer would be heading off some of their inquiries so that soon she could be shot of the whole case and devote her time to the Kowalczyk one. That was not very enticing either.

    She recalled the dust around her living area a few days ago and decided to have a cleanup and polish while waiting for Jonathan's call and, for that matter, any contact by the cops. The latter was very distracting because of the uncertainty of it. Will they or won't they? She would eventually find out. She finished the cleaning by lunchtime and, after some bacon flavored tomato soup – from a can, and some sourdough bread, she settled in to read more of her Astronomy book. The day drifted on and, finally, Jonathan called in the late afternoon. The lawyer had been finishing up a squash tournament which, apparently, took up a whole weekend whether the participants won or lost. He had been on the winning end of things but had lost in the final. Jonathan gave her his contact information, telling her that he was expecting her call as soon as she was contacted by the police. His name was Francis 'Frank' Pederson. He went on to say that he, himself, would be out of town for a few days. He and Cedric would be visiting their friend, Blink Collins, in Seattle who had some problems, as yet undisclosed to Aggie, which they would be addressing. They would be leaving for Seattle the next day, Monday. As late afternoon rolled into evening Aggie received the call. It was Hollis. With little preamble, he indicated that her presence was required in the morning. Aggie asked if she had a choice and Hollis' response was not equivocal. It was very important and it would be advisable, indeed necessary, for her to be there. She was given the address and the time scheduled was 10.00 am. Aggie ended the call by saying, "I will be accompanied by my lawyer."

Hollis was mildly surprised. "Who would that be?"

"Frank Pederson."

Hollis was quiet for a moment. "Really. How did you manage that?"

Aggie responded. "He happens to be my lawyer. See you tomorrow."

The call was terminated from the other end. Aggie immediately called Pederson. A well-modulated, rich voice said, "Frank Pederson."

Aggie said, "Mr. Pederson. Agnes Trout. Jonathan Black said to call you as soon as I heard from the police."

"Hi Ms. Trout. Yes. When is the face off with our friends?"

"10.00 am tomorrow morning."

She gave the address.

"OK. Meet me outside at nine fifty five. Bye."

And he was gone. Short and sweet.

Aggie had no ideas for dinner and so went to the old standby, Chinese take-out. Thirty minutes later, she was taking spring rolls, hot and sour soup and moo shoo chicken out of the ubiquitous brown carrier bag. She opened a Shiraz to accompany what turned out to be a tasty repast. After dinner, although feeling sleepy, she decided to run through all of her notes and to see where things stood. She probably wouldn't receive any information on Strum and Westlake from Jonathan for a few days now because of the Seattle trip. That left her own efforts to go towards running down some research on Kowalczyk's partners and family – not a task that she was relishing. In the end, she decided to relax instead and to watch television, which came down to a 60 minute show on Iran and a financial scam involving medical insurance and a movie called San Andreas. The latter had the most astonishing computer generated city destruction that she had ever seen. She went to bed with a host of those images in her mind, together with random thoughts about what tomorrow's meeting might offer.

The next morning, Aggie was up early, had showered and breakfasted quickly and began choosing something sensible to wear for the meeting. She decided on blue jeans, a light blue tee shirt and a black faux leatherjacket along with moccasins. As usual a shake of the head and a finger comb fixed her hair. A peripheral look at 'Morning Joe' completed her preparation. It was a fresh morning and so she walked to the meeting place, a different precinct building from Jack's. She waited outside for less than two minutes before an Uber car deposited Francis Pederson onto the sidewalk. He had a shock of white, wavy hair carefully combed into a youthful style, partly covering his ears. He had bright blue eyes, bronzed, strong features, was clean shaven and sported a navy blue three piece suit, white shirt and red bow tie. "Ms. Trout, I presume."

Aggie smiled.

"Yes."

"Francis Pederson. Call me Frank."

"Right. I'm Aggie."

They shook hands briefly, his grip warm and tight. As they walked up the three steps to the revolving door, he said, "When you answer questions, pause in case I wish to intervene, which I probably will. Give no extra information. Your answers will be brief. OK?" Aggie nodded. They entered the interview room which had a large letter A on the door. Aggie had, she thought, seen dozens of such rooms but not often from the inside. Hollis and Zhou were standing behind the only table which was of fake, stained wood rather than metal in construction. They indicated that Aggie and Frank be seated on the two plastic chairs provided, which they did. One other person remained in the room after the door had been closed. He was suited, impassive and expressionless, remaining standing by the door. Hollis and Zhou sat on similar chairs on the opposite side of the table, Hollis opposite Aggie. They each had a closed folder in front of them. Both were suited, Hollis with a tie, Zhou with an open necked blouse. Hollis spoke. He said that the proceedings would be recorded both visually and aurally, pointing out the recording devices and switching them on. He named those present, the date and time and, without any further introduction, began.

"Ms. Trout. What is your profession?"
"I am a Private Investigator."
"And, in that capacity, do you know Dwight Forman?"
Frank interrupted.
"Define the word 'know'."
Hollis continued.
"I'll rephrase the question. Ms. Trout. Have you had contact with Dwight Forman in any way?"
Frank nodded.
"Yes."
"In what way?"
"He engaged my services."
"By engaged you mean…"
Aggie remained silent.
Hollis said, "What were the services, Ms. Trout?"
Again Frank nodded.
"He asked me to document his wife's activities."
"Asked you?"
"Paid me to."
"Did you document those activities?"
"I did. I opened a file."
"What was Dwight Forman's wife's name?"
Frank interrupted.
"Why the past tense? Please rephrase."
"My apologies. What is his wife's name?"
"Marcia Forman."
Hollis paused, looked down and then up at Aggie.
"What was the purpose of the file that you opened?"
Frank interrupted.
"The purpose and the contents of the file are confidential."
"Well, in view of your profession, can we assume then, that the file contents are pertinent to grounds for divorce?"
Aggie responded.
"You might assume that but I am not indicating whether it is or it isn't."

Frank spoke with a ghost of a smile to Aggie.

"Let us be clear. We are talking about confidential information here. Ms. Trout is a Private Investigator and so it is reasonable to assume that she is fulfilling her obligations in that capacity. The results of those obligations are confidential and would need Mr. Forman's sanction for release. You could ask him for this information."

Hollis looked irritated as he looked at Aggie, then Frank and back again.

"That information could help us in our inquiries. They are the primary source."

Frank responded.

"Would you please state, for the record, what those inquiries refer to."

Another significant pause, accompanied by meaningful looks. Hollis was not a happy man.

"We are investigating the disappearance of Marcia Forman."

"Thank you. And what does that have to do with my client?"

"At this point, she may have information that is helpful to us."

Frank leaned forward.

"I see. Is my client a person of interest in your inquiries?"

At this Aggie scanned the two faces opposite her. This turn of events– involvement in the disappearance of Marcia Forman – had not crossed her mind. Hollis and Zhou were expressionless, both looking at Frank. Hollis spoke.

"Not at this stage."

"What exactly is this stage?"

"We are making preliminary inquiries."

"OK. Proceed. But, I will advise my client on each and every answer."

Zhou had not spoken. Aggie assumed that she was an observer. Hollis continued.

"Ms. Trout. In order to be engaged or hired by Dwight Forman, you must have met with him."

Frank nodded.

"Correct."

"How many times did you meet with Dwight Forman?"

Again, a nod.

"Three times. At his home, at Starbucks and in Central Park."

"Only three times?"

Frank interrupted.

"You have the answer. Three times."

Hollis again.

"Have you ever spoken to Marcia Forman?"

Frank.

"Don't answer that."

Hollis.

"When you met Dwight Forman on those three occasions," – he emphasized 'three occasions' – "Did you talk about anything else besides Marcia Forman?"

Frank said, "Stop."

He leaned forward and placed both of his hands on the table.

"Where is this going? Mr. Forman is not missing. His wife is, apparently. My client had nothing to do with that. Her private conversations with Mr. Forman are just that. Private."

Hollis leaned forward also which caused Aggie to consider moving back, but she did not.

"We are establishing the relationship between Dwight Forman and Ms. Trout."

"There is no relationship between them. He simply hired her."

"As you well know, Mr. Pederson, we have to look at all of the figures involved in a missing person case. That includes family, friends and who that person knew or met. Like that."

Frank looked at both interviewers in turn and then turned to Aggie.

"We are done here. You don't have to answer any more questions. Let's go."

He stood up and gestured to Aggie to do the same.

He said, "Good morning to you both."

With that he ushered Aggie towards the door which was opened by the fifth member in the room. Hollis called out.

"Sorry you feel that way. You will be back."

Out on the street Frank Pederson smiled at Aggie in an almost paternal way.

"That was a fishing expedition. My feeling is that they want to tie you in to the missing woman's disappearance. Why, I don't know."

Aggie was shocked.

"What?"

"Yes. To do that they need motive. You and Forman are looking like the motive."

"That's ridiculous."

"Of course it is. But it may not be ridiculous to them, especially if they have some kind of evidence. In any event they have to eliminate that possibility."

"I can tell you now. There is nothing there. That's just nonsense."

"So it seems. Jonathan filled me in on everything. Do you have any other information that I should know?"

"I told you. This is or was, a straightforward divorce case. He hired me, we had three meetings for updates. Well, two actually. The third was a strange meeting in Central Park that he asked for. Other than that, nothing else."

"Yes, Jonathan mentioned that meeting. He thought you were being watched or recorded or both. That is a more than strange, if true."

He smiled again.

"Maybe we will find out something about that soon."

Aggie blew out a big sigh.

"What's next?"

"Well, they have a theory. If they find enough evidence to support that theory, we will have work to do."

"How can that possibly happen? I haven't done anything."

"I know. We will have to see that it does not happen, won't we? I do not like surprises. I will make some inquiries, see what's cooking. Meanwhile, be careful who you talk to. I'll be in touch."

He turned and strode away – a tall, trim, well dressed figure, his leather briefcase dangling from one long arm.

Chapter 13

Aggie was soon in her apartment again after a brisk, refreshing walk. The meeting or, more appropriately, the interview still stayed with her. She felt that she handled it well. In fact, she was rarely intimidated by anyone and Hollis certainly couldn't do that, although the content and direction of the questions were unnerving. Having Frank there was looking really sensible now because he knew so much more than her about these kinds of situations, what could and could not be asked and answered. If she had understood the matter correctly, Hollis was liking her for being involved in the disappearance of Marcia Forman. In what capacity she didn't know but it did not sound good. Marcia Forman was now an official missing person by the look of it. She might want to be free of Forman but not her three kids. Forman had said that they did not like her but he was an inveterate liar, just like many politicians these days. There was also an indication that Aggie was in some kind of relationship with Forman, it's nature unclear at the moment. That was straight out of left field, utter nonsense but nonsense that Hollis seemed to be honed in on. She wondered how all of this came about. For a disappearance or a missing person to be associated with her in some way it needed help, say, something or someone pointing the inquiries in the right direction. That someone, Forman in fact, must have laid some groundwork for that to happen, otherwise, she surmised, it just couldn't come about. What Forman was up to would eventually manifest itself. There was not much that she could do about it for the time being. It was just there, hanging over her and she had to ignore it. The next step would, presumably, be a call from Frank when he had more news or something from the cops, moving their case along. She needed some lunch and then she would devote the afternoon to research on Kowalczyk's partners and their families. After the remaining moo shoo chicken and some orange juice she got to work.

By mid afternoon, Aggie had established some information. George Mason and his wife were in their late fifties. She could find no profession or employment for his wife, Susan but Mason appeared to be an artist. He had sold quite a few of his paintings which were highly colored abstracts and he turned them out in prolific numbers. Aggie liked the ones that she saw which were heavy in the blue green part of the spectrum. The three daughters were named after flowers. Camellia, Lily and Marigold in the same way, Aggie supposed, that inspired town planners to name their streets after trees. Anyway, they sounded perfectly normal in most respects. Camellia was in Dartmouth college, Lily in the Peace Corps in Africa and Marigold was a prosecutorial lawyer. Aggie could not visualize any of them being involved in any illegal activities but she thought that she might give them a superficial check. The age of Mason's wife, Susan, took her out of the reckoning as the woman who visited the towing company, at least, according to Steve. Budge Waters kids offered more promise but Aggie was becoming disenchanted with this research. Why would any of these people want to cause Kowalczyk any harm? Was she wasting her time? She didn't know so she had to press on in the hope that something, anything, materialized. Budge Waters and his wife, Maddy, were in their mid-fifties. She was a supervisor in a Real Estate business and he was an electronics engineer in a Space Research company. They appeared to have more than adequate financial stability. They were well off. The kids, Stefan and Cordelia, were late twenties, he dabbling in truck driving, some for Kowalczyk, antique dealing and not much else. She, surprisingly, turning out to be a croupier in a New Jersey casino. Aggie knew that she would also fill in as a driver if Kowalczyk was shorthanded. So, there it was. Water's wife was the wrong age, courtesy of Steve again, and one of the kids was a possibility. Why, though? Aggie thought that at least two people had to be involved in the attempt on Kowalczyk's life but who and why eluded her. Next step, she supposed, was a closer look at Stefan and Cordelia. She had to report something to Kowalczyk by the end of the week. In the late afternoon Aggie did receive a call but not one that she expected. It was Jonathan.

"Hi Aggie. I'm at the airport with Cedric. Got a bit of time before we take off. We are going to have a drink in a few minutes. Fortification, of course."

"Hi Jonathan. Good to hear from you. Everything OK?"

"Yes, we are fine. Got a bit of information for you."

"Thanks. About what?"

"Not much, really but it's about the two guys. The ones at the dealership."

"Great. Anything juicy?"

Jonathan laughed.

"No. Pretty much as we expected. Besides the car business, they run a loan business. All above board as far as I can tell. There have been rumors of something bigger, money laundering, protection and the like but nothing concrete."

"No charges or anything like that?"

"No. Apparently, they have used unpleasant tactics to correct non-payment but, not surprisingly, no charges have been pressed. Westlake has had a couple of GBH brushes with the law but nothing has stuck."

"So, nothing approaching a mastermind in either case?"

"Indeed. That would be a stretch. So that's about it. I hope that it's helpful."

"It is. Thanks Jonathan. Give my best to Cedric and have a safe trip."

Jonathan paused.

"Ah. Before you go. How did Frank do this morning?"

Aggie had almost forgotten.

"He was great. We left long before they wanted us to. The whole thing is looking a bit dodgy. Not sure where it is going but Frank is trying to find out."

"Good. Well, keep me posted. Bye."

He ended the call.

Aggie sat back on her couch and thought about this new information. Although Strum and Westlake were at the scene and had followed Kowalczyk by their own admission, it seemed unlikely that they had been in any of the planning of the incident itself. They were involved for their own benefit, the recovery of monies owed to them by Kowalczyk. That in itself might have eventually become physical in some way, but not this time around. She was now fairly sure that their presence at the possible attempt on Kowalczyk's life had, indeed, been coincidental.

Some progress then. She had now to concentrate on the remaining players in this tableau, knowing that more than one person was involved. She also found herself thinking about what it would be like to report to the person who could be paying her to investigate himself, if he was somehow involved in the truck fire. She hoped that was not the case. After a spare meal of French toast and coffee, it took Aggie very little time to confirm that Camellia Mason was ensconced at Dartmouth and that her sister Lily was in Africa. The lawyer, Marigold worked in Manhattan and so still needed a more definitive check. Aggie would have liked photographs of Marigold and Cordelia to show Steve to see if he recognized one of them but, from his vague description, that would be a long shot. Her next move would seem to be meeting or seeing Marigold, Stefan and Cordelia to try to form an opinion about each of them. Plus, there was the question of insurance which she had not really put under the microscope yet. That information would need to come from one of the three partners. She began to think a little more about the money that Kowalczyk apparently owed Strum. If it was substantial then it could rise to the status of motive for the truck fire. Although, quite how it would figure in was not clear yet. Jonathan had suggested to follow the money, cliché that it was, but it did make sense. The only source besides Kowalczyk himself, was Strum. She wondered if he would be forthcoming. It was worth a shot. Too late tonight but she elected to try tomorrow. She decided to read for a while and get to bed early.

Chapter 14

After a good night's sleep, Aggie had showered and was having cereal and coffee by 9.00 am. When she had finished the cereal, she picked up her cell and called Strum. A cheerful, young voice answered and Aggie gave her name. She was asked to hold. After two or three minutes, Strum came on.

"Good morning Ms. Trout. What's up?"

"Hi. We met last Friday, if you recall."

"I do."

Aggie spoke into the following silence.

"I am still working on Mr. Kowalczyk's case. Looking for as much information as I can get. Background you understand."

There was a brief silence.

"I do. Good for you. What are you after?"

"You did mention, during our meeting that is, that Mr. Kowalczyk owes you some money."

Aggie couldn't help feeling that sounded tacky but there it was. She went on.

"I assume that means that he is behind in some way in his repayment of that money to you."

"That would be a correct assumption. Are you thinking of paying it off for him?"

Some vague humor came through.

"Sorry, no. Look, can you give me a ballpark figure of the amount owed you? It would be very helpful for me to know what kind of debt he is in."

A long silence again.

"I don't know about that. It has nothing to do with you. We just want our investment back as quickly as possible. We are not a charity."

Aggie tried a little further.

"I understand that. It's your business. But are we talking hundreds here or thousands, perhaps?"

Strum cleared his throat.

"Much more than that, lady. Much more."

"Really? Much more?"

"You got it."

Aggie was actually quite shocked.

"How does that happen? It seems so much."

Strum responded with anger in his voice.

"It is. That's what happens when you gamble."

Another shock.

"Oh. That would do it. Well, thank you for being frank with me. I do appreciate it. I hope you get repaid soon."

"So do I. Bye."

He cut the call.

Aggie dropped the cell onto the coffee table. That had been a very useful call. Worth the effort. Kowalczyk was in severe hock to a couple of quasi loan sharks who were not short on intimidation. He must have missed payment by a substantial time factor or those guys would not be pursuing him with some intent. The situation had obviously reached some kind of tipping point. She realized that did not, necessarily, make Kowalczyk a criminal but it certainly gave him a motive if the truck fire was beneficial to him in some way. That meant that the insurance possibility was now looming large. She had to find out if insurance was part of some scheme. That, in turn, meant asking Kowalczyk himself or one of the two partners. She would give that some thought. In terms of photographs, she did manage to track down Marigold in the Justice Department and found a website head and shoulders of her carrying a large smile on an open face which was quite attractive. Usually, young lawyers tended to show a serious side in those photographs or, at least, just to hint at a happy face but Marigold had gone most of the way. Aggie tucked a xerox copy away in her bag ready for her next trip to New Jersey. She was settling on the idea of a surprise visit to the Waters home in the hope of seeing Budge Waters. She did not expect either Stefan or Cordelia to be living in their parents' home at their age but, you never knew these days. She could also drop in on Steve during the same trip, which would have to be towards evening as both Waters and his wife had employment and, presumably, worked in the daytime. She thought that tomorrow might work for a trip. It just felt like too much today. She was almost at a loose end which was unusual for her. Nothing from Frank yet and not much more to be done on the Kowalczyk front. Of course, a call to Kowalzcyk himself might save a lot of time and effort. She could ask him directly about the insurance question. Almost lunch time so why not give it a shot. She called Kowalczyk's cell. He answered quickly and sounded as if he was driving. Aggie wondered if he was in one of the other trucks.

"Hi, Kowalczyk."

He was driving and so, presumably, could not see caller ID.

"Hi. Agnes Trout."

"Hi Agnes. What's up? News for me I hope."

"No, not really. I'm still doing a lot of follow up."

"Oh. What do you want then?"

"Well, I've seen the remains of the truck and I have spoken to a few people which has, in fact, raised some questions that I need to ask you."

"I see. Look, I'm not in a position to answer questions right now. I'm driving. In fact, heading home."

Aggie thought that driving doesn't stop a conversation. It sounded as though they were on speakerphone.

"OK. When then."

"How about meeting up. I live over in Bergen County but I could make it, say, to Fort Lee to make it easier for you."

Aggie liked the idea.

"When are you thinking of?"

"Would this afternoon work? 4.00 pm?"

"Sounds good. Where?"

Kowalczyk paused.

"I know a diner that would work."

He gave her the address and they agreed to meet there. They cut the call. Aggie was pleased with the arrangement. There was a lot to clear up with Kowalczyk. She had expected to have a quiet afternoon and evening but now she would be in New Jersey again in the late afternoon. She found the time for a quick, minor grocery shop and then dressed in her usual casuals – sweats and sneakers with a rose colored tee. She was soon zooming over the George Washington Bridge in the comfort of an Uber cab. Not for the first time, she thought that it would be really easy to slip into traveling everywhere in this way. It was very comfortable, reliable and so simple with her smart phone. Way of the future. The diner was a quite attractive one story building with half a train carriage built into one side of it for those that preferred the illusion and ambience of a train. Kowalczyk was not there and so Aggie asked for a window booth, which was not in the train section, and was soon seated with a view of light traffic in the street outside. She did not see Kowalczyk's car arrive but, after a few minutes, he appeared in the doorway, looked around for her and headed to the booth. He was in black jeans and wore a blue tee shirt under a blue and black check shirt. He had received a recent haircut and shave and looked almost well groomed. His features, especially his eyes, looked very tired and the lines on each side of his nose were indelible.

"Sorry I'm late. Traffic a bit heavy."

Aggie smiled.

"I've only been here a couple of minutes."

"Shall we order something before we talk? I'm rather hungry."

Aggie agreed. She ordered a Portobello mushroom and Blue Cheese topped burger with curly fries and Kowalczyk went for a full throated breakfast meal, even though it was late afternoon. They both also asked for coffee, which was immediately dispensed. Kowalczyk began.

"So, what's all this about?"

"Well, what it's about is, me finding out whatever I can about what you believe are attempts on your life."

"Believe?"

Aggie paused.

"Figure of speech. Something certainly happened to you, maybe even twice. I am still trying to find out who might wish to do you harm."

They sipped their coffees which were not very good.

"OK. What have you got so far? What am I paying for?"

Aggie said, "You haven't paid me beyond my retainer yet."

"I've brought you a check. Thought that you might be asking for it."

Aggie began.

"I spoke to Mr. Steinman a few days ago. He was very helpful. He thought that you were very conscientious about maintenance. He told me about the brake failure a few months ago. I can't say with any certainty that it was an attempt on your life but the possibility is there. Kowalczyk drained his coffee, looking at Aggie over the cup.

"Why the lack of certainty?"

"Your mechanic, Mr. Steinman, had maintained the truck for you – exclusively he said but, after the incident, the brakes were checked and found to be adjusted incorrectly – I'm not sure of the technicalities. Mr. Steinman just assumed that you had used another mechanic who had not done a very good job. There was no discussion about it according to him and so no follow up. It could have been deliberate of course. I just don't know."

"So it could be or it couldn't be. Not very helpful. I think it was deliberate."

Aggie sipped some more coffee which tasted progressively worse.

"I understand that but it is a theory. It was also a rough experience, I'm sure."

Just then the two meals arrived and they started eating for a couple of minutes. Aggie was decently impressed with the burger which was juicy and flavorful. Kowalczyk tucked in with gusto and then put both fists on the table, knife and fork vertical, looking at her.

"Well, it is what it is."

He lifted the fork and pointed it randomly.

"I still think my brakes were tampered with. It figures as the precursor to the fire in my truck which was also deliberate. I am certain."

Aggie had stopped eating, mostly because it was difficult to talk about this and eat at the same time.

"I respect that Mr. Kowalczyk. I really do. But I do work with evidence. I have to."

"OK. Fair enough but bear it in mind. I'm right about this."

They resumed their meals, Aggie down to her curly fries and Kowalczyk mopping up the remains of eggs and ketchup. Aggie resumed, "I did go to the towing company last Friday. Guy called Steve helped me out."

"Right. Big guy."

"Yes. I looked at the cab again. There is a problem there."

"I know there is. A deliberate fire of some kind. It's pretty obvious."

Aggie took a deep breath.

"Someone came and removed all the evidence. That is, all the electrics and burned out bits and pieces. They even cut away some of the cables."

Kowalczyk looked puzzled. His eyes became wary. Aggie thought that there was a good chance that this was not news to him.

"When did that happen?"

"Well, sometime on Thursday Steve said."

"Thursday?"

"Yes. The thing is – the visit occurred within hours of my calling you. I told you that I might be going to the towing company."

Kowalczyk put down his cutlery and turned the tired eyes onto Aggie.

"Wait a minute. You think that I set someone up to do that?"

Aggie returned his gaze.

"You're saying that it was a coincidence?"

"No. I'm saying that I would not want evidence removed. I need it to show how it all happened."

Aggie sighed.

"Unless the evidence showed more than you wanted it to about how the fire started."

There was a long silence while Kowalczyk digested the inference. Finally, he spoke.

"I don't believe this. You are actually saying that you think I started my own fire? Then, of course, I took some pills to knock myself out so that I could be cooked as well."

Aggie responded.

"No. I am not necessarily saying that. I have to look at all of the possibilities. That is just one of them. It is possible isn't it?"

He looked angry but spoke in a measured tone.

"I suppose it is but the idea is ridiculous. I did all of that myself? Nonsense. I'm surprised that you would even go there."

"Let's leave it at that for a moment. Who would want to take away all of the evidence then?"

"Whoever set the fire, of course. It would show that it wasn't an accident."

Aggie sat back in her chair. She had riled Kowalczyk purposely and now wanted to settle things down a bit. The diner was full apart from a couple of central tables but reasonably quiet.

"I've asked this before. Do you know anybody that would want to do you harm?"

Some relief in the features.

"No I don't. Neither do I know why anybody would want to."

"How about a woman?"

"A woman?"

"Yes. The person that went to the towing company was a woman."

"What was she like?"

"It was raining heavily, so Steve did not get a good look."

Aggie saw definite relief in the eyes.

"Pity. That could have been useful for you."

"Yes. She knew what she was doing though. Cutting cables. Cleaning up evidence. She could be connected to the trucking business in some way."

Back to being wary again.

"Well, all I can say is that I have no idea who that could have been."

Aggie had doubts about that but thought that it was time to switch direction. A waiter came to the table and began clearing up, asking about desserts but they both declined. Kowalczyk ordered more coffee and Aggie asked for a ginger ale to try anything but the coffee. She knew that the next questions were not going to be received well either.

"Mr. Kowalczyk. You recall my visit to see you in the hospital?"

"Yes, of course."

"I asked you a few questions and a couple of them were whether you knew or had heard of certain people."

She paused and saw the wariness again.

"Right."

"I asked you if you knew or had heard of Paul Wright and a guy called Strum. Tig Strum, in fact."

Kowalczyk nodded.

"Well, you told me that you did not know either of them."

"That's correct."

"Incorrect, in fact. I have met with Mr. Strum and, it turns out, you know each other rather well."

Kowalczyk paled a little and swallowed twice.

"OK. You've got me. We don't get on at all. I didn't want to talk about him."

"It's a bit more than that isn't it? I understand that there is money involved between you. The result of gambling debts, perhaps."

Kowalczyk looked very uncomfortable.

"He told you that? I can see that he did. This is personal and has nothing to do with you."

"Mr. Kowalczyk. It has everything to do with me. You owe him money. He could get upset enough to do you harm. That is, a motive. Don't you think that is important?"

"Put that way, I suppose it is."

Aggie realized that she had given Kowalczyk some neutral ground.

"As it happens, I don't think that Mr. Strum was involved in the fire incident."

"Why not?"

"For one thing, he would lose his cash cow. For another, I don't think he is bright enough to pull it off."

Kowalczyk looked disappointed and did not respond. Aggie pressed a little as she sipped her ginger ale.

"I understand that the sum that you owe is substantial."

"Some might see it that way. It doesn't seem too bad to me."

No quantification then. She had a good idea anyway.

"I hope that it is something that you can take care of soon. Mr. Strum is not a happy person."

"I'll take care of it. Was there much more that you wanted to ask?"

The check had arrived and Kowalczyk was looking very restless.

"Sorry, this has taken longer than I expected. I do have a couple more questions."

"OK. Let's get it over with."

The first signs of tension were emerging. He had left his coffee untouched and his features had tightened.

"You said that the load in your truck was Home Depot stuff didn't you?"

"That's right."

"Was it damaged?"

"No. It survived very well."

"What happened to it?"

Kowalczyk had already told Aggie that he had removed it or transferred it for security reasons.

"The towing company took it to their place – I went to the hospital, you remember. I had another driver pick it up and deliver it. Late, of course."

"Right. Was the load insured?"

"Yes. It has to be. Too risky otherwise."

"I assume then that your trucks must be insured too."

"Yes."

Kowalczyk was not so forthcoming.

"Would that be a sort of general insurance for the fleet or was that particular truck insured on its own?"

"That's a strange question. Why all this insurance stuff?"

Aggie backed off a little, feeling that an important point had been reached. She smiled.

"Oh, no biggie. I've just been through a nightmare insurance experience. I totaled two cars and had to negotiate my way through all of that. I do not even have a car right now. I came by Uber."

"Two cars?"

"Yes, one was a rental though. I used Geico and they were understanding. Who did you use?"

Kowalczyk was more relaxed now.

"I used The Highway. They are coming through for me."

"Well, that's good isn't it. Tough for business, if you cannot replace the truck."

Kowalczyk did not respond. Instead he reached into the top pocket of his shirt and took out a folded check. With a ghost of a smile he said,

"I have to go. Here's the expenses that you mentioned. Well, that you hinted at, at least. Sounds as though you have been busy."

Aggie slipped the check into her bag without looking at it.

"Thanks. I'll keep at it. You've been very helpful."

Kowalczyk abruptly stood up and slid into the aisle, standing motionless for a moment. Aggie stood also. Clearly he was not a handshaker. Perhaps, just not with women.

Kowalczyk said, "Keep me posted."

With that he turned and strode from the diner. Aggie turned to the window to see what he was driving. It was a truck, probably a Silverado by the look of it. So, not a Cherokee, not that she expected it, of course. She was amused that Kowalczyk stiffed her for the meal. She sat down again, called an Uber and paid the check. Four minutes later she was on her way back to Manhattan. It was almost dark and she had a lot to think about.

Chapter 15

The next morning, Aggie had electronically deposited Kowalczyk's check, which she thought, was more than generous. She was well into her notes and summation of the meeting with Kowalczyk when her cell buzzed. She saw that it was Frank Pederson.

"Hi Frank."

"Hi Aggie. How are you doing?"

"Good. Busy but good."

"Well, I have good news and bad news for you."

He actually sounded cheerful. Perhaps that was always the case when he was delivering news. Aggie felt anxious.

"OK."

"The bad news is that Hollis is building a case against you in the disappearance of Marcia Forman."

"What? That's nuts. He think I kidnapped her or something?"

"Maybe worse. It is not clear at this point. He just seems to be on a roll."

Aggie was shocked.

"All I've done is track her movements over a period of time, looking for evidence of an affair. Sordid I know but it is what I sometimes do."

"Look, forget the guilt complex. It isn't relevant here. We are looking at facts, not emotion. Hollis is using your meetings with Forman as a basis for nefarious behavior."

Aggie laughed, in spite of herself.

"That's stupid. That would implicate him too."

"Mm. Perhaps. In any event, your presence is required at the precinct tomorrow at 11.00 am. Another go-round, I'm afraid."

"So this is serious stuff. Will you be there?"

"Of course. All of this is circumstantial, you understand. Hollis is hoping to squeeze enough out of you to strengthen his case. He's got nada in terms of solid evidence – that's the good news. We play it cool. Any questions?"

"What do I do in the meantime?"

There was a smile in Frank's voice. He sounded so positive. It was disarming.

"Just your usual. Do not speak to any connected parties. Be prepared to say as little as possible tomorrow. Leave the rest to me. See you then."

He rang off. Aggie felt a little stunned. This was a quick and unpleasant turn of events. Dwight Forman was evidently trying to implicate her in the disappearance of his wife. Since his wife seemed to be listed as missing at this point, what could that have to do with Aggie? There could be no evidence of any kind that could show that she was involved in any way. Simple as that. What was Hollis doing then? She didn't know and that lack of knowledge was very disconcerting. Forman's antics, or odd behavior, were playing themselves over in her mind with no clear solution as to what they meant. Not much could be done now. She had to wait until Friday to find out. The trip to the Waters family home suddenly sounded daunting. There did not seem much to be gained by it. They lived near Ramsey in Bergen County which was close to an hour away and so Aggie shelved the idea for the time being. That also meant that she could not show Steve the photograph of Marigold to see if he recognized her as the woman who paid him a visit on Friday. The solution suddenly occurred to her. She was not yet fully integrated into modern technology enough so that her first thoughts in solving problems were tech related. All she had to do was call Steve and text him the photograph or show it on Face/Time. She chose the text method and called the number he had given to her, finding him in his office – she felt like calling it his lair – and explained what she wanted him to do. Three minutes later, with Aggie congratulating herself, he was staring at the photograph. "You know that I didn't really get a good look at her face – just the impression that it was a young face. She was in and out of the office in no time."

Aggie felt her enthusiasm draining away.

"But I do know that this woman here is not the one who came by."

Aggie perked up considerably.

"How do you know that Steve?"

"This one is obviously a blonde. The visitor was a brunette. Right age though."

"Great Steve. You have been very helpful."

"Good. Bye for now."

They broke the connection.

What were the odds that the woman would have dyed her hair? Aggie thought absolutely none for that particular trip. So, Marigold was not the woman who paid Steve a visit. That narrowed the field a bit, assuming that the woman in question was not a complete stranger, which made no sense. In addition, she could not be working alone, at least, Aggie thought it very unlikely. Time for a break. She went to the gym for forty five minutes of kickboxing, her favorite high energy kind of workout. She could never see the point of sitting on a stationary bicycle and peddling frantically to the sound of loud music. It was not too comfortable either. Back in her apartment, she had two yoghurts for lunch – the flip over kind with cereal - and then returned to her notes which she had now transferred to her iPad. The foremost item in her mind was Kowalczyk's insurance payout. Her research had shown her that a cab could cost up to $180K and the trailer $30K and up but they could be insured for more than that. Kowalczyk had given her the name of his insurance company and so she decided to try to find out. She dialed up The Highway Insurance Company but her first two approaches got her nowhere. The information was confidential she was informed, even before she got to the details. Then she had the resourceful idea of posing as a prospective client to see if she could work her way into the system.

This was new territory for her, even the terminology was suspect and so she had to feel her way She began her call with a curt insurance associate.

"I need to insure a semi – an eighteen wheeler which is three years old."

"Value?"

"About two hundred and twenty thousand."

"What? And it's three years old?"

"That is only my estimate. Perhaps about two hundred then."

"Used for what?"

Aggie had a stab.

"General haulage."

"Will any loads be liquid, flammable or inherently dangerous like chemicals?"

"No. Are the loads included?"

"Yes. Unless any of the above. What will be the nature of your loads?"

Aggie was gaining confidence.

"Regular household and commercial materials."

She thought that sounded reasonable.

"Any international work?"

"No. Domestic."

"Will the truck be garaged when not in use and, if so, where?"

"Yes, in Bergen County."

"That's New Jersey?"

"Yes. Look, I just wanted a ballpark figure. You know, for comparison purposes."

"Really?"

"Yes. I have a friend who has a policy with you. He has three trucks and seems very happy with his policy."

There was a pause.

"What's the name of the company?"

"J. K. Trucking. His name is Jakob Kowalczyk."

"Spell it."

Aggie did. The sound of computer keys being tapped echoed down the phone line.

"That's correct. Just lost one of his trucks."

Time for a white lie.

"Yes. Some kind of accidental fire he said. But I think the load was salvageable."

"Yes, it was. You're not looking for that kind of coverage, though, are you?"

Aggie felt cautious.

"I'm not sure. It was fully comprehensive wasn't it?"

"Fully covered, yes. Except for an Act of God, of course. But Mr. Kowalczyk added further personal clauses. The premium was commensurate with those additional clauses. Want more, pay more."

Aggie kept her voice steady.

"I don't have a lot of capital. What overall coverage are we looking at?"

"Close to a million, give or take. But you obviously don't want that kind of coverage do you?"

Aggie was shocked and excited at the same time.

"No. It sounds like the premium would be much too much for me. Incidentally, how long does it take to redeem the insurance policy. What I mean is, how long before a financial settlement?"

"Hm. I suppose that is a valid question. Usually, several weeks I would say. Mr. Kowalczyk's case was expedited by the claims adjuster- the paperwork has been completed and so the renumeration is imminent."

Aggie paused, taking this in.

"Oh. Well that's nice for him."

"Yes."

After another few minutes, no further information emerged and she ended up with an acceptable quote for her nonexistent truck. She said she would get back later and rang off. She was quite pleased with herself. Lucky too. She put her cell down and sat back on the couch. The insurance settlement for the truck was substantial. Enough for a scam? Quite possibly. Or to kill for? It had been done for less. Who would benefit though? Probably the partners were unaware of insurance arrangements because, she assumed, Kowalczyk had paid the premiums himself or hidden the costs somewhere in the accounts. There wouldn't be much in it, anyway, for the two partners, if they were involved. Didn't sound right. No, Kowalczyk was doing something on his own. Aggie was surprised that the claims adjuster who had checked the truck could not have been concerned about the cables being cut and the debris removed, unless it was inspected before that happened. That was probably the case. But then, he, or she, could not have thought that there was anything suspicious about it. She assumed that the inspection must have been cursory, unless, and this was a new thought, the claims adjuster was complicit in some way. Perhaps it had been worth his or her while to be cursory. Plus, not only that, but the assessment conclusions had been expedited. In any case, the possibility of a motive for the fire had now presented itself. The payout was enough to buy another truck and have plenty of spending money left unless the Strum faction needed appeasement. In addition, in the back of her mind she still carried the sight of Kowalczyk being uncomfortable when the topic of the woman visiting the towing company came up. That could be a significant pointer so she kept it filed away. It was this kind of puzzle that Aggie enjoyed.

Gathering critical information and piecing it all together to find an answer, a conclusion. Enough of that for now. It was a big day tomorrow and she needed some down time. A frozen meal, for once, was in the offing along with some wine and an early Charles Todd for reading. She had a long way to go in that series.

Chapter 16

The next day, interview day, Aggie reached her meeting spot outside the precinct at the same time as Frank, who greeted her with a warm handshake and a few words of wisdom.

"As I said before, pause when you are asked a question to give me time to intervene if I need to. When I indicate OK, answer and make it as brief as possible."

Soon, they were once again in Interview Room A, although Aggie assumed that there must be a B and C or more. Hollis and Zhou were behind the table and the same guy was at the door in the same clothes as before. Frank had on a dark brown suit and a bow tie with puppies all over it. Aggie seated herself in a position slightly turned towards Frank to make it easier to see him out of the corner of her eye. Hollis opened up a folder in front of him, went through the same careful introductions and began.

"Do you know what a stalker is Ms. Trout?"

Frank interrupted immediately.

"Don't answer that."

Hollis.

"It's a simple question. I just want to know if she understands what it is."

Frank.

"Assume that she does. Next."

Hollis turned his gaze back to Aggie.

"Your lawyer has indicated that you know what a stalker is, Ms Trout. I am suggesting that you have stalked Mr. Forman for some time now. In fact, since that first meeting at his house when he hired you."

Frank.

"Suggest all you like. My client has no knowledge of that activity."

Hollis.

"Is that true, Ms. Trout?"

"It is."

"How many meetings did you have with Mr. Forman?"

Frank nodded imperceptibly for Aggie to respond.

"I told you before. Three times."

"Yes you did but we have indications that it was more than that."

Frank.

"My client has said three times. What other information do you have?"

"Mr. Forman's sworn statement that there were more meetings. Clandestine meetings, in fact."

Aggie spoke.

"That is absolutely untrue. He's lying."

"Did you go to Mr. Forman's house at other times, without meeting him?"

"Of course not. Why would I?"

"I don't know, that is why I'm asking."

Frank.

"My client has clearly said no."

"Have you followed Mr. Forman, anywhere, outside his home?"

Frank nodded.

"No."

Hollis.

"Where were the other two meeting places that you met with Mr. Forman?"

Aggie kept her composure.

"As I said before, at Starbucks and in Central Park."

"Right. When you met at his home what occurred at that meeting?"

Frank.

"Be more specific."

"What did you discuss at that meeting?"

Frank nodded.

"Mr. Forman told me what he wanted me to do and hired me to do it."

"What did he ask you to do?"

"Monitor his wife's activities."

"With what in mind?"

Frank.

"You should ask Mr. Forman what he had in mind, not my client."

"OK. What specifically, did he ask you to do?"

"As I said, check her movements."

"Spy on her?"

"If you prefer that connotation. Your words not mine."

Frank had an approving look on his face.

"Did you ever meet Marcia Forman?"

"No."

"Speak to her?"

"No."

"No contact with her at all?"

"No."

"You just observed her?"

"Yes."

Suddenly Zhou spoke.

"What else occurred at that first meeting?"

Frank.

"Specific."

Zhou.

"Besides a discussion about hiring you, what else did you do at that meeting?"

Frank.

"Specificity please."
Zhou.
"Did you make a pass at Mr. Forman?"
"What?"
"Did you attempt to commence a relationship with Mr. Forman?"
"No. That is utterly ridiculous."
"Ridiculous? Have you had relationships with clients before?"
Frank.
"Don't answer that. It's irrelevant."
Zhou.
"It could show a propensity for initiating this kind of a relationship."
Frank.
"There was no relationship. You heard my client. If you pursue this line of questioning we will be leaving. We are here to be helpful, not insulted."
Hollis.
"We have a statement from Mr. Forman that Ms. Trout tried to initiate a relationship."
Frank.
"As my client indicated, she did not. Mr. Forman, therefore, is lying."
Hollis.
"Who else was at the meeting?"
Aggie replied.
"No one."
"Was Marcia Forman at work?"
"I've no idea."
"Was the babysitter there. Children were home.."
Frank nodded.
"Somewhere in the house, yes."
"You didn't see her?"
"No."
"Could she have been observing you?"
Frank.
"What's going on here? My client would like an explanation for these questions. As I said, we are cooperating, being helpful."
Zhou.
"We have a statement from the babysitter which indicates that Ms. Trout tried to engage Mr. Forman in a relationship."
Aggie was annoyed and before Frank could intervene, spoke.
"She's lying. This whole thing is a charade."
Hollis.
"They are both lying?"
Frank.
"They are. What else is there?"
Hollis.

"Where were you last Tuesday, say, afternoon and evening? Also, Wednesday morning?"

Frank nodded.

"Take your time."

"Tuesday afternoon I was at home doing some research. Evening, at home too. Wednesday morning I went to a New Jersey hospital with a friend. Didn't get back until lunchtime."

"So, no one can confirm your whereabouts on Tuesday afternoon and evening?"

"Correct. I live alone. I had two lengthy telephone calls during that time though. One in the afternoon and one in the evening."

"With whom were those telephone calls made?"

Frank.

"That's personal. Unnecessary information."

Aggie responded.

"That's OK. The afternoon one was with Jakob Kowalczyk, a client. The evening one with a very close friend."

"Who was that?"

"Jack Coletti."

"Why do I know that name?"

"He's an NYPD detective. We spoke about him when you came to my apartment."

Hollis gave a loud sigh of acknowledgement and leaned back for a few moments. After a minute or so, he leaned forward again.

"Did you see or speak to Marcia Forman at any time on Tuesday or Wednesday of last week."

Frank nodded.

"No."

"You met with Mr. Forman at a Starbucks? What was the reason for that meeting?"

"Just an update. A very brief meeting. One coffee."

"And why did you meet in Central Park?"

"Mr. Forman called me and asked to meet."

"Why? Why in Central Park?"

"He said that he couldn't tell me why until we met. Central Park was my choice because I thought it was a strange request. I wanted public."

"You thought it strange ?"

Frank.

"My client was being cautious because it was an odd request with no reason given for the meeting. She chose a public place."

Hollis.

"And you instigated this meeting."

"I certainly did not. Mr. Forman did. He also behaved in a very peculiar way."

Frank was not happy with the additional information.

"Peculiar how?"

"He waved his arms about, was manic almost. I thought he was on drugs."

"You're an expert on this sort of thing?"

Frank.

"My client is simply saying that Mr. Forman did not behave normally."

Hollis closed his folder and spoke.

"Ms. Trout. We would like you to come next door and look at a video. It is short, just a couple of minutes. We would like to know what you think of it."

Hollis and Zhou stood up as did Frank and Aggie. All stretched and then Hollis lead the way next door with Zhou bringing up the rear. The next room, to Aggie's amusement, was labeled B, although she was not feeling that happy at the moment. This was an ordeal. In the next room, they sat at a table, Hollis and Zhou on one side and Aggie and Frank on the other. At the end of the table, about four or so feet away, was a small screen. Hollis switched on and, looking at Aggie, said,

"Watch this carefully and tell me what you think."

Frank said, "Not without consulting with me first."

There was no response. The lights in the windowless room were low. Hollis began the video. It showed an end court at the tennis facility in Central Park, white hats bobbing around as four older men wrestled commendably with the game of tennis. The camera shot zoomed in on a seat beside the court on which, quite clearly, sat Aggie. A man, viewed from behind walked up to Aggie and sat down next to her. He looked very agitated from his movements as he spoke to her. She appeared basically non-committal as she returned the conversation. Suddenly, the man, clearly Dwight Forman, stood up, gestured with his arms in a demonstratively frustrated way and strode off toward the camera, which closed down. Hollis switched off. Frank spoke.

"That was a meeting between my client and Forman, arranged in some secrecy by him. Nothing more than that, utterly innocuous. What is the point of it?"

Hollis.

"The video was taken by Mr. Forman's babysitter."

Frank.

"So what."

"It was at his request."

"Again, so what."

"He wanted a record of the fact that he was trying to end Ms. Trout's efforts at stalking him. He believes that she is infatuated with him."

In spite of the seriousness of the situation, Aggie laughed quietly.

"That is so preposterous that it's funny."

Hollis looked annoyed.

"If you think that is funny, you should know that Mr. Forman says that you have been stalking him for some time now and that he believes that you are involved in the disappearance of his wife."

Frank.

"Two statements and a video from a pair of patently inveterate liars without a shred of evidence. Is that really where we are?"

Hollis.

"I can tell you that we are taking this seriously and we would like Ms. Trout to make a statement."

"You might like her to but she isn't going to. Are we free to leave?"

Hollis and Zhou did not respond.

Frank turned to Aggie and said, "We are leaving. Let's go."

They stood and left the room with nothing being said. Once outside, Frank turned to Aggie.

"That was nonsense. If that woman turns up dead, though, things might get a little sticky."

"How is that possible? I haven't even spoken to her."

"I know. Chances are that Forman has done something to her and is laying it on you. I am surprised that they are buying it though."

"What's next?"

"Your friend that you mentioned in there? Another word from him wouldn't do any harm. Otherwise, we sit tight. There is no evidence against you, of course. Nothing will happen until Marcia Forman shows up one way or the other."

"Thanks for all of your help. I would not have been confident on my own in there."

"You're welcome. We'll keep in touch. Don't meet with Hollis without me being there."

For the second time in a few days Aggie watched Frank Pederson stride purposefully away.

Chapter 17

Aggie was soon back in her apartment contemplating the last couple of hours. She knew that Forman was up to something but, even so, the way things had worked out was still shocking. She had been called many things in her line of work but stalker was a first. Forman had weaved a carefully planned scenario involving Aggie but to what end? Could he have been planning to do harm to his wife but, somehow, she had taken off or was there something more sinister going on? Either way, Aggie doubted that she would be charged with anything. The case was just too flimsy and Forman's efforts surely too blatant. She would, as Frank had suggested, have to wait and see – not the best of situations and not her style. She thought that she would begin to be proactive and look into Marcia Forman's disappearance herself. That, at least, felt positive. First, a call to Jack was in order. After a few rings he came on.

"Hi Ag. How's it going?"

"Not too bad. How about you?"

"Good. Making progress. That robbery? Looks as though the housekeeper's involved. Shame really – coerced, I think. Still working on it."

"Right. I'm calling because I've had a bit of bother with that divorce case."

"The stay at home dad one?"

"Yes. Well, the two cops that came to my apartment?"

"Yes."

"They have had me in for two interviews already, second one today."

"You're kidding. What did they want?"

"Well, bottom line is I am a stalker, infatuated with the guy and involved in the disappearance of his wife."

"That's absurd."

"I know but they seem serious."

"You need a lawyer to sort it all out."

"I've got one. He's been really helpful."

"Good. Where did he come from?"

"Friend of Jonathan's."

"Oh. Has he been helping?"

"He has but he is on the West coast right now, seeing a friend."

"Right. How can I help then? This whole thing sounds so bizarre."

"It is. Took me by surprise. I've been sort of set up."

"Well, you are not a stalker and obviously not involved in the wife's disappearance so they've got nothing to go on. Do you want me to call them and talk to them again?"

"That's why I'm calling. The lawyer thought that it might be useful."

"OK. I'll get on it later this afternoon. I'll call Hollis again. Make sure that he knows what a great person you are."

"Thanks. I'm sure it will help. See you soon."

"Bye Ag."

They rang off. Aggie was sure that a call from Jack would, indeed, be helpful.

She saw that Hollis was slightly thrown off his game when she had mentioned that she was close friends with a detective. She thought it ironic that she should need a character reference, for that's what it was. She knew, though, that it would not deter him when he thought he was on to some kind of foul play, at the center of which he had placed Aggie. She decided to veg out for the rest of the late afternoon and evening with Indian take-out, a glass of Malbec and some more of Charles Todd. After breakfast the next day, a Friday, she had a call from Jonathan. Aggie asked him how things were going with his friend, Blink and learned that he had, for some reason, gone badly downhill, had been evicted from his apartment and been living on the streets for almost a month. It had taken Jonathan and Cedric three days to track him down. They now had him in a motel, were cleaning him up and figuring out a way to get him back on his feet. Jonathan expected that to take a week or two. Aggie brought him up to date with her own predicament and when he asked about Frank again, she reassured him that Frank had been incredibly helpful. She asked Jonathan if he needed anything done in New York like picking up mail or shopping but he said that he was good.

They ended the call promising to stay in touch. Aggie turned her mind to planning the day and, maybe, the weekend. She could do nothing about Hollis's efforts to drag her into some kind of charge with respect to Marcia Forman. What she could do was to try to track down Marcia Forman herself. She was reasonably confident in her ability to do just that and thought that she would begin later in the morning or after lunch.

Meanwhile, she had to make some solid progress in the Kowalczyk affair. He was expecting some clarity soon, even though, she thought, it might not turn out to be the clarity he sought. Who had drugged him and who had started the truck fire? Presumably the same person or persons. What was the next step? She now had a burgeoning feeling that he was involved in some kind of scam but she needed to establish whether there had been an independent scheme to murder him and, if so, who was responsible. Or, had he faked the whole scenario himself? Had he been planning something nefarious all along? The nefarious part would have been a complex operation, much more so than if others had simply tried to murder him while he was perpetrating a scam. Until shown otherwise, she would accept that no outsider was involved unless he or she, had been hired for the job. Cordelia was the one possibility remaining for the visit to the towing company. If she did turn out to be the primary suspect for all of the planning, she would almost certainly have needed an accomplice and that, unfortunately, could have been anyone in the partners' families or Kowalczyk himself, if it was a scam and not a murder attempt. Aggie thought that she could eliminate the three Mason daughters – two were away and one, the prosecutor, had been cleared by Steve via the photograph, assuming that he was correct and not lying. Also, she could not see the well-off Masons being party to an attempted murder for profit. So, she concluded, she was left with the Waters family and Kowalczyk. As she sat and mulled it all over, she could not shake off the feeling that, in spite of the intriguing challenges, the whole affair was so sordid, petty and unpleasant but she was being paid to get to the bottom of it and she intended to – and quickly. A trip to see the Waters family, or some of them, seemed onerous and, maybe, she could get all that she wanted out of a phone call to Budge Waters. She would have to put some thought into it first to ask the right questions but felt that it could be done, if he was in a compliant frame of mind. By midday, she was well prepared but doubted that Waters would be home although it was worth a try. She picked up her cell and dialed the Waters home number. After many rings there was a pick up.

"Hello."

That one word had enough slur in it for Aggie to know that the speaker had been drinking.

"Hi. My name is Agnes Trout."

Before she could continue the voice said.

"Is it really?"

"Yes it is. I would like to speak to Budge Waters please."

A lengthy pause.

"He's not here at the moment. He's at work."

The words were slow and carefully pronounced.

"I see. What a pity. Who am I speaking to?"

"My name is Stefan. Mr. Waters is my father."

Aggie was quite pleased with this information. Also, apparently Stefan still lived with his parents. Not uncommon these days.

"Oh. Well, that's good. Perhaps you can help me."

"Perhaps I can. What are you doing?"

"I am a Private Investigator. I have been hired by Mr. Kowalczyk of J. K. Trucking to sort out some problems that he is dealing with."

Again, a long silence while processing was in operation.

"He has problems?"

"Yes. I am helping him to resolve some of them."

"What problems does he have?"

"Stefan, I'm afraid that they are personal. I can't talk about them."

"OK."

"I am making some initial inquiries. I have the names of his business partners and their families."

"So this is to do with trucking stuff."

"Some of it is, yes."

"You are on about the fire aren't you?"

"Correct, at least that is part of it. Do you know anything about it?"

"All I know is that Jakob was driving a truck when it caught fire. Lucky to get away with it."

Aggie waited for more but none came. She responded.

"He was lucky. He passed out around the time that the fire started."

"Yes, must have been the fumes."

Again silence apart from a stifled yawn.

"You drive his trucks sometimes don't you?"

"Yes. I fill in now and again. He has a couple of regular drivers who have been with him for a long time."

Aggie continued.

"Does each driver drive the same truck?"

"Yes, pretty much."

"So Mr. Kowalczyk would drive the same truck most of the time? The one that caught fire?"

"Yes. That was his baby. Look, I'm a bit tired. Can you call my father later when he's home."

Aggie glanced at her notes.

"OK. Just a couple more things, please. Have you seen the truck since the fire?"

"No. Why would I want to?"

"Just to see what happened to it, perhaps."

Another pause.

"I drove it once in a while. I don't care what happened to it."

"Are you visiting your parents at the moment?"

He was sounding irritated.

"What? No, I live here."

"Does your sister live there too?"

"Of course not. She lives with her boyfriend. Look, I'm done here."

"OK. Sorry. One last question. What car does she drive?"

"A Jeep Cherokee. Bye."

He broke the connection.

Chapter 18

Aggie put down her cell thoughtfully. She thought that, because Stefan was somewhat inebriated and seemed to lack any obvious deviousness, he was probably telling the truth. That being the case, it was reasonable to eliminate him from being involved in the attack on Kowalczyk. The really interesting new development was that Cordelia drove a Jeep Cherokee and was, therefore, most likely the woman that cleared up the evidence at the towing company. Aggie needed to talk to her or, at least, find out more about her. She realized that she had no phone number or address but could likely dig it up on the ubiquitous Internet. Then she had an idea, picked up her cell and called Stefan again. He picked up straight away – probably, like Aggie, hadn't moved.

"You again. What's up this time?"

"Sorry. I know you are busy."

He interrupted immediately.

"Funny. What do you want?"

"I really would like to talk to your sister and wondered if you could give me her phone number."

"Why do you want to talk to her?"

"Just so that I can tidy things up and finish all of this. She might be able to help me do that."

"OK. Got a pen?"

He gave her the number.

"Do you have her address as well?"

A pause.

"No. Not giving you that. You can be a detective and find it."

"An investigator, not a detective. OK. Well, thank you Stefan, you have been very helpful."

There was no response. Just a click as the phone went dead. Suitable profanities bubbled up in Aggie's mind but she brushed them aside. She was closer to Cordelia now and had to consider what to do next. After a few moments, she began to like the direct approach by phone. The only drawback was that she had not seen Cordelia yet and would like the chance to see her reactions to certain questions. She held the idea in abeyance for the time being. A quick lunch of a couple of yoghurts again with coffee was on the cards before any more planning. After lunch, Aggie did not take long to track down an address, again in Bergen County, for Cordelia Waters. Also listed at the same address was Clement Smith. He turned out to be a mathematician of some note who had taken up teaching mathematics and computer science at a local High School. Aggie was torn between wanting to observe the two of them, preferably together, to see what vibes she could pick up and just making a phone call to glean what she could. Clearly, the first was a better option, especially now that the weekend was here and both might be counted on for being at home, although, maybe casinos had weird hours for their employees – she didn't know. Still, early on a Saturday morning might be a good bet. As she turned the ideas over in her mind, her cell buzzed. She glanced at the number, which was a New Jersey code, and picked up. The voice sounded youthful, relaxed, assured.

"Hi. I am Detective Moses Reede of the Bergen County Major Crimes Unit. I'm looking for Agnes Trout."

Agnes thought that this sounded serious and wondered who she knew in New Jersey.

"You've found her. What's up?"

"Good. I understand that you are a Private Investigator."

"I am. What's this about?"

Reede ignored the question.

"Do you know Jakob Kowalczyk?"

Aggie had little patience for the way that detectives worked in obtaining information and not answering questions, even though she knew that was the way in which she worked too.

"How do I know that you are who you say you are?"

Reede had a smile in his voice.

"I thought that you might go there. Look at my number. It's my cell. I could also give you my office number and you could call me back."

Aggie sighed, still perturbed by the call.

"OK. I believe you."

"Do you know Jakob Kowalczyk?"

"I do."

"How long have you known him?"

"A couple of weeks. Look, do the decent thing and tell me what's going on."

There were a few moments of silence.

"I'm afraid that he was shot last night."

"Oh, no. Is he OK?"

"No, not really. He is unconscious after surgery. Fifty-fifty."

"That's terrible. Where did this happen?"

Reede paused again.

"In a diner car park as he was getting in his ride. Shot twice in the back. Now, as you must know, I need information."

"Of course, but how did you get my name?"

"We found a note in his wallet with your name and number, together with a check stub with your name on it. Now, how did you know him?"

Aggie responded.

"He hired me a couple of weeks ago."

"To do what exactly?"

Aggie summarized the circumstances of the hiring and the reasoning behind it, from the fire to the diner meeting in as spare a way as possible. Reede responded.

"Did you come to a conclusion about his claims?"

"I've gone back and forth on it. I'm at about eighty percent on there being something to it but that could change. I do not yet have a clear idea who is behind it."

Reede paused for thought.

"Well, I think that we can say that it's one hundred percent now, don't you?"

Was that a hint of humor?

"True."

"When you met him this week, how did he seem? Anything unusual about your chat?"

"He seemed fine. I updated him. He seemed good with my progress and he paid me. Told me to keep on with the investigation. This is hard to take in."

"Right. So he didn't point you in a particular direction. Anything like that?"

"No, he didn't. Look, just because he was shot – that is, someone tried to kill him, does not necessarily validate the idea that there were previous attempts on his life."

Reede responded quickly.

"What? Why doesn't it? He told an EMT guy that someone had tried to kill him in the past. Now, they have had another shot, haven't they? Oops, sorry about that."

"Of course. He has just been shot, that's true. But I have not fully subscribed to definitive attempts previously."

"What other solution is there?"

"I am still working on that."

"OK. Let's leave it at that for the moment. Now, supposing that there were previous attempts. In your work on this, who would you have in mind for that?"

Aggie did not want to be too explicit.

"I said that I did not have a clear idea yet. I'm looking at a circle of family members and business acquaintances."

"Anyone in particular?"

"No, not yet. Ongoing, you know."

Aggie felt that it would be beneficial to both of them for a fresh pair of eyes to take a look at this situation. Reede probably understood that too.

"OK. But let's keep in touch. Use this number."

"I will. By the way, what hospital is he in?"

A pause, perhaps because Reede knew that Aggie could find out anyway. He gave her the hospital name.

"I wouldn't visit for a while. It's uncertain as to if and when he will recover."

He disconnected.

Aggie put down her cell and leaned back on the couch. Someone had tried to murder Jakob Kowalczyk for real now. Unless it was a random shooting, the motive and the perpetrator had to lie somewhere in her investigation. She should have asked if anything had been taken from him because, if not, he was the target.

Reede would probably have mentioned it if a robbery had also taken place. The person, or persons, would have had to have followed him to the diner unless he always ate at the same diner at the same time each week, which seemed unlikely for a truck driver, often on the go. Aggie still had that nagging, intuitive thought that Kowalczyk was somehow, himself, involved in the original truck mishaps. That would make this murder attempt a separate issue, unless, perhaps, one incident provoked or instigated the other. This latest development meant great care in approaching Cordelia Waters and this Clement Smith. They were now looming large in her thoughts as possible suspects for all of this with, maybe, Kowalczyk fitting into the puzzle somewhere. A visit to the Cordelia Waters household tomorrow still felt right but, she thought, it might take on an observational bent rather than a confrontational one. She sighed and sat up on the edge of the couch. Time to let all of this settle in her mind and find something else to do in the meantime. She decided to have some coffee and cookies and, of all things, to call her mother in Florida. Her mother often made these calls, usually about every three weeks or a month, so occasionally, Aggie would reverse the family habit as, what she hoped, was a nice surprise. It was about three weeks since they had last spoken. She grabbed her cell and called. It was several rings before her mother picked up.

"Hi. Agnes?"

Her mother never seemed to have mastered looking at caller ID. If she did, she did not always believe it.

"Yes, mom. It's me."

"How are you love? Anything the matter?"

"No mom. Just calling to say hello."

"Oh, that's nice. We were just getting ready to go out. You know, the early bird. Your dad's in the bathroom."

"That's OK, mom. We can talk in a day or two."

"Good. We can catch up. Everything alright?"

Aggie tried to cover all in one sentence or so. She did not tell her parents about her more lurid adventures. It had crossed her mind that, perhaps, she should do that but the thought was unresolved as yet.

"Yes, mom. Still working on cases and having a good time with some of my friends."

"That's good. Well, your dad's on his way – so I'll call over the weekend, perhaps."

"OK mom. Give my love to dad. Love you."

"Love you too."

They disconnected.

Aggie stared at the phone for a while. She and her parents were quite close, she being an only child, and she regretted not seeing them more often. They were very comfortable in Florida. Lots of friends, very fit and healthy but Aggie was a New Yorker. Those were the chips that had been dealt. Still, she should be the one to visit Florida. She resolved to think it through and make more of an effort to see them. Next on the agenda was renting a car for the morning and then some deeper research on Marcia Forman. She had some superficial information from

Dwight Forman and some necessary detail that she had needed for observation for an alleged affair which, she was fairly sure was nonexistent.

Marcia Forman worked as a flight attendant for British Airways and had been with them for three years. She was thirty nine years old and had three children with Dwight Forman, their ages being nine, seven and four years of age.

Aggie assumed that she began working for the airline after the birth of her last child. Dwight Forman was a stay at home dad and, as far as Aggie could tell, had been that way for a long time, maybe since the birth of their first child. The source of his income was not readily available but Aggie had gathered it to be inherited through his immigrant grandparents who had started up some kind of tobacco business after the Second World War. The Formans had employed a live-in babysitter, supposedly for the heavy lifting of parenthood, Marcia being away a lot and Dwight perhaps tired of feeding kids and getting them to school. Most of this Aggie realized was her own speculation plus some intimation from her initial talk with Dwight Forman. That was the extent of Aggie's notes. After reserving a rental car for the following morning, she spent the afternoon and half of the evening researching and trying to confirm Marcia Forman's movements on Tuesday, her dinner being pieces of Cheddar cheese and some radishes with a glass of Cabernet. Five phone calls and extensive internet work did not come up with much. Marcia Forman had left London Heathrow at 10.00 pm UK time with the flight crew and had landed at JFK just after midnight US time. She had passed through the crew airport check quickly and then vanished. She had not gone home according to Dwight Forman and had not called either. He had said that she usually called to say that she had arrived safely. Of course, there was no way of knowing yet whether he was lying. Feeling very tired, Aggie opted for an early night and fell asleep after only five pages of her Charles Todd.

Chapter 19

The next day, a Saturday, Aggie was soon on the West Side Highway heading for New Jersey in a black Camry, her vehicle of choice as well as that of many rental agencies. Jonathan's Highlander was very comfortable but she liked the ease and simplicity of driving the Camry. She drove without music for a change and just under an hour later was approaching her goal, all detailed for her by GPS. She came off Route17 and followed a minor road for about seven miles to a tree lined turn off into a close of town house blocks. The close was fairly small with eight blocks of six town houses each. There were evenly spaced groups of parking spaces spread around the close for spill over cars or visitors, because each town house had a garage and front door on the first floor. There were just a handful of parking spaces remaining. The address Aggie had was the second home in the second block down on the right. She turned into the close and drove slowly to the end, needing a three point turn to reverse direction, as the turning circle was small and obstructed by a parked car. She made her way out of the close, carefully avoiding a look at the Waters home. The minor road was too narrow to just park in order to observe the close which would not be helpful anyway because she would not know which house drivers had come from, unless a green Jeep Cherokee emerged.

She hadn't seen one in the parking areas. Aggie concluded that she had to bite the bullet and park in the close and hope that she would not be seen by anyone in the Waters abode. Anybody else wondering what she was up to did not matter. She drove down the minor road and found a spot to turn around and headed back, noting that the land behind the town house blocks was largely agricultural. Maybe a farmer had sold off part of the farm for building homes. She turned into the close, parking on the opposite side of the close from the Waters home and about half a block down, in one of two vacant spots left in a group of spaces. She adjusted her mirror to see the front door of their house and settled in to watch, taking out a small pad and pen from her bag and trying to look occupied and unsuspicious.

A very long hour and a half passed, during which Aggie saw at least eight or nine cars back out of their parking spaces or come out of their garages and drive off, a couple returning, the drivers unloading and carrying shopping bags indoors. Then her patience was rewarded. The front door of the Waters home opened and a tall, grey haired guy emerged. He closed the front door and walked to the garage door standing by it. A strong ripple of excitement coursed through Aggie's body as she stared at the small image in her Camry mirror with acutely sharpened intensity. She was sure that she recognized the man who, apparently, lived in this town house under the name of Clement Smith. He was Paul Wright. The guy who had helped her to extricate Jakob Kowalczyk from the burning truck.

After a few moments, the garage door began to open upwards, triggered by an internal operating system. Aggie could hear nothing of the opening mechanism from her vantage point. When the door was fully open, a green Jeep Cherokee chugged slowly out of the garage and stopped on the short drive, water vapor spouting from the exhaust pipe at the back of the car. The garage door worked its way down in reverse to the ground and Clement Smith aka Paul Wright, as Aggie was now convinced was the case, climbed into the passenger seat. The car then reversed out of the drive in a large arc into the close almost as far as where Aggie was parked on the opposite side of the close and stopped momentarily. Clement Smith was on her side of the Jeep and so Aggie could not see the driver clearly, although she could see that she was a woman with dark hair, wearing a ball cap. Aggie thought that she would bet a lot on the driver being Cordelia Waters. The Jeep surged forward towards the exit from the close, turned off down the minor road and was gone.

Aggie continued to stare at the image of a closed garage door in the mirror as the full import of the new information took its place in her mind. The two people who showed up at the truck fire, ostensibly by chance, did not do so. Cordelia Waters and Clement Smith were intimately involved and clearly had arrived by arrangement. There was no other way of looking at it. Had they manipulated the whole scenario or was Jakob Kowalczyk part of it? He and Cordelia, although somewhat tenuously, were in the trucking business, so wouldn't an educated guess put him right in the middle of all of this? There was no doubt in Aggie's mind that Cordelia was the woman who showed up at the towing company and removed fire evidence.

That all hung together and Cordelia Waters was up to her eyebrows in either planning the whole fire episode or as an enabler for somebody else. Aggie thought that in the absence of a stronger connection between Cordelia Waters and Jakob Kowalczyk, the fact that they were peripherally involved in the same trucking business was probably enough for her theory to hold water. Something must have gone very wrong, though, for Kowalczyk to have been shot. The intent was to murder him but who had done it? What was the motive for trying to kill him?

Aggie was comfortable with the notion that the way these events had unfolded precluded an outsider being involved. She was also aware that she had developed a soft spot for Kowalczyk and mildly regretted that she was making a case against him. She came out of her reverie, noting that life was occasionally going on around her as cars moved in and out of the close and the odd resident walked by with a dog or was just out strolling in a vigorous healthful way.

Time to move on. Aggie decided that some sort of confrontation with these two people was not a good way to go in terms of finding out something new. As she reached for the ignition key, she saw and heard the Jeep Cherokee at the same time, the image in her car mirror catching her eye. It pulled into the drive and stopped in front of the garage door. Clement Smith hopped out and went to the front door, opened it and went inside. After a few moments, the driver's side door opened and the boot and jean clad legs of Cordelia Waters emerged. She stepped out somewhat athletically, stood for a moment staring at Aggie's Camry and then strode towards it in a discernibly aggressive manner.

Chapter 20

So much for a non-confrontational morning with these people or, for Cordelia Waters, in particular. That thought was history now. A hand with the forefinger doubled over appeared at her window on the driver's side. The forefinger knuckle tapped twice on the glass. Aggie lowered the window a few inches only because, seated in the driver's seat with a fully open window felt vulnerable. She looked up into the face which had lowered itself to her level and noted the dark hair and eyes, sharp features and generous mouth of Cordelia Waters. The ball cap had no logo on it. The mouth twisted into an ugly shape as the words were forced out.

"Ah. I thought it was you. What the fuck are you doing here?"

"It's a public place."

Waters sucked in a breath.

"It's our public place. And you, whatever your name is, are not welcome. Does that seem clear to you?"

Aggie remained calm and did not respond. She stared coolly into the distorted, angry features. The corner of Waters' left eyelid was twitching rhythmically as if to a musical beat.

"You're spying on us, aren't you?"

That word again.

"Spying?"

"Well, there is nobody else here that you could possibly know is there? Why don't you just fuck off."

"Or what?"

Waters stood up suddenly and gazed around her, breathing heavily, and then bent down again.

"Look, why are you here? This is my home and I don't need you hanging around and staring in my windows."

Aggie wanted to turn this down a notch, if that was possible, and to see if anything useful popped out.

"I'm looking into a couple of things for Jakob Kowalczyk."

A fleeting look of naked shock ran across Waters face and vanished.

"Jakob? What's that got to do with me? What does he want?"

Aggie noted the first name use. Difficult to read the hard eyes. Did she know about the shooting? Aggie could not tell. Reede almost certainly had not got to her yet. It would be easy to check with him anyway.

"I'm afraid that I can't tell you that."

Anger returned.

"Oh, nice. You a cop or something?"
"No, I'm not."
"Friend then? Oh, no, not a girlfriend? Checking me out are you?"
Aggie thought this to be an interesting tangent.
"No. I'm not a girlfriend."
Intuition clicked in quickly and she continued.
"You still his girlfriend are you?"
"No. Are you fucking crazy?"
She stole a glance back at her house, where all was quiet.
"That was all over a long time ago. Anyway, none of your fucking business"
"No, I suppose it isn't."
Waters moved her face perceptibly closer.
"What do you really want?"
An edge crept into her voice as she continued to speak slowly.
"What do you fucking want?"
Aggie responded and, as she spoke, fired the ignition.
"Nothing. I'm done here."
"You are. Don't fucking come back."
As Aggie reversed the car, stopped and put it into forward gear,
Waters walked alongside the car.
"Do you hear me? Things can happen."

Aggie did hear her and headed out of the close, glancing in the mirror at the figure standing in the middle of the close behind her as she turned in the direction of Route 17. As she drove back to the city, Aggie put all the new information together in her mind. Cordelia Waters had, by her own admission, had an affair with Jakob Kowalczyk and not a fleeting one at that, it seemed. At the mention of his name, her expression registered shock which Aggie took to indicate her disbelief that an apparent stranger, an unwitting participant in the scam, not only knew about the affair but also was well acquainted with Kowalczyk, hence the girlfriend comment. Waters must have wondered how all of that had come about. She did not know Aggie's name or her profession. Jakob Kowalczyk, then, had been very careful to keep his business relationship with Aggie confidential. Interesting, because it meant that even if he was involved in the scam, he thought, or suspected, that something might happen to him. He had enlisted her services as some kind of back up in case things went south. Aggie smiled to herself as she reflected on the principle of insurance against an insurance scam. Well, things had, indeed, gone south and here she was trying to figure out what happened. Somebody had shot Kowalczyk. Who and why? Had to be about the money. Could Cordelia Waters have done it? Aggie thought that she was perfectly capable of doing so. Coarse, cunning even. But she was either a brilliant actress or she didn't do it. She was, though, living with a man who had given a false name to cops at the scene of an accident. No need for that as far as she could see – unless he had a lot to hide. Not a smart thing to do – they could have asked for ID. It would definitely be helpful to talk to Reede in a day or so to compare notes – if he was the comparing notes type of detective.

Before she was really aware of it, Aggie had dropped off the rental and was in her apartment, having been dragged into currency by working her way through the Johnathan inspired locks on her door. Tossing her bag and jacket onto the couch she thought of Kowalczyk. For several reasons, she hoped that Kowalczyk would regain consciousness soon. His brush with mortality might engender a cooperative mood or, at least, he might feel inclined to share some details with Aggie once she had laid out her findings, suspicions and educated guesses. More than that, on a personal level, she also liked him. He had put a successful business together through hard work in a tough market and had, subsequently, taken a misstep or two in handling his finances. Everything now pointed to his skirting the law, while, at the same time, beginning a relationship with a much younger woman, who might have had an ulterior motive for the liaison. Nothing new in that, of course, and, to be fair, maybe they had something going to begin with. Somewhere along the line Clement Smith had entered the scene. Perhaps he was the catalyst for all of this. A sudden flight of fancy struck her. Mathematician, computer scientist, an affair with a casino croupier. Was there a link in there somewhere? It hardly worked in any way with an insurance scam. Where did their paths cross? Lovers had to meet up somewhere. A school or a casino? Too fanciful. Probably a bar. Food for thought anyway. An extra look at Clement Smith could be fruitful. Plus a call to the hospital to check on Kowalczyk. A chat with Moses Reede too, would go down well. Aggie realized it was mid-afternoon and she had not eaten. Time for cheese, crackers (stale) and coffee.

Chapter 21

After her belated lunch, Aggie brought all of her musings up to date on her iPad and decided to give the hospital a call to see if she could squeeze out any information on Jakob Kowalczyk. She reached someone relatively quickly for a hospital, who declared themself to be a media administrative assistant. Aggie said that she was seeking information on a patient.

"Who are you again, please?"

"Agnes Trout and I am not media."

"I see. Who are you inquiring about?"

"Jakob Kowalczyk."

"Could you spell the second name please."

Aggie did so and also mentioned the 'k' in the first name.

There was a lengthy silence broken only by computer keys.

"Ah. Are you a member of the family?"

"No. I know Mr. Kowalczyk through work."

"An employee or employer then?"

"Not exactly. He engaged my services recently."

Time to push the envelope a little.

"And we became friends."

"So you are a professional of some kind?"

"Correct. And a friend."

"So you do know why Mr. Kowalczyk is here?"

"I do. He was shot."

There was another brief interlude.

"Just so. Well, he is unable to receive visitors because he is sedated."

"Actually, I don't know of anyone who is likely to visit him. Except me."

"That may be the case but he has been unconscious since he was admitted. He has undergone surgery and is in intensive care."

Aggie continued.

"Is there any projected time that he might be able to receive visitors?"

"Not at the moment. It is a day to day thing. You could call early next week. I might add that he has not given permission for the release of any personal information to an outside source."

"Well, he hasn't been in any position to do that, has he?"

Aggie heard a definite sigh over the line.

"True. But the policy still stands. We need his permission to release any personal information."

Aggie wrapped her mind around the word 'personal'.

"Is there an official classification for his condition that you feel comfortable sharing with me?"

"Yes. It is 'critical but stable'."

Aggie responded.

"Thank you. Has it always been that since he came in?"

"No. He was unstable at an earlier juncture. You are not a reporter, are you?"

Aggie laughed.

"No, I can safely say that I am not a reporter. I will try a visit next week then. Thanks."

They broke the connection. Aggie put the phone down on the coffee table and gazed at the window reflectively. Two or three useful facts had emerged. On a personal level, she was relieved that Kowalczyk had made a little progress. There was a lot in that word 'stable'. As far as she was aware, it referred to vital signs which were, presumably, unstable on his arrival and had been steadied up by the doctors. Good news. Plus, he could have been a stage worse than critical too, whatever that was. 'Grave' perhaps or 'extremely critical'. She had heard both terms before and had assumed their relative ranking. So he was improving. He was sedated as opposed to unconscious through trauma. Also, good. There seemed to be some expectation that he would improve enough for visitors. She would keep track of that. Also, intensive care meant monitoring around the clock, so he was being well looked after. She had a sudden thought and looked up the shift times of the nursing staff at the hospital. There was an end to the current shift right now at 4.00pm. Maybe, the administrative folk had similar shifts. Maybe, if she called again she would get a different person anyway. She called again an hour later, caught a different administrative assistant but got all the same answers, except that she was advised to call on Monday morning. All in all, a useful exercise imbued with some relief at Kowalczyk's condition. Aggie felt restless and somewhat fatigued and thought that a down, relaxing evening with Jack would not go amiss so she called him. He answered quickly and turned out to be at home for once.

"Hi Ag. How's things?"

"Good. You at home then? Case over?"

"Yes and no. Still working on it. More to it than I thought."

He seemed rushed and not keen on talking about it so Aggie dropped it.

"Are you doing anything this evening? Wondered if you wanted to get together."

Jack sighed.

"Sorry Ag. I'm doing something tonight. Wish I'd known."

He seemed about to explain but Aggie interrupted him. She did not need explanations. That was not how they worked.

"That's OK Jack. Another time. I'd only just thought of it. We can catch up during the week."

"OK. We'll do that. Is everything OK?"

"Pretty much, although a lot going on. The trucker got himself shot, almost killed."

"Wow, that's bad. How is he doing?"

"The doctors are officially cautious but it looks like he'll pull through."

"Any idea who did it?"

"Nothing concrete, just ideas."

"Well, keep me posted. You know, on how you are doing. By the way, I called that guy Hollis."

"Did it go alright?"

Jack paused.

"I think so. He seemed to resent me calling. None of my business sort of thing. But I told him that I had known you for a long time and that there was no way you were a stalker or anything else bad."

"He didn't like that?"

"No. Bit of a one track mind. We are on the same side when you think about it. Anyway, it had to have helped. Make him think a bit."

"Thanks Jack. Have a good weekend:"

"And you. Bye."

They disconnected.

That was it then. No fun weekend. Happened now and again. No more work this evening. Aggie decide to veg and pamper herself. Soup and two take out sandwiches plus some Chardonnay and television. First part of the evening was, by chance, flipping channels, the life of squirrels. Normally, Aggie was put off by all wildlife programs because they almost always involved creatures or animals killing each other but this program was actually interesting and, although predators, like snakes, entered the story, all principals escaped which was nice. She found out that a squirrel's brain somehow changes in size or capability to accommodate information like where a thousand nuts are buried. Could that be true?

And that the UK red squirrel is diminishing in numbers and becoming confined to Scotland. A woman also reared a few days old baby squirrel into adulthood. Good things and good people sometimes happened in life, which was reassuring. After that, she watched a political channel but gave up after half an hour because it was not so reassuring. An old movie called 'The Bishop's Wife' rounded out an odd evening but it was Cary Grant whom she liked and admired – plus it was a sad, beautiful emotional movie.

Chapter 22

Sunday came soon enough, although Aggie stayed in bed for a while dozing and having no urge to venture into the world until she felt guilty enough to give it a try. A long, hot shower and two cups of black coffee later, she pulled out her iPad and ran through her comments and projected actions, wondering which offered the most enjoyable experience. Thing was, none of them did. So, buttered toast and more coffee filled the void as she considered all of the options. None were appealing but she decided on some research concerning Clement Smith, also known for a brief time as Paul Wright. Two hours later, she rubbed sore eyes or, at least, eyes that needed a rest, and looked at her findings, which were quite substantial. The Clement Smith, who seemed the most likely candidate of a couple of dozen Clement Smiths, was born in Brooklyn to two Middle School teachers and was 48 years old. Perhaps Cordelia Waters liked older men? Aggie found a published resume for him online – one of the strange outcomes of the data gathering universe. Many people found it useful and had no trepidation about confidentiality.

    He had science degrees and a penchant for mathematics which he had used in a variety of jobs from Civil Engineering to Wall Street. Shortly after his spell with the latter he had gone through bankruptcy which was interesting. Aggie wondered if there was a connection through mathematics, investment and casinos. He was probably a gambling man and wouldn't be the first to pit his skills against the casino – and lose. It just felt right. He then became a relatively successful and apparently well liked mathematics teacher in High School, perhaps licking his financial wounds and steadying his life. Old habits die hard though and Aggie could see the possibility of Clement Smith crossing paths with Cordelia Waters somewhere in the environs of the casino where she worked. Mostly supposition but it carried the ring of truth. Could he have begun to imagine again, perhaps, that he could beat the system? Throw a friendly, young croupier into the mix and plans begin to take shape. Perhaps they had been, or were even now, in the planning phase of something profitable at the casino but how did all that fit in with the Kowalczyk business? Aggie rubbed her eyes again. She needed a break and so pottered around the apartment, cleaning and washing up the dishes. It really was a perfect time for the gym and so she put her work out kit together, took her credit card and keys and set off to reinvigorate herself. By chance, even though it was a weekend, she was able to join a Feldenkrais class instead of performing her usual kick boxing routine.

    She rather enjoyed the company and doing something in a group, although she still, basically, kept to herself. She had wondered about taking up a racket sport indoors because of the high intensity relief of tensions that they were supposed to bring about. That was in the future. She bade farewell to those of her companions who felt like communicating and headed back to her apartment. She decided not to shower and baked a couple of jacket potatoes with butter for dinner with some Fiji water. She also decided to take more care about her carb intake after that because the potatoes tasted too good to be good. She spent most of the evening trying to get a handle on some of the financial aspects of Cordelia Waters and Clement Smith. The town house was in the sole ownership of Cordelia Waters who was paying the mortgage and had not missed any payments, most of which went towards covering the mortgage interest at this stage. Aggie could find nothing on Waters' income but assumed that it was a reasonable one in order to cover taking out a mortgage. It would also be reasonable to assume that Clement Smith coughed up a little financial aid for the house budget, as he lived with Waters.

His salary as a suburban mathematics teacher should allow for that unless he was still gambling it away. Finally, just before a well-deserved rest in bed, she looked up some of Jakob Kowalczyk's residential information which, although she had an address in Ramsey, New Jersey, she had not gotten around to doing. It turned out that he lived in a two bedroom apartment in a block of eight apartments, his being one of the ground floor ones with, presumably, some yard access. He had almost no mortgage left to repay, being less than two years away from redeeming the mortgage. The apartment block was situated in a busy area that included several hotels, car franchises, liquor stores and an I Hop restaurant. Plenty of noise and activity then but a desirable place to live for those that liked company. As far as Aggie knew, he lived on his own, except perhaps when Cordelia Waters had stopped over in better days. So, he seemed to be in a solid financial position as far as owning property and part of a trucking company. But, according to Strum, Kowalczyk gambled and owed him a substantial sum as a result. Aggie thought it a pity to rock the boat in that senseless way but each to his own. What was it with all these gamblers? She closed her iPad, cleaned up the kitchen and went to bed.

Chapter 23

Aggie was in the shower on Monday morning when she thought she heard her cell phone ringing. She finished up and, with a towel wrapped around her, stepped into the living area and picked up her cell from the coffee table. The caller ID offered Moses Reede. She wondered, with some amusement, if he announced himself on pick up as "Moses here".

She supposed that doing so would soon begin to grate. Look at Trout. She dialed up to get Reede. Of course, he could see who was calling so no answer to her fantasy.

"Good morning Ms. Trout. Reede."

"Hi. Returning your call."

"Ms. Trout. Do you know a guy named Adam Salter?"

Aggie paused to think.

"No. I don't know the name."

"So, in all of your investigation into the trucking thing, you have not come across this guy?"

"No. What's he done?"

Reede was silent for a moment.

"Nothing. Just got himself shot. He's dead."

Aggie was puzzled.

"OK. Not good. But what has that got to do with me?"

"Nothing directly. But what if I told you that his job in life was a claims adjuster?"

Aggie drew in a deep breath.

"He was THE claims adjuster?"

"Think so. Have to double check, of course. Things are getting a bit hairy, don't you think?"

"Looks that way. How did it happen? You're sure there is a connection?"

"Come on. How couldn't there be? The truck driver and the claims adjuster both shot in connection with the same truck. Wouldn't take much guesswork to put it all together."

Aggie added.

"I thought that the truck assessment was somewhat cursory. No mention or concern about the removal of what could be forensic evidence. So this is a murder/attempted murder investigation now not just a scam."

"That's the size of it, Ms. Trout."

"Please call me Agnes or Aggie. I expect we will be in touch now. At least, I hope you will keep me up to date."

"Well, Agnes, that is a possibility. Call me Moses, if you are comfortable with that."

Aggie wanted to know a little more.

"When did all this happen?"

"Last evening, between nine and midnight. Shot through an open window. Quiet street, no witnesses. Must have used a silencer. At least, nobody seems to have heard anything."

"What will you do next?"

"Follow up in general but concentrate on the cast of characters around your truck case."

"You think one of them did the shooting?"

"Well, that would seem to be the obvious notion. Unless there are other circumstances that we don't know about yet. I'll be covering the bases. Anything new on your end?"

Aggie considered her answer. Reede seemed genuine and helpful.

"I went to observe the couple from the truck scene. The ones that showed up at just the right time. I think that they are involved in an insurance scam, probably with Jakob Kowalczyk."

Aggie suddenly realized that she knew that he had to be part of the scam, something she had been unwilling to accept but there it was. Reede responded.

"They have serious motive here, don't they. Doesn't seem like enough for a couple of murders though. What happened?"

"I got into a set to with Cordelia Waters. She asked me to leave in an impolite way."

"Hah. What did you conclude?"

"That she and her boyfriend, Clement Smith, who lives with her, are in on the scam. That she removed evidence from the truck after the fire. Kowalczyk insured the truck so he must be part of it or they could not get to the money. I don't know who planned the whole thing or how they actually did it. Don't know why they would kill him – makes no sense. He has control of the money. Like you say, not a lot of money to kill for either."

"Right. Well, someone in there did the shooting, whether they planned this whole thing or not. Waters works as a croupier at the casino. She is well paid, has had no problems that I am aware of and is financially stable. She doesn't need to go scamming insurance companies or killing people. I'll see what else I can dig up. What will you do?"

Aggie thought for a moment.

"I'm going to keep in touch with the hospital. If Jakob Kowalczyk comes round I will need to speak to him."

"So will I Agnes. So will I. Keep in touch."

Reede closed the call.

Aggie put down the cell and went to her bedroom to get dressed. It was clear now that, if Kowalczyk survived and was lucid, she would have to speak to him and confront him with several issues, not least of which was that he had engaged her services to cover his actions and that now, she would have to turn over her findings to the cops. Added to that, someone had literally tried to kill him.

Someone with a taste of irony if they had any awareness. That person also had no qualms about cleaning up any loose ends if the claims adjuster had, indeed, been one. She wondered how safe Kowalczyk was in that hospital. She supposed that some hospitals had security issues and some did not. As an outsider it was difficult to know about a particular hospital. She thought about asking Reede about it but felt that it was farfetched. The pool of suspects was very small. As far as Aggie could see, there were only Waters, Smith, Strum and Westlake in that pool. The latter two were not really contenders and, as Strum had indicated, Kowalczyk needed to be around so that they could collect. If either Waters or Smith had done the shootings, would the other have known or suspected something? Could they have done the shootings together? It was hard to visualize Waters being a participant. What would be the point? Money? Love? Neither seemed likely. She probably didn't need either. So, some kind of double cross was in the works, perhaps, and a talk with Kowalczyk, if possible, pointed the way to a solution. On the spur of the moment, she decided to call her newly acquired lawyer. She was a little perturbed by the silence from that side of her recent experience. After a couple of rings, someone picked up.

"Pederson and Frome. How can I direct your call?"

"Agnes Trout. I would like to speak to Frank Pederson please."

"The nature of your call?"

Aggie responded.

"I am a client of his and would like a word."

"Right. Just a moment."

There were a couple of clicks, momentary silence and then Pederson's voice.

"Hi Aggie. How are you? Before you answer that, let me guess. You are waiting for a proverbial shoe to drop. Right?"

Aggie couldn't help smiling. Was it so obvious?

"Hi Frank. Yes, you are correct. Wondering what was up."

"Well, I've heard nothing. I am not inclined to stir the pot by asking. If, and when, they are ready, we will hear from them. I've no doubt that they have been inquiring their heads off but there is nothing there."

"No, there isn't but that didn't seem to stop them before."

Pederson laughed.

"True. But now, to proceed, they need evidence, not just supposition. And there is none. Now, as I intimated before, if Mrs. Forman shows up in a less than alive state, things will begin to hum."

"Yes. I can see that."

"So, as far as we are concerned, we just sit tight and put it out of our minds. Not easy for you is it?"

"No. It's just there, hanging about."

There was a pause.

"Hm. Well, there's nothing stopping you doing what you do."

"What are you thinking?"

"Why don't you check up on this woman? Find her. See what's going on."

He added.

"Might keep you amused. I'm sure you are busy but it may help."

Aggie smiled.

"That sounds good. It had crossed my mind and I did a little digging. As a lawyer, you are a good psychologist. Thank you."

"My pleasure Aggie. Good luck."

And he was gone.

Aggie thought it all through. She had a bit of time. She had to call the hospital to see how Kowalczyk was doing but it was worth having a shot at finding the Forman woman. She would get to that later in the morning. After a quick cereal breakfast, she put in a call to the hospital. This time the experience was a little easier and the response less official. Kowalczyk was now conscious and his condition had been marginally upgraded. He was not yet receiving visitors although, Aggie assumed, there were not many of those clamoring to get in to see him. In another day, perhaps, she might be able to do just that and begin to approach some kind of conclusion with his case which had now mushroomed into a police investigation. Her end of it had diminished somewhat due to the shootings but she could still resolve much of it for her own satisfaction and, maybe, an assist for Reede. Adding a chat with Waters after Kowalczyk would go a long way towards doing that. She wondered if she was in any kind of danger at this point due to her sleuthing. Whoever was behind the shootings must know that she was sniffing around and looking for answers. Not for the first time, she resolved to take a little care. Aggie began sifting through her notes on the iPad concerning Marcia Forman. She had arrived at JFK around midnight on Tuesday going into Wednesday, skipped through customs and vanished. Well, nobody vanishes. As a start she thought that she would call a bunch of hotels around the airport to look for a check in after midnight in the name of Forman. A long shot to find a random hotel, even if Forman used her real name. Aggie decided to eliminate the really upscale hotels. If Forman wanted a hotel for whatever reason, she probably would not go for expensive but clean, comfortable and, perhaps, unobtrusive.

In other words second tier. There were dozens of those hotels and, after three hours of calls with no luck, she took a break and made some buttered toast and coffee. Supposing Forman was not planning to come home but needed an overnight to meet someone or just to think. In the latter case, some downtime in other words. To Aggie, that seemed right. Also, why go to the bother of a name change? According to Aggie's theory, she would not be in hiding but looking for time to herself. A decent hotel would fill the bill. A couple of drinks at the bar and some room service for dinner. Of course, all of this theorizing precluded foul play, but she had to start somewhere.

Her investigatory instincts told her that Marcia Forman was not deceased and she wanted to prove it.

Chapter 24

After another two hours, Aggie was running out of steam. She then drew a circle of about ten miles radius around the Forman address and began calling up hotels in that area. It took less than another hour to get a hit. Marcia Forman had checked into a Best Western just six miles or so from her home and stayed one night before disappearing again. The reservation was for two people and, Aggie, supposed, six miles was as good as a hundred. Two people, one room. Aggie began to think that she had missed something. And now they had gone again or, at least, Marcia Forman had. One good thing about all of this – there was no way that she could be tied to any kind of foul play. What had Dwight Forman been up to with all of that? She wanted to find out. She also wanted to track down Marcia Forman and talk to her. It was already evening and her eyes were too tired for reading so she opted for some banal TV after a can of soup and a piece of French baguette before bed.

The next day Aggie was up early. She showered and sat on her couch in her robe drinking coffee and reviewing her findings. She called the hospital and asked if Kowalczyk was receiving visitors yet. She was told that was unclear just now but, if she left her name, they would call back later in the morning. She gave her name and said that it was urgent for her to see Kowalczyk on a personal matter. In the meantime, there was not much to be done on that front so she turned her thoughts back to Marcia Forman. Without much effort, she was able to obtain a cell phone number for Forman. She knew that it was possible to track smart phones using online forensics and to get a reading on the cell location but she did not know how to do it. She thought that Jack might be able to get somewhere with that idea and so she called him. The call went to message and so Aggie left a message with the cell phone number in case Jack could help. She had barely dressed and returned to the living area before her cell rang. It was Jack.

"Hi Ag. How are you doing?"
"Hi Jack. Pretty good. Making progress."
"Good. Look, I've got some info for you on that phone."
Aggie was impressed.
"Great. That was quick."
"Yes. Not too difficult actually."
"What's the info?"
"Well, your phone is currently heading out of Chicago in a North Westerly direction."
Aggie took in a quick breath.

"What?"

"Yes, it's very busy."

"Wow. Thanks Jack. I am surprised. This is very helpful. I would have had no idea."

Jack laughed.

"I'm good aren't I? It could be on a train or a plane or in a car. The speed will give you a clue."

"Thanks."

"I'll keep tabs on it for a while and let you know what's up."

This was really interesting news.

"Great."

"Of course, it's only the phone. May not be the person that owns it."

"Right. It belongs to the stay at home dad's wife."

"Ah. Still alive and kicking then."

"I hope so."

There was a pause for a few seconds.

"OK. I'll call you in a couple of hours with an update."

"Thanks Jack. How's your case going?"

"Got to go. I'll tell you when I see you. Will that be soon?"

"I'd like that. Later in the week?"

"Great. Would Friday work?"

"Yes, I think so. Around seven? I'll cook up something."

"Perfect. I'll do some vino. Be in touch. Bye."

Jack rang off.

Aggie turned this new information over in her mind. She had had a fairly strong feeling that Marcia Forman was alive and now it looked even more positive that this was the case. What was she doing in Chicago? And now heading who knows where - in a Northwesterly direction. Montana? Canada? What was there? Aggie had also harbored vaguely perturbing thoughts about Dwight Forman. He was devious and a liar and she was sure that he was planning something in connection with his wife. Not something good either. Aggie couldn't put her finger on it but there was something there – he was putting some kind of plan together. Anyway, nothing had happened as far as she could tell. Follow the phone would be what she would be doing for the time being.

Late morning had already materialized and Aggie ran through all of her notes again before pottering around her apartment deep in thought. Eventually, she decided to call the hospital again since she had heard nothing. To her surprise, Kowalczyk had indicated to the administration desk that he would entertain a visit from Aggie. She immediately set it up for the following day at 11.00 am. She found herself quite fired up at the prospect of bringing her end of the case to a conclusion. There was much to resolve and determine in this prospective conversation and she looked forward to clearing up a lot of loose ends.

During the afternoon, she did some more research on Marcia Forman. She was an only child of a middle class family, both parents running a local pharmacy in Southampton on Long Island. She had been a good student and an athlete, playing field hockey for her school and Tufts University where she went to college. With an undergraduate degree in Education, she had drifted into social work, eventually becoming a Probation Officer which, Aggie had always thought, was a tough assignment. That lasted for about a decade before she completely changed direction and joined an airline in the role of flight attendant. Perhaps to see the world Aggie guessed. Somehow, she met Dwight Forman, got married and had three kids. Those were the bare bones of her life, encapsulated up to the present. After dinner, a plate of buttered spaghetti with lemon, she received a call from Moses Reede as she was washing up the dishes. She picked up.

"Reede. Anything new?"

Abrupt.

"Hi Moses. "You OK?"

"Sorry. I've been a bit pressed, er, Agnes."

She smiled to herself.

"Sorry to hear that. My news is that I'll be seeing Jakob Kowalczyk tomorrow. He's probably not in great shape but he agreed to talk to me."

"Wow. I am surprised. It didn't sound good."

"No. It didn't. Truck drivers must be tough."

"Do you think you have a handle on things yet?"

Aggie smiled.

"I think that I have most of it figured out."

"Ah. Do you feel like sharing it with me?"

"I will, but after my visit to the hospital tomorrow."

Reede gave a noncommittal grunt.

"OK. Fair enough. I've spoken with Cordelia Waters and Clement Smith."

"How did that go?"

"They seemed like ok normal people. That's entirely superficial though. I had about half an hour with them."

"Do you think that one of them did the shootings? Assuming that they are linked of course."

Reede took a deep breath.

"Couldn't tell. Neither of them had an alibi for the Salter killing. Smith was out and Waters was home. Both said that they were together at the time of the Kowalczyk shooting. Covering for each other, perhaps? Needs more checking."

"I've never really spoken to Clement Smith. What was he like?"

"Hm. Looks academic but he's not really. I wouldn't trust him with much. He has a devious feel about him. Looks upwards every time he answers a question. Bit weird. Neither here nor there, I suppose."

Aggie responded.

"My impression, not having spoken to him of course, is that he's a freeloader. I could be wrong but I don't think that he puts much into the relationship. Anyway, one or both of them concocted this insurance scam, along with Kowalczyk. That's my take. I'll know more tomorrow. I don't know what to think about the shootings."

"No. The scam is small potatoes really. But somewhere things went sideways."

"OK. Look, I'll call you when I get back from the hospital. What's next for you?"

"Well, I have to check into the Salter killing a bit more. I can't just assume that it's connected to the Kowalczyk shooting. I've got to do that."

"Right. So I'll call you tomorrow then. Bye." Aggie broke the call.

During the evening she reserved a Camry for the Kowalczyk trip and finished her Charles Todd book and, to her mild irritation, failed to pick the baddie. After all, that was her profession, but, there it was – must be the skill of the author. She retired early and had a refreshing, deep sleep. The next morning, after showering, cereal and black coffee, she compiled a comprehensive list of questions for her chat with Kowalczyk at the hospital. They were varied in nature and complexity. She had no idea how receptive or how tired and lucid he would be. The 'receptive' part was somewhat tenuous and she was aware that she was assuming he would be forthcoming. If not, she felt that she could be persuasive enough with all of the information that she had amassed. Nothing like being well prepared. Today, she hoped to approach a full picture of the whole affair and, also, find out if he had any clue as to who had shot him. She dressed in sweats and sneakers with a plain white tee shirt topped with a heavy silver necklace, grabbed the small briefcase carrying her notes, iPad and keys and headed for the rental agency.

Chapter 25

During the trip to the hospital Aggie listened to a radio documentary about Buddy Holly whose songs she had listened to often and enjoyed. Holly was musically talented and had played several instruments as a youngster. His wife talked about their relationship, which was very brief and many of his songs were played or partially played. He had once opened for Elvis with a partner. Sad that his talent was extinguished so early. Within an hour Aggie had parked her rental in the hospital parking lot, which was vast, and was soon at the reception desk. She was directed to Kowalczyk's third floor room and was, within minutes, once again, visiting him in a hospital. She walked into the two-bed room, his bed being next to the window through which the morning sunlight was streaming, and headed over to his bedside. The second bed was occupied by a white haired man who was sound asleep. Kowalczyk was propped against several pillows with tubes attached to both arms and leading up to plastic bottles hanging from a stand. He looked as though he had been dozing. His torso was bulky with dressings, some of which showed through his pale blue hospital garb. His face was pale and drawn, his thin lips purplish in color and his hair tousled and lank. He hadn't shaved in a while, which was understandable, and his features registered faint amusement as he lifted tired but welcoming eyes to Aggie.

"You made it then. Nice to see you – well, sort of."

Aggie felt genuine when she responded.

"Good to see you. How are you doing?"

"I'm doing OK. Close call but here I am."

"Yes you are. Thank goodness."

Kowalczyk reached over to his bedside table with some difficulty and picked up a plastic cup of water. He sipped while looking over the top of it at Aggie.

"Well, I think I know why you are here. It's not just an update is it? You said something like it was important to see me."

"Yes, I did. I've put a lot of things together and I think I've got it right. I would like to confirm as much of it as I can with you."

Kowalczyk looked resigned.

"Oh dear. I was afraid of that."

Aggie reached over for the wooden bedside chair and sat down, her position a little lower than Kowalczyk's.

"Before I begin, I did want to ask you one thing."

"Go ahead."

"Do you know who shot you?"

"No. I've no idea. I had my back to the shooter. I just felt the sharp pains from the shots and heard popping sounds all in a blur. I thought I'd had it and I didn't know why. I still don't. Then I passed out."

"Good job the shooter didn't make sure. You know, a coup de grace."

"I suppose so. I hadn't thought of that. Must have been concerned about being seen."

"Or, perhaps he or she thought that they had done a good job."

Kowalczyk nodded.

"Yes, I was very lucky. They got me in here quickly and saved me."

"No thoughts about who did it then?"

"No. None."

"Not even an inkling?"

Kowalczyk smiled wanly.

"Not even an inkling."

Aggie turned her gaze to the window in thought, taking in the blue sky and copious clouds. She turned her eyes back to Kowalczyk.

"Did you know that someone else was also shot?"

Kowalczyk's face registered instant surprise.

"What? To do with me you mean? Who got shot?"

"You know the claims adjuster who looked at your truck? Him."

"Salter?"

"Yes."

"How is he?"

"Dead. Not as lucky as you. Through a window of his home."

"That's terrible. So two of us got shot. Why? It makes no sense."

"It's one of the things I'm hoping to resolve today."

"What, by talking to me? I don't see how."

Aggie paused.

"We'll see."

Kowalczyk gave a long sigh.

"OK. I don't know about all this though."

"All what?"

"Answering a bunch of questions. I…"

His voice tailed off and he turned his head away towards the window. He stared off into the distance for a while and then turned back to Aggie. She could see that he had come to some kind of decision.

"Before you start throwing questions at me, I would like to say something."

Aggie waited.

"You are a good person and you have gone about this business professionally and in good faith."

"Thank you. Yes, I have."

Kowalczyk cleared his throat quietly.

"In some ways, I feel that I have taken advantage of you. Do you know what I mean?"

"I have a very good idea where you are going, yes. You mean something along the lines of lying to me – a lot I might say, and misusing my services in some way?"

Kowalczyk's features folded in relief and a modicum of regret.

"Yes, I did lie to you and, although I thought that I had to, I am very sorry for that. As for the other, I wouldn't say misusing your services. Using them to my advantage perhaps. Anyway, I've been pretty stupid, I know."

Aggie smiled.

"Semantics."

"OK. The main reason to ask for your services was that I was genuinely concerned about my safety. I really thought that there was a possibility of my being killed. Only a possibility, mind. Having you look into things made me feel safer."

"Other reasons?"

"Well, they, or it really, means me having to admit something."

Aggie nodded.

"Of course it does. I know about the insurance deal that you cooked up."

"I didn't cook it up but there was an insurance deal."

He paused.

"You see, if the insurance company didn't buy the idea of an accident, that would be where you came in."

"I would investigate the possibility of an attempt on your life and, hopefully for you, show that there was one."

"That's the size of it."

Kowalczyk was now fully acknowledging the existence of the scam.

"What about the cops involvement in that case? They would have needed to know."

Kowalczyk smiled wryly.

"I suppose that part wasn't thought out properly. As it happened, things worked out."

"Yes, but now they are involved. They are on the shootings."

Kowalczyk looked at Aggie intently.

"Are you working with cops?"

"Not working with them but in touch with a detective who is working on the murder and attempted murder. I do have to inform him of my findings here, or most of them."

"Ah. I suppose that is inevitable."

"Yes, I'm afraid so."

Aggie thought for a moment.

"What about the claims adjuster? Was he paid off?"

"Yes, and handsomely. So the bases were covered."

Aggie leaned back in her chair, looking Kowalczyk directly in the eyes.

"Me being one of the bases."

He sighed.

"I know, I know. I'm sorry."

"If that's an apology, I accept it."

"It is."

Then, he added.

"Poor Salter. That's very sad."

"It is. There has to be a connection. You might know something that makes sense of it all."

"Not that I know of."

"As I said, we may come up with something today."

There was a prolonged silence as Aggie turned some thoughts over in her mind. Then she spoke.

"How did you get into gambling? You had a good business going and then, at some point, you let gambling get in the way."

Kowalczyk drew in a long breath.

"I suppose the urge was always there but I resisted it. Some people are made that way. They can't hold back. I began by betting on dogs and then horses. I did fairly well. Then I graduated to casinos or, at least, one casino."

"The one that Cordelia Waters worked at."

"Yes. I didn't meet her there, of course."

"You met her through one of your partners? Her father?"

Kowalczyk stared out of the window with sad eyes.

"That's right. I needed help on a long trip. One of my more lucrative truck jobs. She offered to help out. We hit it off. She is a good driver. Much younger than me but it worked out well. At least, I thought it did."

"A good relationship?"

"Yes. Very good. Her father didn't approve though. Too blue collar, he thought but our paths rarely crossed so it was never a problem. I did wonder, at times, what she saw in me. I was older and I didn't work out much, though I kept trim."

There was something endearing about the way he talked of the relationship.

"How long ago was that?"

"Over two years. A long time."

"Sounds pretty solid. Did anything go wrong?"

"Ah, not really. I think I was just too set in my ways. Boring. Things started to pall a bit after a year and a half. I'd got into gambling at the casino quite a bit after going there to see her, didn't do too well. Then, I think, that guy showed up."

"Clement Smith. The one that Cordelia lives with?"

"Yes. Him. By that time I'd borrowed money to cover my losses and Cordelia was not at all happy about that. Throwing money away, she said. She had seen it a lot at the casino and said that I should stop as nothing good comes of it."

"Good advice."

"Right. She did care about me and worried about the gambling."

Kowalczyk paused for a few moments.

"You know, I did take care of her though. The least I could do."

"What do you mean?"

"Financially."

"I don't see how. You were in debt."

"I owed Strum, yes. But I willed my home and my share of the business to her. Plus, of course, the proceeds of the insurance deal which would have been part of my estate."

"Hah. I hadn't thought of all that. Were, or are, you splitting the insurance three ways? A moot point now, I suppose."

"No. Half for me and half for them."

"Them being Cordelia and Smith."

"Yes."

"Let's go back a bit and talk about how all of this came about."

At that moment an orderly came into the room pushing a trolley with two trays of lunches on it. With some surprise, Aggie realized that an hour and a half had passed since her arrival. The white-haired man sat up in bed in response to all the activity and was handed a tray which he put on the mobile table across the bed. He was very thin and quite old but seemed eager to partake of his lunch. The orderly came over to Kowalczyk's bed and unloaded the tray onto a similar table. He turned to Aggie.

"Would you like something? A drink, perhaps?"

Aggie thought that she would have to be in dire straits in order to want hospital fare.

"No. Thanks anyway."

The orderly turned and pushed the trolley back through the door, one wheel complaining faintly. Kowalczyk sat up a little more, adjusting his seating position and began unwrapping the plastic from each of the offerings, yielding a plastic cup of tomato soup, something that purported to be a relative of Shepherd's Pie and was comprised of minced beef, carrots and peas which were topped with Lyonnaise potatoes. It was close enough for Aggie to recognize it. A decent looking piece of cheesecake and a small bottle of water completed the repast. Aggie said,

"Look, Mr. Kowalczyk, you get on with lunch and I will go and stretch my legs. Give you some peace."

Kowalczyk simply nodded.

Aggie rose from the chair, stretched her legs, grabbed her briefcase and headed for the door.

"See you in a bit, then."

The hallway was long and brightly lit, the light reflecting off the polished floor. The walls were painted in cream and pale green pastels and the doors to all the rooms were wooden and lightly varnished. Aggie saw only one white coated figure in the hallway and an orderly pushing an empty mobile bed. Cleanliness echoed everywhere. Aggie took one of a bank of eight elevators to the first floor where there was an extensive waiting area that was only a quarter full. She wondered where all the owners of all the cars in the parking lot were hiding. In the corner of the waiting area Aggie spotted a sandwich and drinks stand and headed over. First she cleaned her hands at an antibacterial dispenser and then bought a corn muffin and a black coffee and sat in an empty row of seats near the entrance.

As she ate the muffin and sipped the coffee she took out her iPad and wrote up all that she could recall from her interview with Kowalczyk so far. She felt that she had made a really good start. She had built up a lot of the background to the case, including the motivation, how the whole episode got started and who all the prime movers were. Kowalczyk had confirmed the insurance scam, not that there was any doubt, and now she needed to see how it was put together. The shooter was a different matter. She had no idea who that was and, not only that, but did the shooter want to finish the job? Was she now, also, in any danger? That was an interesting new thought. In movies, killers seemed to get into hospitals rather easily, finding a closet and a white coat and doing the job. Hard to visualize that scenario here. Nevertheless, not for the first time, the thought fluttered about in the back of her mind. She brought her focus back to the task in hand. There were a lot of questions that she still wanted to ask but, she knew that her time must be limited. Kowalczyk must be wearing down, only days from severe trauma. She drained her coffee with no memory of eating the muffin and headed to the elevators.

When she arrived in Kowalczyk's room she found him fast asleep. The tray was still in front of him. The soup, most of the Shepherd's Pie and all of the cheesecake had gone, been consumed. The water was untouched. Aggie seated herself on the wooden chair and waited. Kowalczyk seemed relaxed and was breathing lightly. His companion in the other bed was also asleep. Aggie did not want to wake him and so sat silently gazing out of the window, collecting her thoughts. Ten minutes had passed when the lunch orderly returned and began to remove the depleted trays from both beds. The clatter and sudden movements caused Kowalczyk to open his eyes and try to focus. He took in the orderly's efforts and turned to look at Aggie. She saw all of the late morning's events flooding back into his consciousness and he slowly sat more upright into a comfortable position.

"Been doing a lot of that lately," he said.
"Not surprising. You've been through a lot."
He glanced at her.
"Where did you go?"
"Down to the lobby. I had a coffee and a muffin."
"Make a lot of phone calls, send lots of texts?"
Aggie was a little surprised by that.
"No. Actually I did not make any phone calls or send any texts."
Kowalczyk seemed comfortable with that and just nodded his head.
Aggie spoke.
"Do you feel able to continue now?"
"I think so. Don't know for how much longer though."
Just what Aggie had expected.
"OK. I'll try to be as brief as possible."
Aggie began to mentally prioritize her questions, assuming that she would not manage to ask all of them. She began.
"I was curious about the so called possible first attempt on your life. Clearly, it wasn't that. So, what was it, an accident?"

"Oh, that ? It was me. I messed with the brake system."

"But why? Nothing had been planned about insurance had it? That was some time ago."

Kowalczyk came close to looking sheepish, embarrassed.

"I did have my own ideas about doing an insurance job."

He looked at Aggie apologetically.

"I was only thinking about it in a vague way. You know, I don't think that I would have done anything."

"But you did, didn't you."

"Yes, but that was when somebody else made up a plan and came to me."

"I see," said Aggie without really seeing.

"I tried out a few things and came to the conclusion that they were far too dangerous for other folk."

"Collateral damage."

"Exactly."

"Very thoughtful of you."

Kowalczyk threw her a reproachful look but Aggie did not respond.

"Anyway, I gave the whole thing up as a bad idea. I was dating Cordelia around that time and had other things on my mind."

A glimmer of a smile crossed his features.

"So, as you say, someone else, presumably Cordelia and this guy Smith, came up with a viable insurance idea?"

"Yes, as I understand it, he had the brainwave."

"Why did he want to do it, do you think?"

"Well, they had met at the casino where he had done some gambling. Not some, really, a lot. He was in over his head."

"He is a math teacher, I believe."

Before Kowalczyk could reply, another episode in the routine of a hospital occurred, one of many that had to be accepted. A nurse came into the room and made a beeline for the Kowalczyk bed. She put a small plastic tumbler containing some pills on the bedside table.

"Time for your meds again, Mr. Kowalczyk."

She picked up his container of water and handed If to him whereupon he dutifully swallowed the pills with a couple of gulps of water. She then wheeled a small computer on a slender stand, which was nearby, over to the bedside and took Kowalczyk's blood pressure, heart rate and temperature, all of which was automatically entered into the computer. He looked at her and since no information seemed to be coming his way, he took the initiative.

"All good, is it?"

The nurse gave him a quick glance.

"Yes. All normal and as expected."

He smiled and thanked her as she went over to the second bed for a repeat performance. Kowalczyk watched her for a while and then turned back to Aggie.

"Getting a bit tired of that. Every four hours, no matter what. Where were we?"

"We were talking about Clement Smith. He being a math teacher."

"Oh yes. He thought that he could beat the system, as many gamblers do. He had worked out some crazy scheme but he couldn't do it on his own. He had tried several schemes, apparently, but they didn't work and he lost heavily. He needed Cordelia to help on the inside as a croupier. Right card at the right time, I don't know. Anyway, she refused to help. She liked her job, got paid well and had a good life. She didn't want to risk it all."

Aggie nodded knowingly.

"Of course not."

"I was concerned for her. Apart from the fact that something was going on between them, I thought he was an opportunist, a sponger."

"My thoughts also but I'm only guessing. I have no evidence of that."

"Well, one night she told me that they were having an affair and during that conversation which went on all night, she told me about his plan for beating the casino and recouping his losses."

Aggie was sympathetic.

"That must have been hard. Hearing about the affair I mean."

"It was. She saw both of us for a while but it was clear that the end was near for me. We stopped seeing each other and he moved in with her. Something I'd hoped for at one time."

"I'm sorry. What happened next?"

"Nothing for a while. Then one day she showed up at my home. That was when she told me about the insurance idea. He had come up with it. Said nobody loses except the insurance company and they could afford it. I could settle with Strum, he could clear his debts and there would be enough cash left over to make it all worthwhile."

"Cordelia told you all of that. Convinced you?"

"Yes. Apparently, she had initially been against the idea but eventually went along."

Kowalczyk flashed Aggie a look of triumph for a moment.

'I got her to pick up with me again for a while."

Aggie said, "Hah, they needed you."

"Yes. The question became how to do it. He came up with several different ideas and Cordelia would come and talk each one over with me. And, you know, we had fun. I don't think Smith knew about that bit."

Aggie smiled encouragingly and actually felt pleased for Kowalczyk, although there was not much doubt that Cordelia was manipulative.

She said, "What was the plan? I've got a good idea but I'm not absolutely clear about it?"

Kowalczyk took a sip of water and continued.

"The main thing was to start a fire just behind the truck cab using a pack with combustible material and an accelerant. It was to be triggered by me from inside the cab using a simple electrical circuit with contacts and a button up behind my head. Smith tried several designs before finding the right one. Then there was the medication, a drug supplied by Smith."

Aggie leaned forward.

"Why."

"It was to knock me out for a short time. It would look good and make everything look genuine. Only a couple of pills, well, three actually."

Aggie interrupted.

"It was just plain stupid. What if they wanted to kill you or they didn't make it in time to save you?"

"I suppose it looks that way now but it seemed sort of clever then."

"Still stupid."

"Well, we did try it out a couple of times, me and Cordelia that is. We didn't have enough to try it too often. It was hard to get. I knew that it wasn't foolproof."

"You're not kidding. It was harebrained from the start."

"Anyway, we kept in touch and we planned to be at a prearranged spot on the road at the right time. I took the meds with coffee while on the road and then triggered the fire. I actually only just made it because I started passing out a bit early."

"And then I came along."

"You did. A good thing too. I was a bit worried that they might not get there on purpose. I suppose I will never know."

"Strum was around too. So you would have been OK."

"Yes. That was a surprise."

"On the other hand, when I got to the truck – and I was the first one to arrive – things had really heated up. You were unconscious and flames were very close to you. I dragged you out with help from Smith who arrived after me."

"So, you are saying a close call."

"Yes. You were lucky."

Kowalczyk smiled openly.

"Seems to be my thing."

Aggie did not respond but leaned back and looked at him.

"That was quite a story. Did anybody else know about it? What about the Masons or the rest of the Waters family?"

"No. Never saw the Masons. Cordelia's brother knew a bit about it, not the details."

"The brother? What, Stefan?"

"Yes. He and Cordelia are close so she told him some of it. I don't know how much."

"Interesting. So, nobody else?"

"No."

"And you said that you paid off the claims adjuster but you still had Cordelia go to the towing company to eliminate evidence of the fire source?"

"You're correct. We suddenly got worried that there was substantial debris left from the pack that Smith concocted for anyone to see."

"Well, I looked and I just saw a burned out mess, all charred up but I wasn't looking for something."

"We just had to be sure, that's all."

Kowalczyk was clearly tiring rapidly.

"A couple more things. Do you know anybody in your group, the group of people involved in this scam, who has a firearm?"

"No I don't. Well not a handgun anyway. You're thinking about who shot me aren't you?"

"Yes. You mean some may have weapons other than handguns?"

"Well the two partners are hunters, so they would have rifles."

"Right. So, Cordelia didn't have a handgun?"

"What are you saying? She wouldn't shoot me."

"Sure?"

Kowalczyk looked agitated, affronted.

"Of course I'm sure. Out of the question"

"OK. Just asking. That leaves Clement Smith. Perhaps he shot you."

"Can't see why. I've done nothing to him. Maybe he didn't like me seeing Cordelia again."

In spite of his increasing tiredness, Kowalczyk laughed.

"That's it. He was jealous," he said jubilantly.

Aggie laughed too. She could see that Kowalczyk was now nearly exhausted.

She said, "We've got to stop. You look very tired. I want to thank you for telling me all this. You have been more than helpful and I really appreciate your candor. Whatever comes out of the insurance business, I will help you wherever and however I can."

Kowalczyk looked truly grateful.

"Thank you. I could do with that. I do feel better for having gone through all of this today."

"Do you need anything now? Can I get you anything or do something for you?"

He smiled.

"No thanks, I'm good."

Aggie stood and stretched her limbs.

"OK. I'll be off then. I'll see you again soon, I expect. Keep in touch. Get better quickly."

They shook hands in an awkward way and Aggie left the room. She wandered down the hallway to the elevator bank, went down to the first floor and out to her car without really noticing that she had done so. It was already late afternoon. She hopped into her rental and chose to drive in silence in order to allow her mind to settle and sift out the nuggets of new information that she had picked up. She was getting close to the George Washington Bridge when her cell chirped up her latest attempt to get an acceptable ring tone. The Stones days and regular bells were gone and she had fallen into experimenting again with nothing yet that she could endure. She also had to get a no hands system for use in a car. She saw that it was Jack calling and quickly told him that she would call in fifteen minutes. About twenty minutes later she was calling him from the depths of her couch.

"Hi Ag."

"Hi Jack. Sorry, I was driving just now. How's things?"

"Fine. Sunny afternoon, so out for a drive?"

"You could say that. I visited the truck driver in the hospital."

"Wow. Was he able to talk much?"

"Yes. It was an amazing chat. I made a lot of progress. I'll tell you all about it on Friday."

"OK. I'm glad it's working out. Well, I'm calling because I have some more news for you. Thought you'd want it now rather than later on Friday. It's about your phone – sorry, that woman's phone – it's having a great trip."

"Why? What has it done?"

"It's half way across South Dakota and still going."

"Wow. Really? That is something."

"Yes. My guess is that it has to be on a train because of the speed. Most likely the Chicago – Vancouver train. It is not necessarily going to Vancouver, of course, because there are lots of stops on the way."

"Thanks Jack. I wonder why she's heading for Canada, assuming it is she that is carrying the phone."

"Don't know. There are lots of nice things in Canada. We should go sometime."

"We should."

"You know, it's about a sixty hour trip and she is somewhere in the middle of that."

"I'm thinking of calling her in a day or so. Wherever she is going, she should be there by then."

"What will you say? If it is her, of course."

"I really don't know. I've got to think it through along with everything else. Thanks for this Jack. It is going to be really helpful for me."

"Good. You're welcome. See you Friday. Bye."

He disconnected.

Aggie sat back as she put her cell down. Marcia Forman headed for Canada. Even if it wasn't Canada, she was going to somewhere in the Pacific North West. Why? Aggie had not uncovered any connections in that area of the country. She had arrived in New York, where her home and family were, after a normal work flight and, after a night in a hotel had abruptly taken off across country. At least, according to her phone. Aggie needed to take all of that in later. For the moment, she needed to summarize the second portion of her talk with Kowalczyk and assess all of the information to date to see what needed to be done next. First, she was very hungry and decided to make toasted cheese sandwiches, the cheese, to her amusement, being four year old aged Canadian cheddar. Before grilling the cheese, she topped it with a drizzle of HP sauce, a British product whose complex flavor she liked. She finished the sandwiches and a bottle of Fiji water while watching some TV politics but found it depressing, capping the early evening by falling asleep on her couch.

Chapter 26

Aggie awoke early the next morning, still in her clothes from her trip and still on the couch. She groaned loudly, stood up and tried to shake out the aches and the feeling of irritation that a lengthy couch sojourn can generate. The bathroom and a very long, hot shower came next along with fresh casual clothing and she began to approach a normal mood, outlook and physicality. Coffee and toast were next on the agenda as she settled in at the kitchen counter to pull up the rest of yesterday's findings for an overall picture.

Clearly, she had established that Jakob Kowalczyk had perpetrated an insurance fraud devised, tested and sold to him by Clement Smith with a largely unknown input by Cordelia Waters. Waters did, however, act as a go between for Smith and Kowalczyk and she did use her relationship with the latter to convince him – maybe not so much convince him because he was amenable to the whole set up but, at least, point him in the right direction. Then, Smith had used his scientific knowledge to put together an ignition system for the fire, although Aggie thought it would not take too much expertise to do that, followed by unscientific and risky tryouts with medication. Aggie mentally rolled her eyes again at that. After that, they had pulled the whole thing together in a fairly successful and inordinately lucky venture on the highway and could, actually, have gotten away with it. Aggie's involvement and the shootings put a stop to that. Nobody else seemed to be involved unless the shooter was not one of them. Aggie had picked up faint hints, or vague references, or undercurrents concerning the possible demise of Kowalczyk as an outcome of the fire. Admittedly, the vibes came mostly from him but his removal would have benefitted Smith in terms of money and even his getting Waters' full attention. No evidence, just feelings. Worth considering though because Smith could be the shooter for those same reasons. Aggie tended to believe Kowalczyk's assertion that Waters would not shoot him. Why would she? If she did not wish to go along with the scam in the first place, why would she escalate to murder? Surely, Kowalczyk's estate would not be enough for that.

Aggie mused that both men were gamblers, one recreational and one committed and obsessional. Both had, or were having, an affair with the same woman who worked in a casino. Both were in debt because of their gambling. Waters was adept at manipulating both of them and probably wanted to move on from both of them. Aggie wondered if any of that fitted in anywhere, particularly with the shootings. She put those ideas aside in her mind for the time being.

Two people had been shot and both of them were intimately connected to the insurance fraud. Why were they shot? At a stretch, the claims adjuster could be called a loose end but only in a minor crime. A very sad end if that were the case. Kowalczyk's estate certainly raised the money stakes in the case but Waters was the beneficiary and very unlikely to be a shooter. On the other hand, Smith, assuming he knew of the will, might have wanted Kowalczyk out of the way and a share in Waters' windfall. The only other person who might fit in somewhere was Stefan but he was not involved in the scam so had no obvious motive to shoot anybody. Aggie did not think so and fully expected him to be a stay at home drunk.

Aggie stared at her review and could add nothing more to it. As far as it went, it was a clear and concise summary of her thoughts on the case. She realized that she had not called Moses Reede as promised but she had been too tired last night and too busy this morning. Well, she admitted to herself that she had not actually remembered her promise either. She decided to call and dialed up his cell number. It went to message where he used his full name and said that he would call back ASAP. Aggie left a brief message and rang off. At least, she had made the effort. She washed up her dish and mug and went to the couch in the living area.

Thinking through the Marcia Forman investigation, she recalled that Forman had stayed at a Best Western for one night with somebody else and had then disappeared. About five or so days later she, or her phone, was in Chicago. Where had she been in the meantime? Of course, she may have been in Chicago all of that time. Wherever she was, what had she been doing? Aggie began to wonder if she had missed something during her investigation of Marcia Forman. She had tracked several of her working days and nights, including random checks just to be sure about any non-routine movements. She had found nothing untoward, nothing at all to support Dwight Forman's assertions about his wife's infidelity. There had been times when Marcia Forman had checked into hotels or airline pads with other female crew members but that had been normal cost saving. In the US her flights had, on the whole, been to the New York airports so that she had been able to make it home. Nothing there. She had made occasional shopping trips and used a local gym but not on a regular basis. Shopping, in itself, had shades of domestic overtones which suggested that the atmosphere at home was not as poisonous as Dwight Forman had indicated. He had also said that the children were estranged from their mother. In fact, they regarded the babysitter as a surrogate mother. How much of all that was true, Aggie didn't know because it was basically hearsay from an inveterate liar. She recalled that Dwight Forman had refused to accept her findings which meant that he knew something that she didn't or he wanted her to keep looking for some reason. That reason had now emerged in that he had put forward the idea that she had some kind of obsession with him which had manifested itself in stalking episodes. All of which, Aggie knew, was nonsense but what was the big picture? He had declared his wife missing and attempted to tie that fact to Aggie's supposed obsession. He had been trying to set her up. If any of this was true, it would have been legally simple to stop Aggie's attentions but he hadn't done that. He wanted her involved at the time of his wife's disappearance which, Aggie surmised, meant that he knew that his wife was about to disappear. So, did he cause her to disappear or did he know that she was about to disappear? Aggie thought that it had to be one or the other. Hollis had entered the scene because of the disappearance of Marcia Forman but her husband must have done some kind of number on him to set him on Aggie's trail. She realized that Hollis could have been following up on more than one possibility to explain the disappearance but it had felt on the personal side when he interviewed her. She wondered if they knew each other but thought that a bit fanciful. She had tracked the cell phone so why couldn't Hollis have done that? Anyway, silence from that quarter was good news. She had to put all of that out of her mind. She decided to go over her investigation again to see if she had, in fact, missed anything. It crossed her mind that she should check more hotels and motels in this and the Chicago area but could not face that just yet. But, Marcia Forman had to have stayed somewhere after the Best Western and Aggie needed to know where and what she had been doing.

Chapter 27

Dwight Forman's grandparents were Dutch immigrants with an ancestral name of Franken or Frankfort. He couldn't recall the exact name and he did not care what it was and nor had he had the inclination to find out. His given name was now Forman and that was that. His grandfather was born in 1910 and his grandmother in 1909 and they had settled in Queens, New York in 1938, starting a tobacco business which mostly manufactured cigars. They had one child who was Dwight Forman's father, Edward, born in 1942. Eventually, they had passed on the business to Edward and his wife, a local woman whom he had married in 1974. She turned out to be a smart, savvy, natural investor in the stock market and, after they had sold the business, she had invested shrewdly and built a fortune. Looking ahead, they had set up a fund for their only child, Dwight Forman who had been born in 1976, so that he would not have to worry about money. He began drawing on the fund at age 21 years, knowing nothing about finance and not ever wanting to know. He was happy to live off the interest and a small amount of capital as designated by a committed wealth advisor. Where it came from and how it reached him did not especially concern him, as long as it continued to do so. He had been told that he could not sell off any of his portfolio because of prohibitive tax penalties. His grandparents had died during the late eighties and his parents lived in Austin, Texas. He hardly ever saw them, the last time being eight years ago, nor they their grandchildren.

He was antisocial in school, bullying and sometimes hurting other kids. He had several years of child therapy and improved somewhat after eighth grade but he was not popular or well liked. Many students gave him a wide berth and chose not to interact with him. He had attended the University of Pennsylvania with moderate success and, once again, lacked the ability to have social discourse of any meaningful kind. He managed a misfit friend or two and an occasional date with a woman but those interactions did not amount to much. He had failed to get into Wharton Business School which had been the goal of his parents for him. He did not take a post graduate degree and drifted around in mostly clerical jobs. He had contemplated the military and the police force but had the good sense to anticipate disaster in those areas. During one of his clerical ventures, his and Marcia Delaney's, as she was known then, paths crossed, she working for Social Services. After an all too brief series of dates, they decided to marry and produced three children – a boy and two girls. Their marriage deteriorated over time to the point where they went from disliking to hating each other, Dwight becoming more and more physically and mentally abusive to Marcia but not to his kids. She found a job with the airlines which took her away from home as often as possible and he took on a 28 year old Taiwanese babysitter, after interviewing a dozen or more candidates. Her name, when anglicized, was Shu-Chen Huang which was much too much for him to handle and so he called her simply Shu. As was his hope, they soon began an affair and Dwight Forman began to think about divorce and to worry how that would look from the point of view of his legacy and their home. They did not have a pre-nuptial agreement.

The prospect of any reduction in his income began to gnaw at his mind until he began to conceive of the removal of his wife. That was the way that he viewed his situation – not the murder of another human being – his wife no less, but the simple resolution of a personal problem. He spent many hours figuring out how he might achieve this, from following her to another country and disposing of her there with nothing pointing to him as the perpetrator and, anyway, long gone, to kidnapping her near home and driving her into a New Jersey lake. All of his ideas seemed too complicated. Even a well-planned accident was not easy to accomplish.

Getting rid of a body too, was quite difficult when it came down to it. He thought that people must do this all the time and not get caught. How did they do it? And then it came to him. The New Jersey lake idea prompted him. Not the lake, the ocean.

In movies, people did it all the time – cement shoes and all of that. Now, he planned with some focus and excitement. He would pick a flight when Marcia was returning home, one that was late at night when it was quiet out or relatively so. One, where she had arranged to meet up with her lover, whoever that was at the time, in the Best Western, her usual choice as he had learned over the last year or so. He had begun to check her cell phone and had seen calls to the Best Western hotel for reservations, usually after late flights into the country.

He had also taken to checking the hotel when she had late flights to see if she had a reservation. Obviously, he thought, she was having occasional trysts but he did not know if it was the same person or several lovers. He assumed that they, or he, were other crew members. It did not really matter. It was more a matter of principle, to catch her with one of them. He planned to kill them both and dispose of their bodies. He was familiar with Montauk on Long Island. He liked it there – the cafes, an excellent diner and a restaurant out at the dock. He had bought a small motor boat some while back to do some fishing. It was really an overgrown rowboat with a motor attached. It was in good shape and he moored it for most of the year on a small wooden pier with about a dozen other small craft. As it happened, he had not used it very often. He had tried fishing, having seen others do it, but it was horribly messy, what with bait and a live fish struggled on the end of his line.

It was too much, gory and unpleasant. He didn't feel that he could eat the fish, having killed it. Briefly, he had entertained the thought that he was something of an enigma. Couldn't deal with killing fish but perfectly comfortable with killing his wife and a random lover. Well, they intruded into his life and the fish did not.

He would now put the boat to good use by using it to take their bodies out to sea and dump them. Nice and clean – no trace. He became totally enamored with his plan and very excited about the clever solution to his problems. There were two things left to consider. One was what weapon to use. He had a small pistol that was over twenty years old but perfectly functional. He had been to firing ranges with it during his loner days and was reasonably adept at using it.

He had also acquired a silencer for it but had not tried it out. This outing would be the first time. He preferred a gun to other weapons – a bit less personal than, say, a knife and more expedient, less effort. Plus, an old gun was good because he did not want a record of him buying a gun in current times.

So, that was easy, settled. The next thing was some kind of backup plan because smart people always had back up plans. He had contemplated hiring a private detective to check on Marcia at a time when he was in full flight with his babysitter, Shu, but he was not sure what Marcia was up to and did not care especially. Then he found out on his own via the cell phone exploits and so he did not need corroboration from a Private Investigator. However, tossing this around in his mind for a couple of weeks, germinated the idea of hiring a female private eye. He needed someone outside of his circle of acquaintances whom he could finger, or at least, generate some suspicion over the disappearance of his wife. He enjoyed using movie terms for some of his proclivities.

He hired Aggie without a reasonable plan in mind. It was not until he saw her that he thought of the stalker idea. It would not be difficult to convince anybody that women might find him attractive and, at a stretch, say, to be modest, become obsessed with him. He liked the whole scenario – a backup plan with utterly plausible content. She was an interesting woman too – attractive, athletic looking, cute and perhaps, dangerous. All very exciting. In addition, he did have a couple of cop friends that could prove to be useful. Both were in homicide as far as he remembered, although one had changed his department a year or two ago. He saw them once a year at a Star Trek Convention where they relived the movies, bought Trekkie paraphernalia and had a few beers. Funny that they were among the very few friends that he had, although he couldn't really call them friends. Sort of fellow travelers would be closer to the truth. Once he had effected his wife's disappearance he might be able to kick things off with one of those cops. All looking good he thought. He had checked his wife's cell before she left on her latest trip and almost out of the blue, but not quite, because he had been vigilant, he discovered the reservation he had been looking for – nice and late at night too – at the Best Western hotel. He had begun to think that she had broken up with her lover, or simply run out of lovers, because there had been no calls or reservations for some time and he had not come up with anything. Well, now he had found something. He also found a call on her cell phone to a local motel. That was puzzling. Maybe the Best Western was booked up or something He called the motel and found out, without much difficulty or subterfuge, that Marcia had reserved a room there too but on the next night and that the motel was fully booked. Only a room, number 22, in her name, nothing more. Could be anything- possible cover for prospective flight delays, adding another venue in case she was being tracked – that didn't sound right – two separate lovers? – no, he dismissed that. He would look at all of that later. For now, the reservation at the Best Western was in Marcia's name for two people – there was the stimulus to throw his plan into high gear. Now for the details. He checked out the Best Western more carefully now because this was the real thing. Slowly at first, but with mounting doubt, he realized that the logistics of his plan were not good. Yes, he might get into the hotel and even find the room and kill his wife and lover. All good to think about but what then? How does one carry two bodies out of a hotel? Over a shoulder in a carpet? Twice? In the ubiquitous laundry basket on wheels? Even if there was a back entrance, it just could not work. Plus, getting into the hotel was not easy either, without reserving a room and he could not do that, even under a false name – too risky.

Why hadn't he paid attention to the details? He felt frustrated and irritated. Alternatives? Kill them and leave them. Were there cameras in the hotel? He did not know. Anyway, he didn't want to leave bodies in the hotel. That would clearly be a murder, two actually. No, he liked the disappearance idea. Nothing definitive about that. No wife, gone for good, everything domestic staying the same, a love struck PI taking the heat for a while until it all died down. Perfect. So, no bodies. Well, what about the motel? Dwight Forman sat in his favorite armchair and mused about the motel. Time was short. Marcia Forman's flight was due in the next night. He would need to speak to Shu about his alibi, being at home for the whole evening and night. Not watching TV either because somebody would ask what programs they watched and what happened. He was too smart for that one. Shu did not know exactly what he was doing but it would not take much reasoning to figure it out over time. He had to reconnoiter the motel. He liked that word and the inference of an adventure. It was dark out as he drove to the motel and checked it out. It was situated between an all-night garage and a warehouse.

The room, reserved by Marcia, was on the warehouse end of the block which was very convenient. He had space between the motel room and the warehouse to park his car and not to be too exposed to the motel office or the garage. It was about as good as it could be. He drove home deep in thought as he checked off all the boxes in his mental plan. Marcia would fly in late at night, spend the night with her lover, neither of them knowing that it would be their last go round, or close to it, depending on their ardor. Then, for reasons as yet unknown, they would transfer to the motel for another bout of love making or discussion or whatever and he, Dwight, would show up and put an end to it all. It had the ring of justice, of comeuppance and utter satisfaction about it. Dwight literally trembled at the thought.

That night and the next day took a long time to go by. Dwight made fairly violent love to Shu who seemed more than comfortable with it all. He explained what she had to do the next night, which was actually nothing, just make sure that she had the story straight in her head. Their story would be that they had spent the evening and night together – in fact, they would actually spend the evening together before Dwight took off so he decided that they would watch television for the evening after all and any questions about it would be quite easily answered and verifiable. They would say that they went to bed then, close to midnight and woke up at 6.30 am ready for the day ahead. Excellent, he had it all figured out.

And that was how it all worked out. They watched American Pickers, a tennis match and a movie, The 3.10 to Yuma, all full of great details so that they could both relate their evening independently and truthfully lending credence to their tale. Finally, the time for action approached and Dwight Forman began preparing himself. He donned black jeans, a black tee shirt and a heavyish black sweater along with black sneakers. He considered using blacking on parts of his face but thought that a little too much. His ball cap was dark brown with a Mets logo, the only suitable one that he had because he did not wear much in the way of headwear. He pulled on some thin gloves and viewed himself in his bedroom mirror. He liked what he saw. He thought that he looked dashing, earnest, athletic. He put on a light three-quarter coat and slipped the fully loaded gun and the silencer into a coat pocket. He did not have much ammunition but there was enough for this assignment. He also had a small set of lock picks which he had acquired at the same time as the gun. He had once entertained ideas of becoming a reputable cat burglar and had practiced on a variety of locks with commendable success but it did not take long for him to become bored with the whole project without a single burglary to his name. To top off his list of useful items for the trip, he retrieved a couple of gym weights from his basement to go along with a handful of bungee cords kept in the trunk of his car. The time was just after midnight. He said goodbye to Shu and headed to his car.

    He drove carefully to the motel pulling into the spot between the motel and the warehouse, as close to the side wall of the motel as possible while still leaving space for him to emerge from the car comfortably. He eased his way out of the car quietly, took off his coat, removed the gun and the lock picks from the coat pocket and stashed the coat on the passenger seat. He fitted the silencer and put the gun in his jeans pocket and then took it out again and put it in his waistband just like gunmen always did. He pushed the door of the car to without making any noise and headed for the door of number 22.

    He had the lock picks in his hand but it felt very clumsy with gloves on – he should have thought of that although there was not really an alternative. The next problem was it was dark and he had no flashlight.

    He felt for the door knob which had the usual single lock in it and using mental diagrams from the book he had used to learn how to pick locks, started work, a tool in each hand. Although it seemed incredibly noisy, it worked and the door slid silently open. He stuffed the picks in his pocket, pulled the gun from his waistband and slipped through the door pushing it almost closed behind him.

    He stood still and listened, his eyes growing accustomed to the darkness, adrenalin coursing through his body. He could hear heavy breathing in the bed over to his right. He moved to the bedside and made out just one figure in the bed. With no hesitation, he pointed the gun at the figure's chest as well as he could and fired four times. The sound of the small gun, even with the silencer, was louder than he expected but it functioned as it was supposed to and he did not think it was loud enough to attract attention. Well, there it was, he had done it.

    He walked over to the only other door in the room and checked the bathroom – nobody else in the room. He left the light on in the bathroom to give some subdued lighting to the main room. He crossed the room to the bed and saw that the occupant was a man. Quite an unattractive man with hair growing out of his nostrils and his ears. Loose lips as well, although he supposed they would be loose if he just been shot. He leaned over and checked for a pulse in the neck. There was none. So, this guy must be Marcia's lover. He was rather disappointed in her choice but supposed that one had to do the best that one could in these circumstances. Marcia. It dawned on him that she must be somewhere. She was not here. She must have had some kind of brief love making episode and then taken off. Could she have gone home? Could their paths have crossed? That was worrisome. He pulled out his cell phone and called Shu to find out. She had not gone home.

Then he wondered if she was coming back to the motel. There was no way to find out. The dead guy was not talking. That meant there was some urgency attached to his current situation. Plus, the whole point of this exercise had been to kill his wife and her lover if he was around. Now the situation was reversed. He had killed the lover and still had a wife. Not good at all. He also had a body to dispose of with no really good reward being offered for all the effort that would take.

All that he would be doing was covering up a crime. He reluctantly turned his attention to that task. He could not leave the victim here because it would not take long for questions to be asked of him, being the cuckolded husband, notwithstanding his own indiscretions. He would go through with his plan of taking the body to Montauk and dumping it at sea. He unwrapped the top sheet and duvet from the bed and rolled the lover's body up into an untidy bundle, the feet sticking out of one end. With great effort because he was not an inherently strong man, he maneuvered the bundle onto his shoulder and worked his way to the door which was still partially open. He eased it open with his foot and, with some difficulty, checked outside for signs of life. It was quiet with only an occasional car slipping by in the night. He walked awkwardly to his car and struggled to open the trunk while balancing the bundle, his knees semi buckling in the process.

The trunk came open and he shrugged the load into the space, pushing the feet down and closing it again. Breathing heavily, he returned to the motel room and checked the bottom sheet and the mattress – blood on the sheet but not the mattress. He took the sheet and, just to be sure, the pillowcase also which had something indecipherable on it. No bullet holes anywhere – he assumed that the bullets had not exited the body and must still be inside it. He went out to the car and tossed the sheet and pillowcase on the back seat, returning to the room for a final look around. He took the personal stuff off the bedside table – a watch and a wallet but left the car keys. He would check the wallet later. He glanced over to the corner of the room which boasted a small alcove with an open curtain in front of it. Clothing hung from a rack above a medium sized suitcase standing on the floor. Nothing of interest. He closed the door of the motel room on the way out and seated himself in his car, running through everything in his mind. Time was passing rapidly. He had to be on his way. He was fervently relieved that Marcia had not shown up. He would have had to kill her somehow and that felt like more than he could manage right now. Her turn would come in due course. He fired up the engine and began his journey to Long Island.

Chapter 28

Marcia Forman gazed out of the dining room window of the small bed and breakfast establishment, at the green, grey ocean waves breaking onto the beach in Hastings, a southern British seaside town. She took in the stationary pockets of clouds partially blocking out the bright sunlight, the rest of the sky a translucent blue. People were out walking, cycling, skating and driving their electrified wheelchairs. She turned her eyes to the person across the breakfast table from her. His name is Bo Schwartz, her personal trainer, who sported a light blue tee shirt and blue jeans, his blue eyes in a handsome face crinkled in a lazy smile.

They had hungrily demolished the prototypical English breakfast which included fried tomatoes, mushrooms and fried bread as well as the usual eggs, bacon, sausage and baked beans. They had arrived in England officially as vacationers but they intended to apply, at least in the first instance, for temporary visas and see where it went from there. Marcia knew that Bo had had a number of affairs with his clients – it seemed to be par for the job but they had hit it off in a big way and both felt that they were headed for a long relationship.

They had initially not attempted to be too secretive about it but, as their liaison progressed through intimacy to a strong commitment, they began to plan. Marcia was well aware of Dwight checking up on her, even had a good idea that he was going through her purse and looking at her telephone. Dwight had taken to being physically abusive to her and life with him was becoming intolerable. It was no surprise to her when she and Bo eventually decided that they would go away together, permanently.

That meant somewhere far away from New York – maybe another country or the West Coast or Texas. Dwight's parents lived in Texas and, although it was a large state, it was not large enough. In the end they thought of England. Marcia had some experience of that country working for the airline. She liked the country and the people but not the everyday food. Some sacrifices had to be made – at least breakfast was good. The idea was to stop seeing each other, unless in secret, to allay any suspicions of a relationship, and then to just go at a chosen time. It would mean Marcia leaving her children and she did not know how she would cope with that. Currently, they did not like her at all. Dwight had seen to that. Her hope was that as they grew up and gained more perspective they would want to see her. That was in the future and somehow she would find a way of dealing with it. Of course, her relationship with Bo was initially primal and physical but, as it progressed, they both realized that they had something special. Bo had fallen in love for the first time with an older, statuesque woman in the mold of Nicole Kidman, who was very smart and entertaining. She found that, apart from his obvious physical attraction, he had a degree in biology and was very interested in working in medicine, maybe as a nurse or an EMT. In any event, they had much to talk about and many interesting conversations. Their plan had been to wrap up all of their personal affairs as best they could and to put together their most cherished possessions in a suitcase each, so nothing of any real size. That meant money and jewelry for Marcia including a pendant and a ring that her grandmother had bequeathed to her. Also, for her, it had to be surreptitious. She had to gather items in the back of a chest of drawers in her bedroom and to have few enough of them to pack in her usual overnight suitcase when on airline trips. Difficult as it was, she managed it. For Bo, it was much easier. He had time and space and a bigger suitcase to help him and actually took some of Marcia's items as well.

They chose a date and arranged their flight times to England's Heathrow airport, all of their paperwork and passports ready and up to date. Marcia would fly into JFK as usual but late at night. They would stay the night at the Best Western, the hotel where they usually snatched a night of love making at those times. The next day they would grab a flight to England to begin their new life together, wherever it took them. If England did not work, then it would be somewhere else.

The point was that they would be together. In case anything went wrong with the flight out or an unforeseen circumstance popped up, Marcia had also reserved a room at a local motel for the next night, assuming that any problem could be solved in less than a day. If necessary, anything else would have to be planned on the fly. As it happened matters had gone really well. Her flight had arrived just after midnight, they had met up in the Best Western for the first time in a few weeks, they had made love until they were exhausted, had slept awhile and had then taken off for England with their somewhat meager possessions. The one hitch, well not so much a hitch but a nuisance, was that Marcia had lost or mislaid her cell phone. She had it in the hotel room but now believed that she had left it on the counter at check out from the hotel. Nothing that she could do about that now.

All of her information, contacts etc. had been lost with the phone so she had begun to write up a list of all the missing data for her next phone. What that would be she didn't know. Did they have the same phones in England? What plan would she use? Time would tell and she had decided to suck it up and forget the whole thing. For now, here they were sipping coffee after breakfast with their lives before them in a new country. At last, for Marcia, life was beginning to work out. She would keep her job with the airlines, some paperwork needing to be straightened out with her new base of operations but Human Resources had informed her that it could be done. This was the first day of their new life together. And, there was something wonderfully poetic about the fact that she was blissfully unaware that, due to the vagaries of fate, she had been within a day or so of being murdered by her husband.

Chapter 29

Aggie suddenly realized that Friday was almost here. She had promised to cook up something for Jack and needed to give that some thought and do the shopping. Usually tiresome, the shopping part, but now it felt like some prospective relief, something she would come close to enjoying, but not entirely. Her cell rang suddenly and revealed the name Moses Reede. He was calling back. She picked up.

"Hi Moses."

Still interesting to say that.

"Hi Agnes. Look, we have to meet. There are some new developments."

"Really. And what are they? Not that I don't want to meet you, of course."

Reede grunted.

"Well, to begin with, Clement Smith has been shot."

Aggie was shocked. She was looking at him as the shooter of two people.

"What?"

"Yes. This morning."

"Is he OK? Not dead?"

"He's more or less OK. He was shot in the phone and an arm."

"Shot in the phone?"

Reede spoke with a smile in his voice.

"Yep. Clean shot to the phone. It was in his chest pocket. Cracked a rib I believe, and it was goodbye to the phone."

"Wow. He was lucky. I suppose that he didn't do it himself?"

"Great minds think alike. I liked him as the shooter and so I was a little suspicious. But, it looks like he was actually shot by someone. He didn't see who did it. At least, not properly. Guy in a hoodie, he said."

"He did say a guy though?"

Reede paused.

"I wondered about that too. He said a guy. Have to ask him again. Thinking he was covering for Waters? I mean in the sense of an arranged shooting by her and then throwing in that a guy did it?"

"I was, yes. I thought she could have done it for him and he then said a guy did it."

"A possibility. Look, can we meet up and compare notes?"

Aggie thought about it for a few moments.

"I suppose we should."

"Well, don't go over the moon about it."

Aggie laughed.

"Sorry. Just taking it in. A bar or a restaurant? Can you come into the city?"

"Of course. You name it. When and where."

"OK. I know a good Mexican place with a bar on Columbus in the nineties. You can park nearby pretty cheaply. How about Saturday at 5.00 pm? I'm seeing a friend tomorrow."

"Sounds good."

Aggie named the place.

"I'll be there. I'll try to guess which one is you."

Reede laughed.

"OK. A challenge. See you then."

He broke the connection.

Aggie was still very surprised at the news. Clement Smith shot. Now, three people had been shot, one of them fatally. It did not make much sense. It would make sense if he had staged the whole thing but it did not sound like it. Who would do these shootings? There was no answer to that at the moment. Meeting up with Moses Reede was a good idea. They could go over their findings together. That in itself was surprising because he was a cop and did not need to share anything, especially with a PI. Perhaps he thought that she had some perspective on the case that he did not. Anyway, time to shop. She had decided on curried vegetables. A lot of work but worth the effort. Cheesecake would follow, a cop out but a tasty one. She set off for a Whole Foods store, promising herself to fit in some more research on Marcia Forman's whereabouts in between her cooking efforts. Part of that, in the next day or so, would be a call to Forman's cell phone which should have reached its destination soon. She expected Forman to answer and she hoped to clear up a few things if Forman was amenable to that.

Chapter 30

Dwight Forman drove as quickly as he dared through the night to Montauk. The last thing he needed for this trip was to be stopped by the traffic cops for speeding, with the cargo that he was carrying. He had kept his gloves on because it seemed to be the right thing to do. He had put the personal items from the motel room in a plastic bag and put the bag and his gun in the glove compartment. The gun would have to go, of course. He was pressed for time and was finding it difficult to think straight. Finally, he arrived in Montauk and drove to the pier area where his boat was moored. He could not get the car closer than a hundred yards or so and had to park on a pebble filled pathway which narrowed towards the moorings. He got out of the car in faint starlight and walked uncertainly to where his boat was moored, nestling with the other small craft. The boats were at right angles to the pier and each one had a narrow wooden platform alongside it for additional mooring.

He would have to get the body along the platform section to tip it into the boat which was going to be a taxing task. The nearest house was over fifty feet away and in darkness, his footsteps sounding unnaturally loud as he crunched the pebbles. It was dark, no question about that, the moon hidden behind clouds. He cursed his lack of foresight once again. He should have brought a flashlight. He made his way back to the car and stood listening for a while, the only sounds being a light breeze rustling some bushes and faint lapping sounds of nearby water. He opened the trunk and leaned in, groping around to get a good purchase on the bundle. He eased himself backwards dragging the bundle out of the trunk gradually until it suddenly came out in one motion causing him to sit on the pebbles with the bundle laying across him. He pushed it off and climbed to his feet, realizing that he had to kneel down again, which was painful on the pebbles, to get the whole package over one shoulder. He lurched to his feet, his knees buckling slightly, and stood there, adjusting the position of the bundle closer to his neck for the most comfort.

He began to move towards the pier, using a staggering gait, dragging cold air into his lungs as he went. After about forty yards, close to halfway, he tripped and fell, the body partially rolling out of the bundle and away from him.

His knees felt skinned and he had hurt an elbow but he gathered his wits and rolled everything up again mostly by touch because of the darkness, hauling it back onto his shoulder.

He made it onto the wooden pier and up to his boat without further incident but gasping from the effort. He dumped the body onto the pier at the junction with the mooring platform. The idea was for him to go along the platform alongside the boat and drag the body after him, which was easier than pushing it, and then rolling it into the boat, that level being a little lower than the platform. He thought about getting into the boat and pulling the body in after him but he was worried about the boat tipping up with both of them on one side. He stepped over the body onto the narrow platform, stooped and tugged on the body, dragging it parallel to the boat on the edge of the platform. He made sure that the boat was up against the platform and then shoved the bundle into the boat. He could see in the weak starlight that half the body was in the boat but the top half was in the water in a gap made by the boat drifting away from the platform. He knelt down on painful kneecaps and reached into the water up to his elbows, heaving the dripping bundle into the boat, the head and one arm uncovered. Shaking the cold water from his sleeves and gloves, he stood up and headed back to the car.

He grabbed the remaining sheet, pillowcase, weights and bungee cords, along with his gun and walked back to the boat. He was feeling cold and miserable, fully regretting this whole episode but knowing that he had to see it through. He climbed into the boat over the body and tossed the gun and linens onto the body. He seated himself next to the motor and pulled on the starter. The engine fired up straight away and he was thankful that, at least something was working. The motor sounded extraordinarily loud in the night air but he didn't care as he unmoored the boat with some difficulty due to the gloves and his cold hands. He made his way past some other boats and along the headland, which had very dim lighting here and there, and out into the relatively calm ocean. He knew that he had eaten up a lot of time so far and that was fast becoming a serious issue. He had to get back home at an acceptable time. He chugged out into the darkness for a few minutes, not knowing exactly where he was and becoming more and more agitated. When he thought that he must be in at least ten feet of water he cut the motor and drifted to a halt. He had no way of gauging the depth of the ocean at this point but had vague recollections of going out to sea about this far when he had attempted fishing a long time ago. This would have to do.

If only he had thought of bringing a flashlight. He just could not deal with anything else going amiss. He squatted down in the boat and struggled in the darkness to wrap up the body again. When he had finished he could still make out the paleness of a foot sticking out. He managed to force it inside the bundle and then, scrabbling around, found the bungee cords and began hooking them around the bundle to tighten things up. Success, it was a decent job.

He then positioned the gym weights under the bungee cords and also added a can of gasoline which he had found while poking around for the weights. All that was left was to get the whole lot into the ocean. He knelt down yet again and got both arms under the bundle, his gloved fingers numb with the cold. He gave a mighty heave and the bundle went over the side, he almost going with it, his head and shoulders going beneath the ocean surface, hands grabbing at the side of the boat as it tipped and bobbed alarmingly. He flopped in the bottom of the boat, snorting seawater from his nostrils and with one hand feeling for the bundle. It had not sunk so he pushed and prodded it down until it silently drifted down and away beneath the surface. He had to hope that it was going down. It had to once all of the bedding was soaked. He fell back, unbearably cold and utterly exhausted. Crossing his mind was the thought that after all of his planning it had come down to this debacle, out in the ocean wrestling with a dead guy with very little in the way of achievement.

With some effort, he found his gun and reluctantly threw it as hard as he could out to sea. He heard the soft plop in the darkness as it found its way to oblivion on the sea bed. He started the motor with dead fingers and drove the boat in a wide arc in case the bundle was still near the surface and headed back towards the mooring. There seemed to be more light on the way back and so he made it to the mooring pier comfortably and tied up. As he got out of the boat and walked back towards the car, he felt stiff and awkward and his knees stung with pain. In the car he started the engine, took off his gloves and turned the heater on. He pulled at the clothing stuck to his arms with the wet and freed them, shook his head which was still dripping water and checked the time. He had lost well over an hour in his planned schedule and would have to warm up on the drive home. His teeth were chattering and he could feel only his thumbs and forefingers.

On the way back he began to recover and started to think things through. He had to be positive. He had, at least, taken out his wife's lover and gotten rid of the body, no mean feat. She wouldn't know where he was and would assume that he had dumped her. That made him feel much better and dimmed the thought that he had, at times tonight, panicked during the execution of his plan. He took the chance of driving fast, not encountering any traffic cops and stopping once to toss his gloves into some bushes. Yes, he had covered all the bases arriving back at 7.30 am. The kids were getting cleaned up in the bathroom before breakfast and he made it safely to his bedroom, without being spotted, to begin his own clean up. He had to decide how much to tell Shu but that could come later. For now he needed to regroup.

Chapter 31

Aggie was well into her machinations about Marcia Forman and was beginning to prepare vegetables for the following night's dinner when she was startled by her cell ringing. She picked it up and saw that it was Frank Pederson. That did not feel good because she thought that he was only going to call when something was up with Hollis.

"Hi Frank."

"Hi Aggie. Look, I've got some interesting news. Nothing to worry about."

Aggie laughed.

"You mean Hollis is not about to arrest me?"

"Ha. No, nothing like that. Did you get anywhere tracking down Marcia Forman?"

"I did. She booked a room for two the night that she flew in. It was in a Best Western about six miles away from her home. Then she vanished the next day. I'm not sure where she is except she might be heading for the Pacific North West."

Pederson paused.

"What?"

"Well, I've been tracking her phone or, at least, my friend has, and it has been heading in that direction for a couple of days."

"That's interesting. Do you think that it is her?"

"I don't know. But I will soon. I'm going to call her. What's your news?"

Pederson cleared his throat.

"Well, the body of a man has turned up in the ocean near Montauk on Long Island. Been in the water for a while."

There was another pause before he continued.

"Nobody we know or, at least, I don't think so. Do you know a Chester Berman?"

Aggie thought briefly.

"No. The name is not familiar at all."

"Well, this guy was shot- murdered, and dumped in the ocean. He washed ashore along with a pile of debris. Bedding stuff like duvet, sheets, pillowcase and all that. Also the remnants of bungee cords, you know, the things you use to strap luggage onto car roof racks."

"Yes. But what has that got to do with me – us?"

"Nothing on the face of it but the cops on the case, whom I happen to be familiar with, told me that the sheets had been traced to a motel through their laundry marks."

He named the motel which was quite close to the Best Western to which Aggie had traced Marcia Forman. "Interesting but no connection that I can see, except proximity."

Pederson sounded minimally excited.

"Right. Well, here's the kicker. Marcia Forman reserved a room at that same motel."

"Really."

Aggie ran through the implications of that but before she could speak, Pederson added,

"This guy was in the room that she had reserved."

"Oh-Oh. Her lover?"

"I don't think so. The motel was fully booked and, since Marcia Forman had not shown up, they gave it to this guy."

"And then he gets himself shot."

"Yes."

"Was he shot in the motel?"

"Seems clear that he was. Guy was a pharmaceutical salesman from Milwaukee. He was traced through his credit card. The motel folks were wondering why a guy would leave the motel with all the bedding and yet leave his car behind."

Aggie digested some of this.

"Couldn't be a coincidence could it. But, if someone wanted to kill Marcia Forman, they couldn't confuse her with a man, could they?"

"Who knows? I'll find out what more I can. Looks like somebody went to the motel, shot this guy and dumped him in the ocean. Cops are bound to talk to Forman, which, I suppose, will lead to us."

"Thanks for the heads up Frank. I'll keep looking at my end too."

"Good. OK, bye."

He disconnected. Aggie put the cell down and stared out of the window as she tried to absorb all the ramifications of this new information. Marcia Forman had checked into the Best Western with someone else. Boyfriend? Maybe. Aggie assumed that it was a lover in spite of the fact that she had not discovered one. OK, a night of bliss. What then? Go home? No, she didn't think so because Forman, or her phone, had taken a trip across country. Why the motel? She didn't go there so, perhaps it was some kind of back up. Mix up the places to stay at in case she was being tracked. She hadn't needed the motel so, whatever plans she had cooked up, they must have been OK. That would be the trip to Chicago and beyond. Presumably, since there were two at the Best Western, both took off to Chicago together. The motel might have been there in case there was a hitch, one could go and one couldn't, something like that. Aggie felt even more strongly that Marcia Forman was alive and probably looking for happiness somewhere else. Without her kids, though. Not a good thing, much too selfish, unless she had other plans for them.

That seemed to be Aggie's best summary of events so far. The murder of the salesman was more puzzling. It looked like wrong place at the wrong time. Mistaken for Marcia Forman or for her lover? Who would do that? Obviously,

Dwight Forman. The cops would go there too, which would lead to more questioning all round as Frank had said, especially if Forman had an alibi. First, they had to be sure that Chester Berman was not the actual target. Once that had been established, Aggie's life would become more hectic to say the least. She now thought that Dwight Forman could be a dangerous individual. If he had murdered the salesman in a case of mistaken identity, then he would stop at nothing to kill his wife and her lover. They were probably unaware of the danger they were in. If, for no other reason, Aggie felt that she had to find Marcia Forman. She assumed that the cops must surely be thinking along the same lines as she was. After all, everything seemed to be pointing in that direction. If, somehow, Dwight Forman did offer a cast iron alibi – and that was not beyond him- then life could, indeed, be quite interesting for Aggie. He had already tried to implicate her in his wife's disappearance and there was no reason for him to stop. All that Aggie had to do, though, was show that Marcia Forman was still alive because there was no way that she could get caught up in the murder of the salesman, was there?

    Aggie spent the rest of the late afternoon and early evening preparing dinner for the following night. Curry was always better after a day in the fridge. She had added garlic and ginger root, in small amounts, to the vegetables because of their beneficial effect on the body's immune system, not that she thought much about that, day to day. To mash or chop the garlic for the best taste? She chopped it minutely with the ginger root and added it to the mix. She made up some crudités for herself with some blue cheese dressing for a dip and topped that with some chocolate and a glass of Sauternes. Nice treat for a change. She began a Malcolm Mackay book based in Glasgow, Scotland to round off the evening before bed.

Chapter 32

The next morning, after showering and black coffee, Aggie checked the vegetable curry, tasting it cold from the fridge and felt fairly pleased with her efforts. She thought that it would go down well with Jack that evening. She would take that and the cheesecake out of the fridge during the afternoon, ready for dinner. She also checked her notes and thought that it was time to call Marcia Forman to try and clear up a few things. She was convinced that Marcia was alive. Would she have her lover with her? That might shed some light on the salesman murder. How was the motel involved? Was she gone for good? Would Aggie have to keep her whereabouts confidential on a personal level? She was, after all, trying to get away and had done nothing wrong. What about her kids? That was a sticking point for Aggie, although she had no real idea how they felt about their mother. Aggie sighed as she began to see a mass of questions that needed to be answered with no guarantees that they would be. She picked up her cell and dialed Marcia's number. It rang several times with no response. She rang off and tried again. This time there was a response.

"Hi."

The voice was female and neutral.

Aggie said, "Hi. Are you Marcia Forman?"

"No. Who's she?"

"You don't know anybody called Marcia Forman?"

"No. Who are you?"

"I am a friend of hers."

"So why are you calling me?"

"I'm not calling you. I'm calling the phone."

There was a long silence.

"The phone? You funny or what?"

Not very bright then.

"No, I'm not being funny. Is that your phone? The one you are using?"

Another long silence.

"I don't have to talk to you."

"No you don't. I appreciate it that you are talking to me."

Aggie tried again.

"Is that your phone?"

"No. I found it. It was lost. I didn't steal it or anything."

"Of course not. But it does belong to somebody. In fact, it belongs to my friend. Marcia Forman."

Aggie surmised that this was not new information. It would be easy to see who the phone belonged to. Just another liar.

"Who are you again?"

"As I said I am a friend. She would like her phone back."

A sly tone entered the voice.

"How much is it worth? To get it back that is."

Aggie responded.

"Nothing."

Indignation.

"What? Nothing? It has to be worth something to whatshername."

"Maybe to her but not to me. You should return it."

"I will but I want something for it first."

Aggie sighed. This was going nowhere and was a bit of a waste of time.

"I told you. It is worth nothing."

"I'll put all the data on the Internet."

"Do that and you will be in trouble with the cops."

"Ha. They would have to find me first."

Aggie smiled, taking a chance on the train journey's end.

"You are in British Columbia. The phone is being tracked as I speak. Your whereabouts are known by the cops."

"What?"

"I can give you an address. Send it and you won't be in trouble."

There was a pause.

"Fuck you."

The connection was broken.

Not a stellar conversation but Aggie thought it was about as good as she could have done. The phone had been stolen or someone had seen an opportunity and taken it. Still a theft. So, Marcia Forman was somewhere else, without her phone. The thief would likely dump it after that little chat and that would be the end of that. Aggie wondered whether, if Marcia got a new phone, she would keep the old number. She doubted it. Back to square one now. One possibility was credit cards. She had no access to them but, if Marcia used them, perhaps Jack or Jonathan might be able to help. She would bear that in mind. Not much else to do today. There were a couple of work related inquiries to deal with but, the Forman case was on hold until she could track down Marcia and she would be meeting with Moses Reede tomorrow about the progress in the Jakob Kowalczyk case. That was really just about catching the shooter of three people whomever that was. She would also have to wait to see what happened in the salesman killing. Frank expected that scene to arrive at their door sometime soon. So she decided to clean up the apartment and then read and veg out until Jack showed up.

Mid-afternoon, while she was in her quiet time period, her cell rang. She saw that it was Jonathan. She picked up.

"Hi Jonathan. How's things and how's the patient doing?"

"Hi Aggie. Things are going well. We hope to be back in a few days.."

"Oh, that's good."

"Yes, it is. I was just checking in to see how you are doing. Frank still doing a good job?"

"Yes. He's been great. Stopped me making a fool of myself. There's not much doing on that front. He might have slowed them down. They need something solid but there's nothing."

"That's good. He's the best. So nothing is going on there, then?"

Aggie laughed.

"Well, something is going on. It hasn't involved me yet. A guy got himself murdered."

Big intake of breath from Jonathan.

"What? You have a way of just tossing things out there. A murder?"

"Yes, long story. Seems like wrong place at the wrong time. I think the Forman guy is in it up to his neck. Time will tell."

"Really. Well, don't be annoyed with me when I say please be careful. Take great care where this guy is concerned."

Aggie smiled. She was getting used to being cared about.

"I will. So how is your friend doing?"

"Oh, Blink's doing well now. We've got him a place to stay. Very small one bedroom, a converted space really, but OK for now. He's on antibiotics at the moment. Couple of things he picked up. And we are getting him to a dentist tomorrow – quite a bit of work to be done. He's not at all happy about that. He had two front teeth knocked out and needs a root canal or two. Amazing how teeth go downhill so fast."

Aggie ran her tongue over her own teeth. She took good care of them but hated dental trips.

"He's lucky he has you guys."

"Yes, I think he is. We have a long history together and this is just the latest installment."

"And, of course, you will tell me about it one day."

Jonathan laughed.

"I will. We are going to find a job for him next and then we are done. Bit of financial support I suppose but that's it."

Aggie had wild speculation in her mind when she asked the next question. Maybe Blink was a spy or a hitman.

"What does he do?"

"He restores art, believe it or not."

Aggie thought not.

Jonathan added.

"Not many places lining up for those skills. Maybe an upscale auctioneer or a museum."

"Oh, that's interesting. How about teaching?"

"Possible. We'll see. First things first. How's the trucking business?"

"Progressing but complicated. I'll tell you when I see you."

"That sounds really good. I've missed our conversations and dinners."

Aggie said, "Me too."

"Call me if you need to. You know that."

"I will, thanks. Bye Jonathan."

"Bye."

They rang off. She hadn't asked about the credit cards. It didn't seem to be the right time. Anyway, that could come later.

As the time for Jack's arrival approached, she took out china plates instead of paper ones, because it felt good to have a change, plus some decent flatware and laid all of it out on the coffee table with a couple of glasses, tumblers rather than wineglasses, which sometimes felt precarious, although aesthetically more pleasing. She put on the curry with a very low heat, stirring it minimally now and again and the apartment was soon imbued with the pungent aromas of good curry. Jack showed up close to 7.30pm, looking tired and rumpled. They hugged in the doorway briefly and Jack put his bag of wine purchases on the floor next to the coffee table.

Aggie said sympathetically, "Long day?"

"Yes. Tell you about it later. I've brought a couple of reds and a Sauternes."

Aggie poked in the bag and came up with the Sauternes.

"I'll put this in the fridge for later. Why don't you have a shower and clean up. We have plenty of time. I've got a robe or a tee and sweats if you want."

Jack perked up visibly.

"That would be great. A hot shower would feel perfect. Don't think your sweats would fit me."

"Open bottoms. You could try. Shampoo's in there. Conditioner if you need it."

Jack shrugged off the leather jacket he was wearing, along with his shoes and socks and headed for the bathroom. After about ten minutes of the sounds of running water, Aggie turned off the curry and some yellow rice she had been preparing, went to the bathroom and tapped on the door.

"Think I'll do my hair too. Can I come in?"

She heard the shower curtain rails rattling along the rod they were on above the bath.

"Of course. Come right in."

It was nearly 10.00 pm when they sat down on the couch with a plate of vegetable curry and yellow rice each accompanied in each case by a large glass of Shiraz. Jack was wearing an old tee shirt of Aggie's and her sweats which came down to just above his ankles. She was in her robe. Both had wet hair which was still exhibiting tiny droplets of water. They ate for a while in companionable silence which Jack eventually ventured into.

"This is really good. Delicious. Hits the spot."

Aggie smiled as she took a large pull of Shiraz.

"Thanks. Good for you too. Loads of vitamins."

They finished up their curries at just about the same time and flopped back on the couch.

Jack closed his eyes.

"What happened with the phone thing? Did you call."

Aggie rested her head on the back of the couch and turned slightly towards Jack, her hair, which had grown longer recently, flopping towards her eyes.

"I did call and the phone was stolen."

"Stolen? Someone else had it?"

"Yes, a woman had taken it with her all the way to British Columbia and wanted money for it."

Jack turned towards her.

"You paid?"

"No. Told her it was worthless and she threatened to run all the data on the Internet."

"Not nice."

"No. I basically asked her to send it back. After an expletive or two, she rang off. She will probably dump it or sell it."

"I expect so. Not much cash in it. So it was a sort of en route theft. Opportunist."

"Looks like it."

"You are back to square one then. No nearer to finding this woman. It sounds as though it would be useful to find her, to say the least."

Aggie sighed deeply.

"I just know that she is alive somewhere. I don't know where. She's gone off with a boyfriend, I'm sure. They did an overnight and took off. Also, the husband is still up to something."

Jack tutted.

"What's he done now?"

"I think he has murdered some guy that he thought was his wife's lover."

Jack sat up in shock.

"What? You didn't tell me about that. He murdered someone? When?"

"Last week."

Aggie told Jack about the murder and discovery of the body and Frank's call with the connection to the motel where Marcia Forman had booked a room.

Jack said, "So this guy was the lover? No, she's gone off with him, you think. So who is this guy?"

"I think wrong place at the wrong time. Bad luck."

"Forman just murdered him and dumped the body?"

"It's what I think. The cops may have a different take. I don't know who is on it but Frank does."

"He must have some kind of alibi because, otherwise, it's a bit obvious. A guy books a room that Forman thought his wife was in and then gets murdered."

Aggie added.

"He is very devious and an outright liar, so who knows what he is saying."

Jack responded, a very concerned look on his face.

"I can see what I can find out if you like. Bound to come to you at some point. Good policing. Hollis will have to update the inquiry. All of that."

"Yes, I know. It's OK. I'll sit and wait on it. I do want to find Marcia Forman though."

"You've tried all the airports?"

"No. I suppose I'll have to. How about some cheesecake?"

They cleaned up the plates and cutlery. Aggie did not have a dishwasher. Seemed extravagant for one person and too finicky. Easier to rinse the dishes. She put the left over curry in a container in the fridge and prepared the cheesecake. They were soon back on the couch with a plate of cheesecake and a glass of Sauternes each. Aggie sipped her wine before tasting the cheesecake.

"Jack, is there any way that you can track credit cards? It might help me find Marcia Forman."

Jack said, "With the right information, yes. It would be more of a favor than an official look because of privacy restrictions. She is not a suspect, at least not currently, so above board would need legal paperwork."

"That's OK. I don't want to cause problems."

"You're not. I'll see what I can do."

"It would help me to prove that she is alive."

"Well, it won't, will it? It will prove that her credit card is alive."

"Yes, but it is a start."

"Right. I'll do my best."

They devoured the cheesecake rapidly and each sat, glass in hand, savoring the wine and the moment. Aggie broke the silence.

"How's your break-in case going? Or would you rather not talk about it?"

"No, I'll talk about it. What about your trucker?"

Aggie laughed.

"Your turn first, me later. How is the robbery doing?"

Jack drew in a deep breath.

"Well, all three are going down."

Aggie was surprised.

"All three? The housekeeper as well?"

"Yes. She's turned out to be part of it. The two guys are barely out of college. Idiotic idea to get some quick cash."

"They are college kids?"

Jack nodded with an expression of some consternation.

"Were college kids. Not too bright. No jobs. Like I said, a bit of quick money. The housekeeper may have recruited them. Don't know yet."

"Interesting. Unlikely to be the first time then. I thought that she had been roughed up."

"She was slapped around a bit. Probably more than she wanted to be. Remember I mentioned the bruising on her upper arms and a hospital trip. One of the guys was a touch too enthusiastic."

Jack leaned forward, fingering the neck of the tee shirt as he spoke.

"I'm talking to one of our guys in Nashville at the moment. Sounds like our housekeeper was active there. We can't figure out if she is a loner or part of some larger operation. Either way, she didn't take much persuasion to shop the two gallant lads."

"She might get some leniency?"

"Possibly, but not if she is some kind of crime organizer on a small scale. We don't know how big this is, how much stuff has been stolen, where it's gone, that is, and if it has been fenced and who by?"

"So, a lot of work to do. She has to meet her protégés somewhere, doesn't she? A bar or a night club? And more than a few times when you think of it. She can't just walk up to them and ask them to be robbers."

"That's true. We did wonder if she picked them up somehow, met them that way."

Aggie gazed down at Jack's bare feet. He had just about perfect toes, all the right sizes, no buckling or bending. She didn't like her own very much. Not bad but the odd bend and callus. All that crazy footwear which she had long given up.

"It's as good an idea as any. Who will be interviewing?"

Jack smiled.

"It's up to me. Sometime tomorrow."

He glanced at Aggie.

"Now, what about the trucking guy?"

"Oh, it's late now, well after midnight in fact, and you have a busy day ahead."

Jack leaned over and kissed Aggie's hair.

"That's OK. Just an outline then. And then we'll go to bed."

Aggie said, "OK, then, just an outline."

She leaned back with a sigh, marshaling her thoughts.

"The trucking guy is going to be in a lot of trouble, apart from getting himself shot, that is."

"Of course he is. He's a scammer. Scammed an insurance company."

Aggie looked conflicted.

"Yes, he did, along with his two enablers."

"The casino woman and her boyfriend?"

"Yes but I can't help feeling sorry for him."

Jack sat up.

"Why? He committed a fraud. Planned it. Took part in it. Was fully involved in it. Open and shut."

"I knew that you would see it that way but I think that he was manipulated, especially by the woman or, the other guy, through the woman."

Jack sighed loudly.

"OK, you liked him but it doesn't really matter. You know that."

"I do know. But it's the way I feel. I can't help that."

"I know, I know. We are coming at it from different directions. Perhaps it's because he got shot. By the boyfriend wasn't it?"

"That's not clear any more. He's been shot too, now."

Jack looked suddenly alert.

"What? He has? Is he dead?"

"No. He was shot in the phone."

"In the phone? Oh, I see, lucky shot for him. That can still hurt a lot. Even be fatal. Didn't do it himself did he?"

"Someone else asked that. Do people do that sort of thing regularly, then?"

"People will do anything if it helps them. Believe me. So, who is wandering around shooting people if it isn't phone man?"

"I'm not sure. Can't be the woman. At least, I don't think so."

Jack waved a hand as he spoke.

"So, you have three shootings and no clues? Who is looking into it?"

"Jack, it is not like that. I have ideas, suspicions. I just haven't resolved them yet. There is a guy from New Jersey, looking into it, as you say."

"Who is that?"

"His name is Moses Reede. I'm going to compare notes with him tomorrow."

"Ah, I don't know him. You are going to compare notes?"

"Yes, I hope so. Why?"

"Unusual, that's all. He would have plenty of resources."

"That occurred to me also. I think he is just covering the bases, being thorough. I can probably save him some legwork."

Jack sat up, looking a little ridiculous in the sweats and tee but concerned also.

"Look, sorry, Ag. I'm tired. I've been a bit touchy. I shouldn't have gotten into it like that a few minutes ago. It's not fair, I know."

"That's OK. I understand. Let's finish the wine and go to bed."

Jack lightened up immediately.

"Let's just go to bed."

Chapter 33

They were up early the next morning even though it was a weekend. Jack had a long day ahead so Aggie set up some coffee, toast and cereal for their breakfast while he monopolized the bathroom. He was soon at the counter with Aggie, nibbling on toast and looking reflective, ready for work, apart from his jacket. Aggie was still in her robe. He put down the toast, sipped some coffee and said,

"Do you ever think of having kids?"

Aggie was startled.

"What brought that on? Are you going domestic on me now?"

Jack smiled briefly.

"No, I'm not. The thought just suddenly pops up out of nowhere and hits me. That's all."

"The thought pops up or is it some kind of atavistic bell starts ringing?"

"I don't know. It just happens."

Aggie sipped her coffee, looking at Jack over her cup.

"Hm. Having kids is almost beyond my comprehension. Well, having them is not. That's easy. The rest is the hard part."

She continued.

"It is not even worth considering without the idea of being one hundred per cent committed. Otherwise, what's the point? What's on your mind Jack?"

"Nothing. I sometimes feel a primal urge to have heirs. Kids. Why? Perhaps to have someone carry on my way of thinking, my perspective on life, build on my values."

The look on Aggie's face told him what was coming.

"That's absolute nonsense. You might feel that but kids are human beings, so there is no reason at all to think that they would assume any perspective that you might have. They will form their own – probably the opposite of yours."

Jack's look was rueful.

"I suppose so. It's a romantic idea isn't it. With my work, I would be a terrible dad. Always absent."

"You could change your job and have kids."

Jack drew in a quick breath.

"Oh. That's a little harsh."

"Sorry. Just being practical. I'm not sure that I even like talking about this, kids that is. It feels too emotional right now."

"You mean right now or in the general sense of things?"

Aggie sighed.

"In general. Look, I'm dealing with serious stuff with these cases. I can't get my mind around anything else with any depth to it."

"Enough said, then."

"No. I'll talk it through with you at some point soon. That's perfectly fair and reasonable. We will do it."

"OK. Deal. I'd better get going."

They finished up the coffee and toast in silence. Then Aggie stood and cleared up as Jack put on his leather jacket. They kissed lightly and Jack said,

"I'll do what I can on the Forman credit card front."

Aggie said, "Thanks. See you soon."

And he was soon off down the stairs. Aggie sat at the counter for some time before setting off to the bathroom and a hot shower. It was barely mid-morning when Frank Pederson called. Aggie had been preparing for her chat with Moses Reede later in the day at the Mexican restaurant. Frank had a tinge of resignation in his voice.

"Hi Aggie. Hope things are good with you."

"Because you are about to change all of that?"

She paused.

"Sorry, Frank. It's my cynical side. I feel a little vulnerable at the moment for some reason."

Frank cleared his throat.

"Well, let's say that a modicum of cynicism is not quite out of place right now."

"Oh dear. What's up?"

"Our friend Hollis has been talking to an investigative team – well not a team really – a couple of guys looking into the motel killing."

Aggie sighed loudly.

"So things are coming to a head."

"You might say that. They have positively confirmed, as best they can, that this guy, the salesman who got himself murdered, has no connection to anybody's case. As you correctly surmised, poor guy put himself in the wrong place at the wrong time."

"So that means, if they are on the ball, that these guys must be on to Forman."

Aggie was feeling the beginnings of concern pushing its way into her consciousness. She added,

"He is obviously the way to go."

Frank continued.

"Yes, to a point. They have questioned the motel people who saw nothing. They have talked extensively to Forman and his babysitter who have a pretty good alibi but it is mutually inclusive."

"What does that mean?"

"They are basically alibiing each other."

"So one or both could have done the deed."

"Exactly. That is on hold at the moment. They are following other leads, including boat people at Montauk and, of course, you."

Aggie gave a derisive half laugh.

"What could I get out of it? More stalking or whatever?"

"Well these guys have called me and, at some point soon, we will have to talk to them. I've got them on hold for the time being but a routine chat, at least, is on the cards."

Aggie sat down, realizing that she had been walking around her living area.

"Frank there just isn't a sensible motive for all of this. What on earth are they thinking?"

"Here's the thing. The direction they are moving in is that the guy in the motel was killed by mistake as we have thought all along. But the killer did not know that until the killing was over. He, or she, discovered their mistake and dumped the body."

"So?"

"Well, just suppose that if the killer thought that it was Marcia Forman, then her removal is still pertinent to the original case touted by Mr. Forman."

"What does that mean?"

"They haven't gone there quite yet but the murder could have been done, in error, by the obsessive stalker."

There was a long silence before Aggie muttered one word.

"Me."

Chapter 34

Aggie fell back on her couch, slumping against the back. Her concern had magnified measurably. This affair would not go away. Forman is guilty for all to see but nobody seems to be able to see it. Hollis has a one track mind which appears to be centered on her and now, she was sure, he was poisoning the minds of the murder investigators. Well, they must be experienced and would have the know how to figure out that Forman was their guy. He had committed a cold blooded murder and body disposal. There had to be clues lying around by the handful. She had to put it out of her mind and get ready for Moses Reade. That case, at least, was coming to fruition. Today should help to put the wraps on that. Her part of it was over. She had been hired, seen it through, been paid and now the Jersey guys could solve the murder and attempted murders and close up shop. That felt good from the case closed perspective but she had residual empathy, misplaced or not, for Jakob Kowalczyk.

She would, indeed, help him where possible. As she was deciding what to do next, Moses Reede called her to make their meeting an hour or so later, closer to 6.30 pm because something had come up. That done, she decided to tidy up her files and iPad notes while thinking things through, making sure that she was up to scratch with everything and ready for that meeting. When 6.15 pm rolled around, she threw on a bunch of casuals, grabbed her bag, put her iPad in it and headed for the Mexican restaurant. When she arrived there was nobody at the long round bar that could be Reede so she decided at the last moment to find a table. There were several free tables for two, most diners being among two large groups towards the back of the restaurant. She picked a quiet table near the doors leading to the front terrace.

A waiter brought her water, tortilla chips and a long thin tray of several salsas. She said that she was waiting for someone but ordered a margarita straight up with ice which, when it came, was very large. She sipped it carefully and tried the green salsa with a chip which was tasty, in fact, delicious. Just as she was thinking of checking around the restaurant in case she had missed Moses Reede, she became aware of a presence beside her. Looking up she saw a big man, dark features, heavyish face, hair trimmed to a stubble as was his beard, large expressive eyes and a generous mouth. Nothing like she imagined but then, when is that ever the case? He wore a tan suit, open necked blue shirt with a white tee and silver Cuban necklace showing. She caught a sideways glimpse of desert boots.

He said, "Agnes, I presume."

Following that with a smile.

"Makes me feel like Henry Morton Stanley."

Aggie stood and they shook hands, their grips firm.

"Yes. So you are Moses. Do you want to join me here at the table? I thought that it would be better than the bar."

"Wonderful. I like it here thanks."

He sat down opposite, lowering his large body athletically into the seat.

"What are you drinking?"

Aggie looked down at her glass.

"I've got a Reposado margarita straight up with ice."

"I'll get the same. I think that Tequila is among the top ten but, I suppose that it depends on who is rating them."

A waiter appeared at the table and took Reede's drink order. He helped himself to a couple of tortilla chips and dipped them in the red salsa before eating them.

Aggie said,

"Would you like something to eat? Just something light to keep us going."

He smiled easily.

"Any suggestions?"

They finished up by deciding on a large bowl of guacamole and an order of cheese quesadilla each, plus some more tortilla chips. Reede's drink arrived and they completed their order. He raised his glass and said,

"Nice to see you."

Aggie replied.

"Same here. You haven't brought any notes with you? I mean, no files."

The smile again.

"It's all in my head."

She gave him a quizzical look part way between we'll see and disbelief.

"I do hope that this will be a fair exchange of information. My guess is that you don't need to do this."

"There is some truth to that but I intend to keep my side of things. I also must admit that I thought it would be interesting to meet up with someone in your line of business."

Aggie sipped her margarita and smiled.

"You must have met many PI's in your time. Why me?"

They dipped the chips in the salsa as they spoke, occasionally sipping the drinks.

"Well, let's say I was curious. You sounded efficient, determined I suppose."

Aggie fingered the base of her glass.

"Nice to be efficient and determined."

Reede shifted in his seat.

"Now I've annoyed you. I meant that you seemed to have made a lot of progress. In areas that I would not be able to get to until later. I had the claims adjuster murder and two attempted murders to deal with. You had a lot of background. Perhaps insight is a better word."

Aggie smiled.

"Getting better all the time. Pushing the faint praise envelope now."

The guacamole showed up with a wicker basket of tortilla chips, almost unnoticed. They both dipped into it in silence for a few moments.

"This is really good," Reede commented.

Aggie added, "Yes, I come here now and again, usually at the bar. Drinks and food are pretty good. Convenient place too. So, why are you a cop?"

Reede offered a reluctant sigh.

"Long story. Do you really want to hear it?"

"Of course. That's why I asked."

"OK. I'll give you the abbreviated version."

He took a pull at the remains of his margarita.

"Folks tend to think that my parents were overly religious due to my name, but not so. There have been plenty of jokes over the years but it was not a misplaced sense of humor on their part. They were a circus double act and made no money to speak of. I came along and so things had to change. They became magicians but there was no money in that either. From what I gathered; they had been having a great time but not much income."

Aggie broke in.

"Worth the story already."

They drank up and ordered another drink each, barely noticing that they had cleaned up the guacamole and most of the chips. The restaurant was also filling up rapidly.

"Shortening things up a bit, they ended up after two or three years of odd jobs here and there – and I mean odd jobs- as a script writing team for a sitcom in Minnesota. They are still there, semi-retired but writing a bit. In case you wondered, my father is Haitian and my mother is Japanese. I am an only child and had been dragged around all over the place early on in my life. I eventually made it through college and became a cop for stability. Much better than the military."

Aggie had been genuinely engaged in the story and was about to speak when the quesadillas and drinks arrived. Reede continued.

"I'd like to hear your story now but I guess we should do a bit of that sharing info business."

"That would make sense. My story is nowhere near as interesting as yours, though."

There were six quesadillas in an order and they each ate the first two in companionable silence before Aggie spoke.

"I'll start then. I'll do a broad outline and then you can zero in where you think it works."

"Great. Thank you."

"When we last spoke about the case, at least my case, I was about to go and see Jakob Kowalczyk in hospital after he had been shot. I had put the shooting down to Clement Smith or Cordelia Waters, really liking Smith for it. Anyway, that can come later. After a long chat with Jakob, I…"

Reede interrupted.

"First name terms?"

"Not really but I sort of liked him and empathized a bit. He pretty much admitted the whole scam. In fact, he did admit it. The three of them were in it. It seems that the idea was conceived by Smith who used Waters to sell it to… Kowalczyk. They had had a longish affair which ended when Smith arrived on the scene. Waters resurrected the affair to convince Kowalczyk to go along. To be fair, he did not need much convincing. Are you interested in how they did it?"

"Yes, to an extent because it shows each one's culpability. You are interested in that too, right?"

"Yes. Well, they used an ignition system from inside the cab to start the fire behind the cab and drugs to knock Kowalczyk out at the right moment for the right amount of time, so that the whole episode would look authentic to an outsider, as it did to me, I might add. I showed up in the middle of it all. Smith and Waters showed up, also at the right time, to rescue him and hopefully have the truck destroyed. The fire didn't get to the load, as it happens."

"What a crazy, misbegotten scheme."

"It was."

"Why did he hire you?"

"Cover in case it did not work. A sort of backup plan to verify the idea that someone was trying to take him out. It did cross his mind that the other two were going to kill him or let him go up with the cab. There was a good reason for that which I'll come to in a bit."

Reede sighed explosively.

"Keystone cops if you ask me. Where did the drugs and ignition system come from?"

"Smith designed the ignition system, which worked quite well. He also supplied the drug. I don't know what it was. They tested it a couple of times. That part was a really bad idea. Dangerous, to say the least."

"The reason for all this was just to get cash. Gambling debts, I gather."

"Yes. Smith got in deep trying to crack the casino and Kowalczyk did some regular gambling. He owes a loan shark with a front of a car dealership in Jersey."

"Who are they?"

"Strum and Westlake."

"Yup. Heard of them. Small time. Westlake is the heavy. Not worth the time of day."

"They showed up at the fire too. They were tracking Kowalczyk."

Reede started eating again.

"Probably going to apply friendly persuasion somewhere."

Aggie took some more of her quesadilla.

"Not according to Strum."

"You spoke to him?"

"I went to see him and he eventually came through with some details."

"Wow. He is not a friendly character and I would have thought that he would have turned you down."

Aggie smiled.

"I paid him a surprise visit and it did not go that well to begin with but he came around."

Reede looked at her in mild admiration.

"Interesting."

Aggie laughed.

"Yes. Gave me coffee too."

She continued.

"Back to the fire. Kowalczyk had misgivings, I think, because during his relationship with Waters, he willed his estate to her. When you add it all up, it is substantial."

"Even though he had debts?"

"Yes. That would have been a fairly small nibble."

Reede stopped eating.

"So, those two would have gotten his estate and the insurance settlement."

"That would have been the idea but the timing was not good in terms of the insurance. All processed thanks to the dead guy, who was paid off, but not yet cash in hand. I don't know if they knew that."

Reede shook his head barely perceptively.

"Getting so sordid isn't it. Starts off with a dumb scam but escalates into betrayals and murders, or one murder and a couple of attempts."

Aggie nodded and they finished up the quesadillas. After draining the dregs of his drink, Reede began.

"What would have happened if you had not arrived on the scene?"

"Not a lot different I don't think, because of the chance arrival of the loan sharks. Serendipity in action."

"Well, the three of them will be charged soon for the insurance fraud. It will be up to lawyers to help their clients as best they can. Smith certainly seems to have been the prime mover and planner of the fraud, while Kowalczyk performed the act. The extent of Waters involvement will become clearer during all of the interviews. I still am not entirely convinced that Waters and Smith did not arrange his shooting between them."

"You mean he could have shot himself with her help or she could have shot him. Staged it somehow?"

"That was my thinking at first. Not at all easy to do. It could have gone seriously wrong. Just more stupidity if they did it. Anyway, fact is that somebody here shot three people. We have just established that all three were shot with the same gun. It's feasible, I suppose that Waters and Smith could have both done the shootings. One, Kowalczyk, one the claims adjuster and then a staged shooting of Smith."

A waiter came by and cleared away most of the table. Aggie ordered some more tortilla chips instead of dessert and they decided to have a last drink. Aggie said, "You know, the interviews of Waters and Smith might come up with an answer to the shootings. One might turn on the other."

"That's a definite possibility and it would prove very fruitful. Save us a lot of time too."

Their drinks and tortilla chips arrived and they both ate a few chips in contemplative silence, which Reede broke.

"You know, the pool of suspects for the shootings is very small. It has been difficult to come up with a decent motive outside our two prime contenders. The shootings have to be about the scam and other cash involved. You'd think that Waters and Smith would have the gumption to wait until Kowalczyk was waving a check around before either of them tried to kill him. That is a bit of a stumbling block for me."

"Yes, I did contact the insurance company and established that the settlement had been approved but not yet sent to Kowalczyk . That was odd, I thought, unless, Waters thought that she would get it as part of his estate."

Reede continued.

"The whole thing seems badly organized. Anyway, what I was getting to, was that I paid a visit to the Waters family or part of it. I wanted to get a sense of who they were. Just after lunch yesterday."

Aggie sipped her drink, getting quite a buzz by now.

"And did you?"

"Did I what?"

"Get a sense of them."

"Oh. Well, I met the father and the son together. The mother was out. Waters senior said she was at her Real Estate business. I do not know why the father was home – he is apparently an engineer in some kind of space company."

Aggie added.

"Yes, I researched both the partners' families. The mother is in real estate and the father is an electrical engineer. Apparently they are reasonably well off financially."

Reede continued.

"Really. Well, I had about half an hour or more with them. Both a little weird I thought. The son seems to be a layabout and has no employment that I could discern and lives at home with his parents. The father seemed a little eccentric, world weary and, at times, aggressive. They said they knew nothing about the shootings, they were sorry that Kowalczyk had gone through all that but the son no longer drove any trucks and neither had seen him in some time. They, especially the father, disapproved strongly of the relationship between Kowalczyk and the daughter. Or even the one with Smith for that matter. While we discussed the relationships, the son just stared out of the window the whole time. Very odd."

Aggie added.

"I spoke to the son on the phone. He wasn't so much odd as uncooperative and a little rude. He had been drinking early in the day but did give me some information about his sister. That was how I found out that she went to the towing yard and removed bits from the truck. He gave me the make of her wheels."

Reede said, "Thinking back on it, he didn't seem to like any discussion about his sister. Seemed uncomfortable. They were also concerned for her safety with both of her boyfriend's getting shot. I did not discuss the scam. I intimated that I was there in connection with the shootings."

Both Aggie and Reede sat back in their chairs and took long pulls at their margaritas, reflectively. Eventually, Reede said,

"Well, I guess we are up to date with everything. I still have a lot of work to do on the shootings, though."

Aggie responded.

"You know, I think I would like to have a word with the son in person. Just for my own satisfaction. I know that my end of this is pretty much done but I want to get a solid opinion of him. My instinct tells me that there is something there, below the surface. In the end it may help your case if I find out anything."

"When do you think that you would do that?"

"Well, tomorrow is Sunday and I imagine that everyone will be home. So, perhaps Monday or Tuesday. That way I might catch him on his own with a surprise visit. Thing is if nobody is home then it will be a wasted journey. I'd have to chance that. It should be a surprise visit."

They finished their drinks and Aggie asked the waiter for the check. She said, "Wow, do you know that over three hours have gone by?"

"Time flies and all that," laughed Reede.

They were both feeling the effects of substantial margarita consumption. The waiter arrived with the check and diplomatically placed it at the center of the table.

Aggie said, "Share this one?"

Reede replied, "My treat, if you don't mind."

Aggie said, "Oh, I don't know about that. Are you sure?"

"I am. My pleasure."

He placed his credit card in the folder with the check and the waiter duly retrieved it. Reede added.

"Look, if you do make that trip to the Waters home, please let me know when you will be doing it."

Aggie smiled.

"Do I detect some concern for me there?"

"Perhaps. But it would make absolute sense to take precautions. We don't really know a lot about this family, especially the men in it. I was not overly impressed when I spoke to them and certainly would not trust them."

Aggie responded.

"OK. That's fair enough. I will do that."

The waiter appeared again and Reede signed the receipt and took his credit card.

Aggie glanced across the table at Reede.

"Thank you for that. Very generous. Look, you can't drive back to New Jersey after all that drinking. You're a cop. I've got a couch; you can have that."

Reede looked at her, undecided. She continued.

"This is not some kind of date. I just think you should be careful, judicious, if you like. Or, how about a phrase I heard recently. It makes absolute sense to take precautions."

Reede laughed.

"You've got me. Thank you. I'll take you up on it."

"Good."

They rose from the table in unison and made their way onto the street. The evening was cool and pleasant as they walked the five blocks to Aggie's apartment block and climbed the stairs, mostly in silence.

Reede commented at the door.

"High security I see. Take some getting into."

"Long story. Not for this evening."

Once inside, Aggie indicated the couch and dug out a couple of blankets and a pillow for Reede.

She said, "Do you want to watch TV or have a coffee?"

"No thanks. I'm good. It's been a long day."

"OK. Water, drinks are in the fridge. I'll use the bathroom and leave it for you. I've got some spare toothbrushes so I'll leave one out and a towel."

Reede said, "Thanks for all of this. I've had a good time."

Aggie was soon in her bedroom and reading in bed for a short while. She felt perfectly safe leaving her door not fully closed and soon went to sleep. She awoke reasonably early the next morning and was surprised to hear activity in her kitchen. She slipped on her robe and went out into the kitchen. The smell of coffee and toast drifted to her nostrils as she took note of Reede, in shirt and tan pants and bare feet, pulling bread from the toaster.

Aggie said with a smile, "Wow, you are up early."

He responded.

"I'm an early riser. Part of the job I suppose."

He put slices of toast on a plate next to some butter and a knife.

"How do you want your coffee? I assume that you drink it because it's here. I didn't butter the toast because I didn't know how you take it."

"Black, please. Well, this is a bit of a treat."

He smiled as he poured the coffee and handed a mug to Aggie. They both took a seat at the counter.

Aggie said, "Did you sleep OK? Looks as though you slept in your clothes."

"Well, some of them. I didn't want to upend your bathroom by taking a shower. This was easy. Coffee, pot, mugs, all out there. Nice apartment. Light and roomy."

"Yes. I like it. Been here a while."

They sipped their coffee and ate some toast, Aggie's dry, Reede's buttered. Aggie ruminated on the fact that she was having coffee at her kitchen counter with two different men on consecutive mornings. Life had strange twists sometimes. She said, "What's your day going to be like?"

Reede said, "I'll do some more follow up on the shootings. As we talked about last night we are at a bit of an impasse at the moment on that. We need a breakthrough. I made a couple of calls this morning and it's a go for picking up Kowalczyk, Waters and Smith. I'm hoping something will get kicked loose when we interview Waters and Smith."

"One might turn on the other."

"That would be helpful. What will you be doing?"

Aggie sighed deeply.

"I'm working on another case and am waiting for a call to go into the precinct for an interview. On the opposite side so to speak. Well, I'm not waiting for a call but I am expecting one."

"What's that about, if you can tell me?"

Aggie gave a broad outline of the Forman case with no interruption from Reede, who listened intently.

He said, "It sounds as though you have a good lawyer. There seems to be no evidence of any kind to support this guy's accusations and, clearly, there wouldn't be any, anyway. This guy Hollis might just be pushing buttons to see what happens. He can't genuinely believe those stories. I'm going to be doing the same thing later today. You might check whether this guy is an abuser. I would think it quite likely, given his weird behavior. On the face of it, I would say that nothing is going to happen as far as you are concerned. I could check to see if I know the detectives on the murder investigation. It might help to know what they are thinking."

Aggie began to feel tired just talking about it.

"Thanks, but I'll be OK. I will be trying to track down the wife of this guy Forman. If I can find her, that will put an end to my involvement right there."

She wanted to change the subject.

"So, are you married?"

Reede was taken by surprise.

"Boy, you know how to switch directions don't you. No, I am not. I have been married twice. My work seemed to drain away all of my emotions, the good ones anyway. There just weren't enough to go around. It seems funny to think of a finite amount, I know, but that was how it felt. I suppose that it is another way of saying I was always busy and had no time for life at home."

Aggie said, "Children?"

"One boy from my first marriage. He is a sophomore in High School now. I've been working on managing a good relationship with him and it's working very well right now."

"That's good."

Reede looked at her directly.

"How about you?"

"Me? I've never been married. I like my independence. My life is relatively simple, unencumbered if you like and it allows me to make the best of my ability as a PI. I enjoy the regular challenges."

"So, you are happy at what you do. That is so important."

"You could say that. On the other hand I am living in the present, the status quo, and I should be trying to peer into the future. You know, get a look at where I'm going and if I want to go there."

Reede nodded and, after a longish pause in the conversation, said, "I have to be off shortly. I really enjoy talking to you. Do you think we could try it again sometime?"

Aggie laughed and found herself in total agreement.

"Yes, of course. I think that would a fun thing to do."

"Great. Well, I'm going to put myself together and be on my way."

Aggie returned to her bedroom to give Reede some privacy and tidied up a few things. After a few minutes, he called out and Aggie came out to see him off. As they shook hands, he asked again that she let him know when she planned the Waters trip, thanked her for the evening and hospitality and then left.

Chapter 35

During the day, Aggie amused herself by researching some of Frank Pederson's past, of which there was very little. He appeared less flamboyant these days than in an earlier photograph that she found at the time when he had been a federal prosecutor, involved in various wide ranging criminal investigations. These days, he ran a two man law firm, was married to an older woman and had two daughters, both of whom were in the medical profession. It was well into the afternoon when his call came. With heightened curiosity, Aggie picked up her phone.

"Hi Frank. What's the news?"

"Hi Aggie. We have to go in for a chat tomorrow if you can make it. I say that because there is no legal reason that you should comply if you don't wish to yet."

Aggie responded after only a few moments.

"I'd like to get it over with. You know, see what they are going to say to me. I suppose that they did not tell you."

"No. They were tight lipped but surprisingly conciliatory. They would like a meaningful discussion, following significant developments in the case. Now I am no clearer as to what that means than you are. There was no hint of an explanation – not that I didn't try for it- as to what the meeting is for or what the developments are."

Aggie responded.

"A little odd in phraseology isn't it. I mean, a meaningful discussion."

"It is. I am assuming that it is not some form of legal stunt being enacted for our benefit, at least, I don't think so."

Aggie had gathered much more of a sense now that Frank Pederson had substantial clout.

"You mean that you don't think that they would try that on with you?"

"Precisely. What goes around comes around. That is particularly true in the legal system. That being the case, I am curious about tomorrow."

"So am I. So, I guess we just grin and bear it. Or I do."

"We both do. The meeting is at 11.00 a.m. OK with you?"

"Yes. I will be glad when it is all over. Thank you Frank."

"Me too. See you then."

He broke the connection.

Aggie was just clearing up after a dinner or, at least, a meal of soup and a cheese and tomato sandwich, washed down with some smart water that she was trying, when Jack called.

"Hi Ag. Little bit of interesting news for you."

"Hi Jack. Thanks. Something good I hope."

"I think so. That credit card belonging to the woman you were tracing? It has been used three times. Once for a car service to JFK, once at Heathrow airport and once at some place called Battle."

"Wow, Jack. You have come through big time. Thanks so much."

Jack laughed, delight in his voice.

"Least I could do."

"It gives me something to work on. Battle is in England. I know of it. This is really helpful."

"Good. I can't go any further with that. That's it I'm afraid."

"This is really good, thanks. How's your day going."

"Oh, very busy. We have info on the housekeeper. She has been operating in Tampa and Chicago, as well as Nashville. The only good thing is that it looks like she is a loner. One operation – hers. We are looking for the fence or fences now. First time that she was the housekeeper. She recruited illegals that were housekeepers in the other places."

Aggie was pleased for him.

"Sounds like a lot of progress. Hope it goes on that way."

"Me too. OK. Got to go."

"Thanks again Jack."

They rang off. Aggie ran through the implications of what she had just heard. Marcia Forman, if the credit card was in her possession, was nothing, if not resourceful. It looked as though she had not only found a good relationship – there had been two people in the Best Western room – but had gone to fairly extensive lengths to preserve it by leaving the US. The assumption here was that she was not coming back. This was not just an exciting or liberating vacation. It made complete sense to Aggie. This news could help her considerably in the get-together tomorrow. Of course, the motel murder was still hanging out there but there could be no connection to her because there just wasn't any. It remained to be seen what, if anything, the investigation was trying to attribute to her.

The one problem she had was that she felt an obligation not to reveal Marcia Forman's whereabouts. She had made the break and clearly would not want Dwight Forman to know where she was. Aggie thought that she would have to find a way of preserving that confidentiality. She decided to see where the town of Battle was in England to see if she could make any sense of why Marcia Forman was apparently staying there or passing through. A map on the Internet showed Battle to be very close to the south-east coast of England about 55 miles south-east of London. Her curiosity about the town name was satisfied when she discovered that the Battle of Hastings had been fought there in 1066. She knew the date and battle, of course, but not that a town had been named after it. The abbey there had been built to commemorate it and the altar was purported to be at the spot where King Harold died. The town was once known for its fine gunpowder and clockmakers. All very interesting but what was Marcia doing in a town called Battle, with a population of under ten thousand people? The answer was, Aggie thought, that she had passed through it on the way to the coast, somewhere on the coast being the obvious destination. The coastal town of Hastings was so close to Battle that Aggie's educated guess was that Marcia Forman was staying, or had stayed, in Hastings, England. She eventually went to bed with all of that new information churning in her mind, as well as wondering what the next morning would bring.

Chapter 36

Aggie was up and showered by eight on Monday morning. After some thought, she decided on somewhat formal attire – for her anyway, a faux leather jacket, blue tee shirt, Zuni necklace that an admirer had once given her, jeans and sneakers. She put all of it together on her bed in readiness. Even though her hair was longer these days she still finger combed it. Breakfast was bananas, yoghurt and three cups of black coffee, enough she thought, to sustain her for the meeting. Just after 10.30 am, she dressed quickly and was greeting Frank less than half an hour later. He had a couple of brief comments to make to her, after an enthusiastic greeting.

"As before, do not say anything but the bare minimum. Give me time to respond on your behalf when necessary and check with me to see if you should answer tricky questions. We do not know what this is about so I want us to be prepared. No charges have been made and if there is no caution made, you are not obliged to answer questions that you do not wish to, or even stay."

He paused for a moment looking at Aggie directly and then continuing.

"Of course, all that may change when we get inside and you may be officially cautioned. I don't, however, feel that that is where we are going."

Aggie forced herself to keep her irritation in check.

"The whole business involving me in any way is preposterous. There are no grounds for any of it. Just the word of a liar and, probably, a lying accomplice."

Frank looked serious.

"Correct Aggie. But, remember, they may be pursuing several lines of inquiry. You are aware of only one, the one in which you have a part. It could even be minimal in comparison to others. We don't know."

He smiled widely.

"Or not."

Aggie found it difficult to see any humor at this point. Frank continued.

"In fact, they should be following up on other leads. It would be unusual not to. They should be covering all the angles looking for an informed solution."

Aggie responded.

"Then, let's hope that I am not that informed solution."

She added, "Frank, I have one bit of news. I think that I know where Marcia Forman is or, at least, has been recently."

"Really. How do you know that?"

"I tracked her through credit card use. I do not want to give her away."

Frank smiled.

"You are very resourceful. Don't tell me where she is. We'll see how things go in there before we consider sharing."

At that, nothing more needed to be said and they turned together and walked through the door into the building, all of it seeming uncomfortably familiar now to Aggie. They were met by an average looking fortyish guy in an average suit with a grim face who led them along two long corridors to a room with an open door and nobody present. It was obviously a conference room with one curtained window and not either interview rooms A or B. Aggie immediately wondered if they were trying to lower her guard in some way with an ambient change in the scenery and a reduction in the intimidatory atmosphere, perhaps. The average guy asked them to take seats at the table in the center of the room, which was, unusually, circular in shape and then he left the room. Aggie and Frank took side by side seats at the table more or less facing the door. Aggie muttered to Frank.

"A bit odd isn't it?"

"It is. Well, this is clearly not a grilling or even an interview. I can see that. It must be that meaningful discussion, whatever that turns out to be."

Before Aggie could reply, they heard footsteps in the hall outside and the average, grim looking guy entered the room, followed by Hollis. Hollis carried a file. Nobody else appeared. Hollis closed the door. There was no recording equipment which was interesting. Hollis and the grim faced guy, whose expression had not changed, sat opposite Aggie and Frank, slightly towards his side. Hollis cleared his throat and opened.

"Good morning. Thank you for coming. You both know me."

He turned slightly towards the grim looking guy and said,

"This is Detective Caleb Davis. He will largely be observing our meeting today."

Of course, there was no change in the facial expression of Davis. Aggie and Frank waited expectantly. Hollis looked down and opened the file and cleared his throat again.

"As you will recall from two previous meetings, Marcia Forman went missing almost two weeks ago under what might be described as suspicious circumstances. My job was to try to locate her, whether she was alive or deceased. I had been apprised of the untoward activity of Ms. Trout here by Marcia Forman's husband, Dwight Forman."

Aggie was about to jump in when Frank signaled not to. Hollis continued, glancing at Aggie.

"He intimated that because of your obsession with him, you might well have done harm to his wife."

Aggie managed to control her burgeoning anger. Hollis again continued.

"As a missing persons investigator, I would not be doing my job if I did not follow all the appropriate leads presented to me. You, Ms. Trout were one of those leads."

Aggie ignored Frank and responded.

"Yes, and you were very aggressive towards me. You must have known that I had no part in any disappearance."

"Not so, Ms Trout. I kept an open mind. That is how I operate. It was, if you like, a means to an end."

"Well, it did not seem like an open mind to me. It felt as though you were zeroing in on me."

"That was the idea. I needed to apply some pressure to get some results. I am working several cases at the same time. If there are any genuine short cuts that I can take, I will take them."

Before Aggie could respond further, Hollis added,

"Before you continue down that road, critiquing me, please hear me out. By the way, we are still unsure of the fate of Marcia Forman."

Frank decided to intervene as Aggie struggled to control her annoyance with Hollis.

"Can we assume that Ms. Trout is no longer a person of interest at this stage?"

Hollis responded.

"I believe we are headed in that direction, yes. That will approach some finality when we locate Marcia Forman but, whatever that outcome, Ms. Trout is not, I think, being accused of anything."

Hollis glanced at Davis, who nodded imperceptibly.

"Now, in asking you to attend today, I mentioned a significant development. The team of investigators working on the murder at the motel of which, of course, you are aware, interviewed the Forman babysitter at length. The upshot of that interview led them to acquire legal access to the Forman home and car. They had also conducted extensive interviews on Long Island, where a boat belonging to Mr. Forman was moored, and staff at a motel and Best Western hotel."

Hollis paused and leaned forward slightly, both arms resting on the table.

"A man's watch and wallet were discovered in the Forman car. They turned out to belong to Chester Berman, the murder victim from the motel."

There was a shocked silence at that statement by Hollis. Frank glanced at Aggie and both established eye contact with Hollis. Aggie spoke with a touch of sarcasm.

"I would say that that is a significant development. Looks that way to me."

"I understand your feelings and sarcasm but the latter is misplaced here."

"You mean that you did not think that I put the watch and wallet in Forman's car?"

"It did occur to me, yes. Initially, but then other circumstances negated that idea, including forensic evidence obtained from Forman's boat, that I won't go into here. Subsequently, Forman has been arrested along with the babysitter who was complicit in all of his activities."

After a short silence during which the import of Hollis' remarks sank into Aggie's mind, she said,

"Did he say why he killed the guy in the motel?"

"He did. He had hoped to murder his wife and her lover but assumed that he had just gotten the lover. He seemed proud of his efforts and was happy to describe them all."

"That poor guy in the motel. What terrible luck."

"Indeed."

Hollis drew in a long breath.

"In the interests of full disclosure, I asked Detective Zhou to take up most of the initial investigation because I knew Dwight Forman. Not well, you'll understand but our paths had crossed two or three times in the past. However, I was in charge and responsible for how the investigation proceeded."

Aggie had the feeling that this was some kind of half-baked apology but did not comment.

Frank spoke.

"Do you mind telling us how your paths crossed or is that privileged?"

Hollis straightened up in his chair.

"No it's not. We met at Trekkie conventions."

Aggie and Frank wore their best impassive facial expressions in the following silence.

Hollis glanced directly at Aggie.

"Ms. Trout, do you have any information on the whereabouts of Marcia Forman?"

Frank spoke quickly.

"You don't have to answer that."

Aggie responded.

"I don't think that I can answer that question."

Hollis took the hint well. The unwritten statement that gave the answer and lessened his burden. He had several other cases. Marcia Forman seemed to have escaped an unpleasant situation and she had not committed a crime. So be it. Once again, he looked directly at Aggie.

"If by some remote chance, you should manage to track down Marcia Forman, you might bring to her attention the possible plight of her children. They do not now have a father, mother or babysitter available to take care of them. Our Childcare Services Department is currently attempting to find solutions within the Forman family structure."

Aggie replied.

"Without question, that is something I will be working on."

"Good. Well, I think we are done here. Do you have any questions?"

Aggie was experiencing some relief at this huge change in events. She felt no urge to prolong her stay in this room. Frank obviously had similar feelings. Aggie answered.

"No questions.."

"Right. If our paths cross again, I do hope that it will be under better circumstances."

Aggie and Frank rose together, neither responding. Hollis remained seated. Davis indicated that he would show them out. They trooped out of the room, along the corridors, through the lobby and out into the early afternoon air, Davis not speaking or saying goodbye.

Once outside, Aggie and Frank stood facing each other. Frank spoke.

"Well, that was totally unexpected. How do you feel about it all?"

"A bit overwhelmed. I didn't know what to expect. I guess utter relief is what I'm feeling."

Frank looked thoughtful.

"Look, let's have a coffee and talk a bit. There's a Starbucks a couple of blocks away."

They turned and headed for the coffee shop. Aggie discovered that Frank was a quick, agile walker, nothing being said on the way. They were soon seated with a Grande Latte each. Frank said,

"I imagine that you might be called on to testify at some point. Fill in some background. Forman should plead guilty but who knows. We'll have to see."

"Yes. I hadn't thought of that. What do you think that guy Davis was doing."

Frank thought for a moment.

"Probably just what Hollis said. Observing. I suspect he was part of the murder investigation, checking on how our performance fitted in."

Aggie was beginning to feel calmer and getting her mind around what had happened. She sipped her coffee reflectively.

"I'm feeling some urgency now about finding Marcia Forman. She needs to be informed about her kids as soon as possible. Of course, she will hear about all this eventually but that may be too late to help the kids."

"Good idea. How will you do that?"

"I'm not quite sure. If she is in that place – and I can tell you now –Hastings in England, I need to find her and speak to her. I have to find a way of doing that without flying to England. At the moment, the only way that I can see is to call all of the hotels and that would take days. And then, she might be in a bed and breakfast. All very hit and miss."

Frank glanced at her over his cup as he came to a conclusion.

"I know somebody in London. He's a freelance investigator and very good at it. I've used him several times. I could speak to him."

"That would be wonderful, Frank."

"OK. I'll do it. No names, though. This guy likes incognito. You do realize that you are about to blow up Marcia Forman's best laid plans."

"Yes, I know. But in a good cause. It will be her choice in the end. I hope she does the right thing."

Frank smiled engagingly.

"Right then. I think we are approaching the end of our relationship."

Aggie returned the smile.

"I'm so grateful for all of your time and expertise. I can see now that I might not have done too well on my own. I have to pay you for all of this. How do I do that?"

"You don't. Jonathan has taken care of it."

"What? How could he? He's away in Seattle."

Frank smiled again.

"We go back a long way. We help each other whenever we can. We are close friends. So, no reparations needed."

"Are you sure? I feel so lucky."

"Of course. Jonathan must think a lot of you."

Aggie nodded.

"Yes. We have become good friends."

Frank sighed and finished up his coffee.

"Time to face the world again. Give me until tomorrow on the English matter. I'll call you."

"That fast. Thank you."

They rose and shook hands. Frank turned and headed for the door. Aggie sat down to put the day's events together with another cup of coffee. Things seemed to be moving very fast.

Chapter 37

By the time she made it back to her apartment, it was late afternoon. She toyed with the idea of calling a few hotels in Hastings but knew that it made sense to wait until Frank called. She decided that she would head out to the Waters house the next day. She wanted to chat face to face with him to see if anything shook loose. With Kowalczyk, Waters and Smith facing imminent charges, she actually had nothing more to work on as far as that case went. The shootings were the province of Moses Reede and her work for Kowalczyk was complete. Perhaps not in the way that he had envisioned but done. The chat with Stefan Waters and whomever else was at home was pure curiosity on her part. She reserved a rental car for 10 a.m. in the morning and called Moses Reede, as agreed, to let him know of her plans. The call went to message, which was convenient because she was in a reflective mood and did not want any conversations at all. She left a brief message for Reede with her trip information. At a bit of a loss for a dinner, she decided to stew some tomatoes and mushrooms together with some spices, something she had not done for a while now. It was just about ready when her phone rang. It was Frank.

"Hi Frank. Everything OK?"

"Everything is fine. I've got some news for you."

Aggie perked up at that.

"Not about Hastings?"

"Indeed it is. My friend took less than half an hour to do my bidding."

Aggie was shocked.

"That's amazing. I wonder how he, or she, did it."

Frank laughed.

"I don't ask him. He is very experienced. OK, look, Marcia Forman is staying at a place called Durham House. It is what is known as a boutique hotel. Basically a bed and breakfast. Apparently it has views of the ocean, or sea, as it is more often called there."

Aggie grabbed a pen and scribbled the name down as Frank spelled it out.

"So, she booked it in her name?"

"Yes. Surprising, perhaps, but she thought that she had got clean away, I imagine."

"No mention of other names."

"No. Just a room booked at that hotel."

Aggie was excited.

"Thanks so much, Frank. This is great for me."

"You're welcome. Catch up with you soon, I expect. Bye."

"Bye."

They broke the connection.

Aggie pulled up Hastings on the Internet. It did not take long to find Durham House. If was on the westerly end of the seafront, partly away from the bigger hotels in an area where there were several car parks between the hotels and the beach. Aggie looked closely at the map. So, there it was. Inside that hotel, or bed and breakfast, Marcia Forman was beginning her new life with someone, as yet unknown. Aggie noted the hotel telephone number. She could not call this evening because, in Hastings, it was pushing midnight. She had to call soon, though, in case Marcia Forman moved on. Her life, just beginning to settle, might undergo an unexpected upheaval as a result of that call. Her children would need her and Aggie hoped that she would need her children. In the end, she might finish up back in the US with her children and nobody else to interfere with their lives. So, it could end up well. After the quick repast along with French bread and a glass of Shiraz, Aggie turned her thoughts to Jonathan. She had not heard more from him and so, decided to call him for a change. It was mid-afternoon on the West Coast. To her surprise, he answered on the second ring.

"Hi Aggie. Everything OK?"

Aggie smiled to herself.

"Yes. All is well. The Forman thing is pretty much over. He's been arrested, I'm not involved anymore and I am now tracking his wife."

"Wow. Slow down. That's a lot to take in."

"Sorry. Yes, I've been a bit excited. It's a really long story so I'll tell you when you get back. That's why I'm calling. Any news on that front?"

"Ah. OK. Quick change in direction there. We are doing well and expect to be back about midweek."

Aggie laughed.

"That's great. So your friend is good then."

She had not adapted yet to the name of Blink.

"Yes. He has recovered well, teeth and all. He has a part time job with a well-known Seattle auction house. Not much restoring but he has an excellent knowledge of artists and will be very useful to them for the evaluation and assessment of paintings So, with luck and he will need plenty of that, he is on the right track. He has promised us that he will do his best to stay on that track."

"Really good news then."

"Yes. I think we will have to check in now and again, though. Are you free now, cases all done? What about the trucker?"

"Oh. That one is all but done too. Just a couple of loose ends to wrap up. Maybe we can meet up towards the end of the week. I'll do dinner."

"Wonderful. I'll look forward to that."

"Give me a call or text when you are ready. I expect you will need a bit of time to adjust and catch up on things."

"I will."

They rang off.

Aggie decided to relax a bit for what remained of the evening. She flopped on her couch with the Malcolm Mackay book, enjoying the sheer escapism of

Glasgow gang life and the unique style of writing. After a couple of hours she took to watching some Mixed Martial Arts on television. If was a program being broadcast from Australia. There was a time in her past when she had enjoyed the sport, especially the grappling skills of the contestants, many of whom were very inventive and had an uncanny spatial knowledge of where every part of their body was at any given time. She found that she missed the big names of past practitioners like B.J. Penn, Matt Hughes and Forrest Griffin. Fighters these days seemed to be more inclined to trash talk than previously and, she thought, the less skillful were greater in numbers. The positive side included the fact that the number of female fighters had substantially increased. She really liked Daniel Cormier but wanted him to retire while at the top. In the end, she took her book to bed with her, set the alarm for 5 a.m.in the morning which would be mid-morning in Hastings – a good time to call – and fell asleep amid thoughts of Marcia Forman and Stefan Waters.

Chapter 38

Aggie struggled into wakefulness when her alarm went off the next morning. She recalled vivid dreams that were non-threatening and enjoyable for a change. She made a quick cup of black coffee and, as she drank it, considered her call to Marcia Forman. Of course, she would be lucky to catch her in but thought she might be in her room following breakfast at that time in the Hastings morning. In fact, there was not much to say – just an appraisal of the situation of which she would be unaware. All decisions on the future would be entirely up to her at that point. Also, Aggie had to hope that Marcia Forman did not simply put the telephone down and take off to other parts. Aggie picked up her telephone and dialed Durham House in Hastings. She asked reception if she could speak to Marcia Forman, saying that she did not have the room number and, within moments the room telephone was ringing. It was answered after three rings with a very quiet, cautious British greeting,

"Hello."

"Hi. My name is Agnes Trout." Aggie began, worried that her accent would be an immediate giveaway. "Please do not hang up. I have very important and critical information for you."

There was a silent, pregnant moment during which Aggie hoped that Forman would stay on the line. She continued.

"Are you Marcia Forman?"

There was a long silence.

"Yes, I am."

Aggie realized that Forman could hear her out and then disappear. That would be up to her.

"Good. I have some vital, personal news for you."

"Who are you again?". The voice was stronger. "Do I know you?"

"My name is Agnes Trout," Aggie repeated. "I doubt that you know me. Your husband tried to involve me in your supposed disappearance."

Marcia Forman gasped.

"Oh, no. I don't want to do this."

Aggie jumped in quickly.

"Marcia, he has been arrested."

Another loud gasp.

"What? What for?"

Aggie needed to hold her attention.

"He is alleged to have committed a murder."

"Oh, my God. I don't believe this. How did you find me?"

Aggie continued.

"That's not important. The point here is that, since he and your babysitter, have been arrested, your children have no one to look after them."

There was an intake of breath at the other end of the line.

"They've both been arrested?"

"Yes."

"When was this?"

"A day or so ago. I believe that the local Childcare Services are trying to locate members of your family to look after your children. Nobody knows where you are, except me."

There was a modicum of relief in Forman's voice, perhaps because Aggie had obviously not divulged her whereabouts to anyone else.

"I can't take all of this in. It's too much. It's so sudden."

Aggie filled the vacuum quickly.

"Marcia, take your time. I can answer all of your questions."

Aggie heard a man's voice in the background.

"What's going on?"

Forman responded in a whisper.

"Not now, Bo. I'll tell you later."

She took a deep breath.

"Who is Dwight supposed to have murdered?"

"It was a man unknown to him or you." Aggie ventured. "It was, or seems to be, a case of mistaken identity."

"Mistaken for whom?"

A significant moment had arrived.

Aggie said, "Well, mistaken for your partner, the person that you are with. Traveling with, that is."

Forman's voice registered the shock she was feeling.

"What? How is that possible? I don't understand. I don't think Dwight even knows who I am traveling with."

"Marcia, he kept track of your movements. He knew where you stayed when you checked into the hotel with a friend. He checked up on you."

Forman interrupted.

"How do you know all of this? Where do you get all of this information? Are you a cop or something?"

"No I am not a cop," she said. "I am a Private Investigator. That is why I am keeping your whereabouts confidential."

"You don't have to do that. Why are you?"

Aggie sighed quietly.

"We can get into that later," she said. "There are more important things to consider."

"But, does everyone know about the rest of it? You know, the hotel, my friend and all that?"

"Yes, I'm afraid so. The murder saw to that."

Forman sounded more agitated at that.

"So, how is this murdered guy connected to my friend?"

Aggie heard a whisper in the background.

"Who's been murdered?"

Forman said, "Not now, I'll tell you later."

Aggie continued.

"You remember that you booked a room at the Best Western?"

"Yes."

"Well, you also booked the next night at a motel."

"Yes. We needed a room as a backup in case our flights didn't work. Just a precaution really. I didn't like to stay in one place more than one night, anyway."

Just as Aggie had surmised.

"Your husband knew about both the reservations that you made and assumed that you would be in both places," Aggie said quietly. "I suppose that he made some kind of choice between the two places you were staying in, or intended to stay in."

The implications were reaching Forman.

"You mean he thought that I was staying in the motel."

"Yes. He went there and murdered the occupant, under the impression that he was your friend. He must have thought that you were out or had gone on ahead."

There was a long silence during which Aggie could hear Forman's heavy breathing.

"So, we missed being murdered by my husband by a day, a single day."

"You did. Fortunately for you and unfortunately for the guy he killed."

Shock and sympathy resonated in Forman's voice.

"I still can't believe it. Poor man. What terrible luck. He was really going to kill me?"

"Yes. It appears that he had the whole thing worked out, including using his boat to drop you off in the ocean near Montauk. The babysitter was his alibi."

Forman said, "Well, I knew something was up with her. It became obvious after a while. I didn't care. I thought that it stopped him from abusing me."

She went on.

"Why kill me? What's wrong with a divorce?"

"We can't really go there," said Aggie. "It will come out eventually. There are serious decisions to be made."

There was a huge sigh from Forman.

"Yes. I suppose there are. I can't think at the moment. I feel so overwhelmed."

Aggie felt that she had to spell it out for Forman.

"Look, I wanted to find you for a couple of reasons," she began. "I wanted to clear my name. Some cop thought that I had somehow murdered you or, at least, caused your disappearance."

Forman interrupted.

"Why would you do that?"

"He knew your husband. That's where it started. Beyond that, I don't really know why he came after me."

She continued in the following silence.

"I was also worried that you were still in danger. That your husband would try to find you. But, that's over now."

Aggie now approached the crux of this call, the part that worried her the most. She thought that most mothers would have jumped in before this but Forman had not. Perhaps, being found and then hit with all this news had blunted her maternal instincts.

"Marcia, your kids are in a bit of a limbo. As of now, I don't know how the search for family members to look after them is going. Is there anyone who would take them for the time being?"

Another long sigh as the situation strengthened in Forman's mind.

"There are plenty of family members, yes. Our parents, cousins and so on. I need to think this through."

Aggie knew that she did not need to press the point, that Marcia Forman needed to go back and take care of her children.

"OK. Let me give you my number. You can call me at any time. Do you have a number for me?"

Aggie wondered if she would get one. She did. That was a good sign.

"Yes, I have a new phone."

They exchanged numbers. Forman could dump the phone and run, of course, but Aggie had the feeling that she would not.

Aggie said, "Do you want me to inform anybody that I have found you, Childcare Services, for instance?"

Only a slight pause.

"You can tell them that you have found me but don't say where I am. I need time to work things out."

That comment alone was promising. Forman had indicated that she was probably going to be moving in the right direction.

"Fair enough. I'll leave it up to you, then. Please let me know what you will be doing when you have made a decision."

There was no reply. Forman just broke the connection. Aggie thought that the whole conversation had gone well. Marcia Forman had to decide whether she would give up her newfound freedom and return to her children. To Aggie, it seemed like a no-brainer but then, she wasn't Marcia Forman. When it came down to it, she could have her cake and eat it. She could return to her home, be with her children without the presence of an abusive husband, maybe keep her job and also keep her boyfriend in tow. Didn't seem like a bad deal. Aggie hoped that she would decide soon. It was still fairly early in the morning. Time for a shower, breakfast and to face the day.

Chapter 39

Marcia Forman slapped the house telephone into its holder and flopped onto the bed, lying on her side with one arm across her face. Bo Schwartz, concern on his handsome face, gazed at her, waiting patiently to hear about all of the revelations of which he had only heard one side. He was anticipating, with some anxiety, that this exciting venture that he and Marcia had launched themselves on was coming under some kind of threat. He wanted to know what kind of threat. Marcia Forman dragged herself into a sitting position with a loud, long groan and looked at Bo.

"My husband and our babysitter have been arrested for murder."

She continued before Bo could turn his shock into articulation.

"That means that my kids have no parent to take care of them."

A double whammy in two sentences. Bo just sat there on the bed looking for words. Eventually, some came to him.

"What are we going to do?"

And then, an afterthought.

"Who was murdered?"

Marcia responded.

"Some guy that Dwight mistook for you. He was going to kill both of us."

"What? Kill us? Why?"

"Good question. He's nuttier than I thought. Couldn't be jealousy, that's for sure. He is vindictive but not enough for that. I don't know."

Bo gathered himself a little.

"Where did all of this happen and when?"

"In the motel. We were booked in that second night. He thought that we were there."

Bo's face once again registered shock.

"We just missed being killed off then."

Marcia nodded.

"That's the size of it. Amazing, isn't it. We could be dead now. We are supposed to be at the bottom of the ocean somewhere near Montauk."

Bo was still struggling with this news.

"It doesn't seem possible," he murmured. "What do we do now? Go back?"

He was sounding reluctant and saddened.

"Well, that's an option, of course."

Bo put on his earnest face.

"Our only option really."

Marcia remained quiet. She found herself in two minds. The maternal, right thing to do one and the profligate, enjoy life one.

" What do you think Bo?" She said. "What do you want to do?"

Bo was not overly bright but his heart was in the right place.

"I think that you have no choice. It's not so much what we want as it is the right thing to do. Your children need a mother."

Marcia sighed loudly.

"You're right. We could still be together though, couldn't we? There will be changes but we still have each other."

A flash of doubt crossed Bo's face as he considered dealing with three children in his life. He didn't even like children.

"Yes, there is that."

Chapter 40

Aggie got the call as she was walking to the car rental franchise for her Camry. Marcia Forman had decided, rather quicker than Aggie had expected, to return to the US in a few days. She was going, it seemed, to have a final English fling with her companion before doing that. Aggie thought that utterly reasonable. She would have done the same. She called Childcare Services to keep them informed – something of a relief for all, apparently. Forman would have to go through some assessment interviews and formalities but Aggie thought that it should work out. She also left a message for Hollis, a somewhat cool one, but he deserved to know. She was soon on her way with Radical Face echoing through her car.

She felt upbeat for the first time in a long time. Most of her current investigations were over, the weather was decent and it felt good to be on the road. After an hour or so, she approached the Waters family home. It was on a tree lined semi – rural street with homes secluded behind high hedges and bushes. Cypress trees were rampant along with redbud and birch trees. She found the entrance from the street in between high privet hedges. There was no gate and a sandy, pebble drive crunched under the car wheels as she went up the short drive to a double garage, the doors of which had seen better days, much better days. She parked a couple of feet in front of the garage and climbed out of the Camry. The house was a rambling ranch style building that had been extended considerably on both sides of the main entrance and, from Aggie's angle of observation, there were more areas of increased floor size towards the back of the property. The Waters family had obviously decided to expand their home in a committed way, rather than effect a trade up. Probably, because the surrounding area was rather attractive, wooded and settled. She walked slowly towards the main entrance, or front door of the property, taking in the surrounding trelliswork. There were plentiful remains of clematis fronds hanging from the trellis. She pulled on a surprisingly old brass bell pull which looked incongruous at the side of a relatively modern door. She heard no sounds of jangling bells but assumed the inside had been electrically modified to produce a normal ring. After a wait of about a minute, she tried again and stood back from the door in case someone needed to see who was calling. Eventually, she heard movement behind the door and it opened, revealing a man of about her height, wearing grey slacks and a yellow sports shirt with a Polo insignia on it, as well as several brown stains. He was bare footed. The face was heavy, pudgy really, a drinker's face. He had a full head of wiry, light brown hair, combed straight back above dark eyes, heavy brows, an aquiline nose and a small mouth. After looking Aggie up and down, a set of good teeth were exposed in a grimace rather than a smile.

"Hi."

"Hi. My name is Agnes Trout. We spoke about a week or so ago on the phone."

The dark eyes focused on Aggie's.

"Did we?"

"Yes. I asked about Jakob Kowalczyk and your sister. You must be Stefan."

The eyes looked up at the sky momentarily.

"Oh. Yes, I remember. What do you want?"

"I'd like to talk with you, if you have the time," Aggie said. "Ask you some questions."

"We're talking already."

"Yes we are but there are questions that I would like the answers to."

"So what? I don't see any reason to talk to you or answer your questions. Just because you show up on my doorstep."

He made a slight move backwards as if to begin to terminate their exchange.

"Stefan, things have happened. Bad things. I need some answers."

He paused and locked eyes again.

"What things?"

Aggie returned his gaze firmly.

"For a start, as you probably know, Jakob Kowalczyk has been shot."

Waters did not seem at all surprised because Reede had spoken to him.

"Yes. Is he doing OK, now?"

Aggie's reply was careful.

"Not really. He's been in the hospital for a while."

"Too bad. What's that got to do with me?"

This meeting was beginning to feel very awkward, standing at the Waters' front door. Aggie began to look for a way in.

"Perhaps nothing. But you might know something that would be helpful to me."

"I don't know anything."

Aggie began to feel the pangs of frustration.

"You might think that way. But, it is surprising what one can remember sometimes."

"Not me. I've got nothing to remember."

Time to try.

"OK. But, can I come in and give it a shot? You never know. It could help me a lot. If not, then nothing has been lost." She added, "I'm helping in the shooting inquiry."

Waters stared at her at length, looked up at the sky again and come to a conclusion.

"OK. Come in."

Aggie stepped over the threshold, past Waters and waited for him to close the door and lead the way. They went along a wide hallway past a couple of rooms with closed doors to a room towards the back of the house. It was dominated by a large wall-mounted television in front of which was a leather armchair with a small side table next to it. There was an open bottle of beer on the table along with a family sized packet of popcorn. A desk was lined up against one wall with a desk chair in front of it. There were sliding glass doors leading to a sunlit patio outside. Trees, grass and bushes could be seen through the glass doors. Waters pointed to a small easy armchair with its back to the opposite wall for Aggie, while he flopped into the leather chair.

Aggie smiled and said, "On your own today, then?"

"What? Yes. My parents are in Mexico."

He sniffed loudly and continued.

"OK, what's up? Get on with it," he said unceremoniously.

Aggie began, without preamble.

"Have you ever heard of a man called Adam Salter?"

Stefan Waters showed no change in expression.

"No. Who's he?"

"He is, or was, a claims adjuster for an insurance company."

"Was? Did he get fired or something?"

Aggie fixed her gaze upon him.

"No. He was shot in his home, just a few miles from here."

Still no change in expression.

"Shot? You mean deliberately?"

"Yes. Murdered, in fact. A friend of mine is looking into that shooting."

Waters looked away, glancing out through the glass doors momentarily. He crossed and recrossed his legs and returned his gaze to Aggie.

"OK. A couple of people have got themselves shot. What's that got to do with me?"

"Nothing, I suppose," Aggie said. "I thought that, if you had heard of Adam Salter, it could be useful."

"Useful? Why would I have heard of him?"

"Well, he was the claims adjuster for the truck that got burnt out. The one driven by Jakob Kowalczyk. So, you can see that he has, or had, a connection to the company."

Waters sat forward in his armchair.

"Right. So, he would have approved the insurance payout or, at least, kicked it off. Fine, but I still don't see where I fit in."

Aggie thought that Waters was being unduly defensive.

"Well, you might not fit in anywhere. I'm just giving you the information that I have in case you know anything that could help me."

"OK. But I don't know anything about this whole truck thing. I'm not even in the company. I used to drive a bit. That's all."

"Understood, of course," Aggie said. Time for a shot in the dark.

"I expect you know that there may not be an insurance settlement now. It's basically up in the air at this point."

Waters looked askance, concerned. She had his attention.

"Why?"

"Well, the cops are investigating the whole thing as insurance fraud. That means that a settlement is unlikely, is my guess."

Waters leaned further forward; consternation written all over him. He looked genuinely shocked.

"What? I didn't know about that. Does that mean that my sister might not get anything?"

Aggie picked up gently on the comment.

"It wasn't for your sister anyway was it. The settlement. It was for Jakob Kowalczyk. It was his truck, not your sister's."

Waters looked confused, trying to gather himself.

"Yes, but they were an item. She would have shared in it wouldn't she?"

Aggie opted for mild condescension.

"They stopped being an item. You must have known that."

"Well, Yes. But they got back together didn't they."

He was getting agitated, uncomfortable.

"She lives with Clement Smith now. You know that. You told me."

"Yes, of course I know that. But she still sees Kowalczyk. He takes care of her."

This was an interesting road to go down.

"What do you mean? Takes care of her."

Waters discomfort noticeably increased.

"Well, you know," he muttered. " Money and that."

Aggie wanted to know if he knew about Jakob Kowalczyk's estate.

"What money?"

A crafty, furtive expression suffused Water's face.

"I don't know exactly. But he saw that she was alright. Financially, like."

"Gave her money, you mean?"

Waters turned vague.

"Maybe. I don't know. I think so."

Aggie paused and then studied him for a reaction.

"Did you know that Jakob Kowalczyk put her in his will? She is a beneficiary of his estate."

Water's face registered shock, anger and neutral one after the other. Not much doubt about his knowledge of that tidbit.

"I suppose I did. I'd forgotten that," he said softly.

A hint of anger returned. Aggie continued.

"So you see, Stefan, if Jakob Kowalczyk had been killed by the shooter, your sister would have benefitted. Quite a substantial windfall, in fact."

"Surely, you don't think that my sister shot him. She would never do that. She is a peaceful, loving person. That's nonsense."

Anger and frustration appeared in Water's features. Aggie had struck a nerve.

"You are right. I don't think that she shot anyone. But, somebody did. Can you think of anyone who might have done the shooting? Of Jakob Kowalczyk, that is."

His face looked tight. He did not speak for a few moments as his eyes turned to the ceiling as if reading something there.

"Can't imagine who would do that, no."

Aggie thought that it was time to change direction. Before she could speak, Waters interjected.

"Look, I let you in here to ask a few questions. I think that I have done more than enough of that. I don't like you or your questions. I think it's time for you to leave."

Aggie looked for her apologetic, soothing tone, which was in short supply.

"I'm really sorry, Stefan. I know that you have been very accommodating and that it hasn't been easy for you. Nobody likes answering personal questions. I would appreciate it if you could manage just a few more. Then, I'll be on my way."

She managed to find an earnest expression and looked hopeful. An offer of a coffee would have helped but there was no effort on that front. Waters wrestled his way through a torrent of thoughts, ranging from the murderous to abject self-pity.

"Oh, alright. But keep it short. I have things to do."

"Thank you. I appreciate that."

Aggie's next topic was, she thought, touchy too, so she looked for a way to approach it.

"Does your sister still drive trucks?"

"No, I don't think so. She could if she wanted to but her job keeps her busy."

"At the casino?"

"Yes. She likes it a lot."

Aggie wondered if she would be able to keep it now. It depended on the outcome of the investigation.

"Do you get on well with your sister?"

"What? Of course I do."

"Just asking. So you are close would you say?"

"Close? Yes, I would say that we are."

Aggie sensed discomfort again.

"So, you have always been good friends. Never argued."

"Well, everybody argues don't they? We've always done well."

"Do you travel a lot together?"

An aggressive glare now.

"What do you mean?"

"Nothing. It's often cheaper to travel with someone you know. If you don't have friends, family is good."

Waters leaned forward again on the edge of the armchair.

"These are weird questions. What's all this got to do with anything? I have friends."

"Sorry. I was just curious. I thought you might be protective of your sister. You know, make sure she is happy. I don't know what that is like. I don't have siblings."

Waters was surprised by this and looked relieved.

"Well, Yes. I look out for her when I can."

Aggie felt that she was reading him correctly. Far enough down that road. She changed direction.

"I mentioned Clement Smith a short while ago but you didn't blink. You must know that he has also been shot."

"Course I knew. It didn't seem relevant."

"Your sister's live in boyfriend. Not relevant?"

Waters' dark eyes looked irritated.

"No. We weren't talking about him. Look, I've had enough. You are not a cop. I don't have to talk to you or answer any more stupid questions."

"No, you don't. You were helping me and I appreciate that."

Aggie moved to the edge of her seat as a prelude to standing and added,

"Three people shot. All connected to the trucking business and your family."

Waters looked tense. Aggie continued.

"So, you can see why I would be concerned about your safety and, perhaps, your sister's."

He looked very confused at this, trying to figure out where Aggie was going. She said, "Strange isn't it?"

"What is?"

"The way that this whole affair ties into your family somewhere."

"Does it? I don't see it. The company has quite a few members. I can't see what you are getting at."

He stood, somewhat unsteadily, and walked over to his desk, speaking as he went.

"I think it's time you left. I've done more than enough to help here."

He slid the roll top lid of the desk open and reached inside, turned around and pointed a gun at Aggie.

"On the other hand, I think you should stay. Stay exactly where you are Ms. Trout. Don't move."

Aggie had to admit that she was taken aback by the turn of events. She knew that she was rattling Waters but that was the point. This was a bit of a surprise. She sat upright on the edge of her seat, her hands resting on the end of the arms. She indicated the gun.

"What do you think that will achieve?"

Waters seemed suddenly confident, almost light hearted.

"It will achieve exactly what I want it to."

Aggie decided not to ask him what that was.

"You don't think that I came here without telling anyone do you?"

Waters smirked.

"That is immaterial. I'll take my chances."

Aggie realized that she had to keep him talking while she figured out what to do.

"So, you're the guy. All this time and, in the end, it turns out that you are the shooter."

Waters allowed himself a facial distortion that approximated to a smile.

"I am the guy, as you put it."

"Why?"

"None of your business."

"How about some truthful answers, then. It couldn't do any harm now."

He looked puzzled.

"What?"

"Make a change wouldn't it. Telling the truth."

Aggie began surreptitiously tensing her muscles trying to stimulate blood flow. Waters sat on the arm of the leather chair facing Aggie, not three feet away, the gun pointing directly at her as he stared at her.

"Shouldn't have thought you had any questions left. Be quick, then. I am looking forward to shutting that mouth of yours. It will be a pleasure."

Aggie didn't like the sound of that. It sounded matter of fact, genuine.

"OK. Just three or four questions. I wouldn't want to hold up your fun. First question, why did you shoot Jakob Kowalczyk?"

Waters smiled faintly.

"Two reasons. I knew that his estate went to my sister. I wanted her to get it. Simple as that."

"Looking after your sister."

"That's right."

"The second reason?"

Waters' face registered anger, and something more. Jealousy, perhaps.

"I didn't like her seeing him."

"You mean dating him? Sleeping with him?"

Waters looked away, not responding.

"OK. Why Adam Salter?"

"Just a loose end. Nothing more. A dead claims adjuster doesn't talk much."

"That really wasn't necessary. He had a very small part."

"I have a tidy mind. Just felt right. Felt good."

Aggie sensed the coldness and paranoia in Waters' mind.

"What was wrong with Clement Smith, then. Your sister seemed happy with him, didn't she?"

"Exactly. She was."

"You didn't like that?"

"No. None of your business. Enough."

Aggie tensed her muscles, ready for a desperate move when the time was right. She needed to distract him.

"Not much of a shot with that gun, are you?"

"What? What do you mean?"

"Well, you only managed to kill one of the three people that you shot."

Waters leaned forward slightly and waved the gun as he spoke.

"I am a good shot. I could have won prizes."

Aggie struck. Taking her weight on both palms on the arms of the chair, her left foot lashed upwards contacting Waters' wrist that held the gun. Several things happened almost at once. Waters screamed at the pain in his wrist, the gun went off with an eardrum shattering sound in the small room as it hurtled towards the ceiling. A bullet struck the wall behind Aggie as her right fist struck Waters' temple, causing him to fall forward into the knee which crushed his nose and knocked him to the floor. He had no inkling of what Aggie's physical capabilities were, an egregious underestimation. Almost immediately, there was a loud crash in the hallway which signaled the front door being broken down and within seconds, Moses Reede stood in the doorway taking in the scene. Another guy stood just behind him. He produced a big smile.

"Heard a shot. Was worried about what had happened. Are you OK?"

Aggie nodded, turning her gaze onto Waters who was blubbering on the floor and covered in blood.

Moses said, " Did you shoot him?"

"No. Just broke his nose. He's the guy, your shooter."

"Yeah. I was getting there. Had to be him. You sure you're OK?"

"Yes. Bit shaky. I think I'll go outside for a while?"

"Good. I'll tidy up in here and then I'll join you."

Aggie walked slowly out of the room, down the hallway and stepped over the remains of the front door, glass crunching as she did so. She stood in the afternoon sunlight briefly before taking a deep breath and walking to her car. She sat in the driver's seat with the door open, watching birds flying in and out of some nearby bushes and taking in the blue sky flecked with intermittent clouds. This chapter was over at last. It had taken a long time to figure out that Stefan was the shooter. She hadn't really known when she drove out here. She had wanted to poke the bear and see what happened. The sudden appearance of a gun was a shock and just goes to show that you shouldn't poke bears. It was hard to tell how much danger she had been in. Stefan had been very convincing and so, could well have shot her. She was fairly sure that he and Cordelia Waters had had an incestuous relationship but she did not know if it was still current. He was certainly touchy and jealous which had been part of the reason for trying to kill Jakob Kowalczyk and Clement Smith. She figured that Moses Reede would work on that and figure it all out. In due course, Cordelia's lovers would find out who had shot them. Aggie wondered what they would make of that. Moses Reede appeared in the drive and came over to her car.

"Hi Agnes, my partner is dealing with that mess in there. Waters has a badly broken nose. Going to take a while to clean that up. Pretty useful with the martial arts aren't you. How are you doing?"

"I'm good, thanks. I'll be on my way soon."

He smiled and leaned down towards Aggie.

"Can we meet up sometime soon and catch up?"

Aggie smiled back.

"Sounds good. I'd like that. I'll call you in a few days."

"Great. Take care."

He turned and walked back to the house. Aggie fired up the engine of the Camry, reversed out of the drive and turned for home. She was in no mood for music, or any sound for that matter. She needed quiet and reflection.

Chapter 41

Back in her apartment, Aggie ordered out for a Chinese meal and decided to accompany it with a bottle of Blue Boy Shiraz. Expensive but really good and she was going to demolish as much of it as possible. When the food arrived she put on the television and watched a British mystery series called *Midsomer Murders* while she ate leisurely and sipped the wine. She had read somewhere that in this mystery series there had been over two hundred murders so far in one village. It was fun, though, and well-acted.

When it was over, she switched off the television and ruminated on the trucking case. Her best guess was that Stefan Waters would spend the rest of his life in prison, Jakob Kowalczyk would probably do some time along with a spell of substantial probation, provided he found the right lawyer– as promised, she was going to help where she could – Clement Smith would also spend time in prison while Cordelia Waters would probably have no charges to face. All in all, quite a case in the end.

Time for bed and a decent sleep. She looked forward to Jonathan being back in the next day or so. She would need to rustle up a fun meal. Tomorrow would be a good time to start and do the shopping. She was too tired to think about it any further. She would call Jack too to bring him up to date and see how he was faring with his case.

The next couple of days passed quickly. Jonathan returned and they arranged to have dinner at Aggie's apartment on Friday. On Thursday evening, she received a call from Marcia Forman. She would be returning to the US after the weekend to take up her maternal duties, via Childcare Services. Aggie was delighted to hear about that. It was something of a relief. Forman hinted that her companion, whose name was Bo – Aggie wondered who would be named Bo and what it was an abbreviation of – seemed equivocal about the state of step fatherhood. Too much responsibility in one fell swoop. The chasm between lover and a readymade family seemed too great a divide to cross, at least for the time being. Aggie smiled to herself. It would all get resolved in due course.

Epilogue

Sukhbir Singh stood at his small apartment window, on the outskirts of Bergen County, watching the heavy traffic rushing by on Route 17. His parents had emigrated to the US from the Punjab and had carved out a living in New Jersey, his father working in a deli and his mother in a dry cleaners. They had worked hard all of their lives. He felt that he was a dutiful son and spent as much time as possible with them. He was, in fact, proud of their hard earned success. He was married to Aad and had a four-year-old daughter, Bhao. He was a truck driver with J.K Trucking and had been for a while. It was a steady job and earned him just enough to support his family. For the past three years, he had bought lottery tickets in the New Jersey Lottery and had regularly drawn a blank – until today. In his hand was a lottery ticket which, he had just learned, would pay him six million dollars. As the tears rolled down his face, he wondered at how the good and bad things happened in life. Sometimes it seemed so random.